Colin Bateman was born in Northern Ireland in 1962. For many years he was the deputy editor of the *County Down Spectator*. He received a Northern Ireland Press Award for his weekly satirical column, and a Journalist's Fellowship to Oxford University. His first novel, DIVORCING JACK, won the Betty Trask Prize. His other novels have all been highly acclaimed.

MURPHY'S REVENGE

Detective Martin Murphy investigates when someone starts to kill the killers — who happen to have been under the surveillance of Confront, a support group for relatives of murder victims . . . Suspecting the group of revenge killings, Murphy goes undercover and joins them. But Confront are one step ahead and the group is forcing him to face his own harrowing history . . . Now Murphy must come to terms with the past and bring the killers' killer to justice. The problem is he's starting to think that the killer may have a point. After all, revenge is sweet . . . isn't it?

Books by Colin Bateman
Published by The House of Ulverscroft:

MURPHY'S LAW
THE HORSE WITH MY NAME

COLIN BATEMAN

◆

MURPHY'S REVENGE

Complete and Unabridged

ULVERSCROFT
Leicester

First published in Great Britain in 2005 by
Headline Book Publishing
London

First Large Print Edition
published 2006
by arrangement with
Headline Book Publishing
a division of Hodder Headline
London

British Library CIP Data

Bateman, Colin, *1962 –*
 Murphy's revenge.—Large print ed.—
 Ulverscroft large print series: adventure & suspense
 1. Police—England—London—Fiction 2. Undercover operations—Fiction 3. Detective and mystery
 stories 4. Large type books
 I. Title
 823.9′14 [F]

 ISBN 1–84617–248–9

Published by
F. A. Thorpe (Publishing)
Anstey, Leicestershire

Set by Words & Graphics Ltd.
Anstey, Leicestershire
Printed and bound in Great Britain by
T. J. International Ltd., Padstow, Cornwall

This book is printed on acid-free paper

For Andrea and Matthew

Prologue

Spot the killer on the Tube. Which one is he? Is it him? Is it him? Is it him? Is it him?

No, it's me, and you wouldn't guess in a million years. How could you? Look at me. I'm so normal. Like butter wouldn't melt in my mouth.

But you would.

Yes, you.

No, don't look away.

His favourite time for picking them out was rush hour, in the evenings, after work. He could hang on the strap next to them, all crammed together, and it was no more or less than anyone else in the packed carriage was doing. Sometimes if he decided against them, he didn't mind making it obvious — he would just stare down their cleavage or brush erect against them as the carriage threw them from side to side. Then his target would blush and look away, or stare and glare; some would try to move away but couldn't, trapped until their stop, or they might decide to get off *now*. Then they had to squeeze past him and he'd press his head close to theirs so that he could smell the congealed mess of their

1

perfume and sweat and fear. Even then he almost always moved his arm so that his elbow dug into her as she passed, or twisted on the strap so that part of his upper body rubbed along her breast. He would know, and she would know, but she always pressed on, saying nothing.

When he actually picked one out, then he was more careful. A subtle appreciation of figure, of race, of beauty, keeping his distance at the end of the carriage, watching. She was almost always deep in a book, oblivious to her surroundings, or wore an MP3 player, battling to drown out the clatter of the train. He had a folded newspaper, or a book; sometimes he pretended to be asleep. If the carriage became too empty then he changed his mind because she might remember him and he didn't want that, because it was the stalking which was the fun; the killing was just the icing on the cake.

She was always young. He had no time for older shop-soiled women. They were too easy. He glanced around the carriage this September night and thought how wonderful it was that beautiful women always lost their looks as they got older, it was God's revenge on Eve to turn her haggard and dry. His eyes fell on a woman with short, dyed-blonde hair; their eyes met for a fraction. He smiled, she didn't.

She returned her attention to her fat romantic book. That's it, dear, he thought. Find your sex in there because I wouldn't touch you with a bargepole.

Alistair Scott kept looking, and eventually he decided on the young Eurasian girl. He guessed she was maybe nineteen or twenty, but you couldn't really tell with Asians; she could be thirty, they always looked young. But she appeared *fresh*, and that was important. She was Chinese, or Japanese, or Korean, or Thai, he wasn't sure. It was early days yet. And he would find out. He didn't think she was a tourist — they usually travelled in pairs, and her clothes were a little bit too smart for that. But she was new in town. He could tell by the way her eyes earnestly followed the progress of the Tube stations and then compared them with the map on the carriage wall, silently counting off the stops.

At Victoria she got off and bought coffee, and he stayed close enough to her to hear her first ask for it in her own language, and then she remembered where she was and asked for it in English. Her voice was soft, quite high, and she smiled when she spoke. He liked that. But then she bought tickets for the Gatwick Express, and he cursed because he thought for a moment that she *was* a tourist, who was going to the airport to catch a flight home. But she'd definitely bought two tickets — so she was coming back. And she had no luggage. She could have sent it on ahead, of course, but if she was going to China or Japan or wherever, she would have had more hand luggage than the little leather bag that swung from her left shoulder. She'd have books and sweets and an inflatable pillow and moisturiser and . . . Perhaps she worked there — at the perfume counter in duty free, or at the check-in desk for China Air or Fly Thai or whatever the hell they were called.

Alistair followed her as far as the train, but then stopped. He didn't want to go all the way out to Gatwick, and besides, he could hardly justify the expense. He had only been in his new job for two weeks, and his first pay cheque wasn't due for another fortnight. He stood on the platform, nevertheless, and watched her take her seat. She was beautiful. Now she was reading a newspaper — an *Evening Standard* someone had left behind, and as she read she formed the words with her tiny red mouth and he thought there was a hint of a smile on her face, as if she found this strange language so *funny*. An attendant in a purple blazer asked Alistair if he was getting on the train, but he shook his head. 'Just seeing someone off,' he said, but the man had already walked on, ushering the last stragglers on board.

When the train began to move, she finally looked up. She met his eyes. He smiled. She smiled.

A pity.

Because that was the end of it.

She would be here tomorrow night, at the same time, going in the same direction, but she would be alone. She had noticed him, and in noticing him, without knowing it, she had chosen life over death.

★　★　★

Alistair rented a room at the top of a large terraced house off the Fulham Palace Road. He'd been there for two months. He always took a room as opposed to an apartment, because with an apartment you lived in your own little world, which wasn't healthy, but with a room there was a better chance to interact with other people — there was a communal kitchen, at the very least, and sometimes a communal bathroom. This time was a bit different, though; he'd made a conscious effort to keep temptation at arm's length — what was that expression, about shitting in your own nest? — by renting off an elderly, retired couple. He made them cups of tea in the mornings and sometimes toast at night, and once or twice they'd invited him down to watch a movie with them, because they knew he only had a small portable, and what way was that to watch *The Searchers* or *She Wore A Yellow Ribbon*. Movies were like music, Alistair thought. You stuck to your era, and anything else was rubbish.

In his last house, there'd been two guys and two girls, each with their own room, and two bathrooms, so there was always a fair chance that you'd bump into one or other of the girls in their bathrobes first thing in the morning, or better, last thing at night, when they were coming home drunk and forgot to lock the door and you timed it just right so you could walk in on them having a pee. Once or twice he'd caught himself preparing to pounce on them sitting there, oblivious to the fact that they were half-naked before him. But no . . . *no*.

Slow down. Take your time.

So he moved out and found the Blairs and they were nice and friendly, treated him — well, not like their son, but like their son's best friend. He enjoyed it. He could relax.

He let himself in the front door, carrying a Chinese takeaway he'd bought on the corner. His stomach was rumbling and he just wanted to get upstairs and eat it, but Adele came out of the lounge at the end of the hall, so he said, 'Hello, Adele, it's getting a bit chilly out there,' and went to move to the stairs. However, Adele said, 'Alistair, can I have a word?' and he stopped with his foot on the first step. 'Of course. I'll pop down after — '

'No, now,' Adele said. She turned back into the lounge.

That was the way they were. Adele wore the trousers, Jack sucked on his pipe. It stank the house out. Alistair hated the pipe and could have rammed it down Jack's throat with great pleasure, but he'd told them he loved the smell. It reminded him of his dad. They liked that. It made him seem even closer to their son — the son they never saw from one year to the next.

Alistair walked down the hall and into the lounge. Jack was just getting up to switch the TV off.

So it was serious. The TV was never off.

They stood together, in front of the TV. Big news. Maybe one of them had cancer.

'Thing is, Alistair,' Adele said, 'we're going to need the room back.'

'What?'

'Aye,' said Jack. But Jack wasn't looking at him. And Adele, she was trying to make it look like she was looking at him, but actually she wasn't; she was looking just beyond him, through the open door, into the hall.

They knew. Somehow, they knew.

At the last house they'd got together and had a vote and told him he had to go. They said he didn't fit in and they had a mate who would fit in and they'd spoken to the owner who was one of their mates as well and he said he had to go — so, he had to go. And the place before that, the widow with the teenage daughter, he'd only been there about a week when she decided it wasn't working and had his bags sitting outside the front door when he got home from work and a big heavy guy he'd never seen before standing in the driveway in case he tried to cause any trouble.

Now Jack and Adele.

'But I was just settling in! I thought we — '

'Aye, well,' said Jack.

'Our son's coming to stay for a while. He lost his job, needs somewhere to stay . . . I'm sorry, Alistair.'

'Aye,' said Jack.

No, no, no . . . *lies, lies, lies.*

But *how* did they know? It wasn't as if he kept all the details on his computer and had accidentally left it switched on and password enabled. It wasn't as if he kept grisly mementoes in pickle jars around his room.

He was careful, *very* careful. *My God, if I hadn't been careful the police would have thrown away the key by now.* He'd been arrested twice in the past three years. But each time, even though they knew they had their man, they'd had to let him go.

Now Jack and Adele knew and they were lying badly.

'Well, I'm sorry he's lost his job. You've been very kind to me. If you could give me a couple of weeks I could — '

'Needs to be the end of this week,' Adele said curtly. 'He arrives on Friday.'

Alistair conceded. 'OK.'

He smiled and nodded, then walked back out into the hall and lifted his Chinese from the bottom of the stairs. He climbed to his room. He was still hungry. He would find somewhere else. There were a million rooms.

★ ★ ★

Alistair was in his third week of designing software at Malcontent Games. It was a nice, bright, modern building in Tottenham, and although he was a couple of years older than most of the people it employed he seemed to connect with them pretty well. On his second week there he was invited by the boss to go and watch Spurs — the company had a

9

half-share of a box at White Hart Lane — and although he was a little disappointed to find half a dozen of his colleagues there as well, it was a good day. They all got drunk and went for a meal afterwards. He liked it at Malcontent; the pay wasn't brilliant but he hoped he would stay there for a while. His last job, at Mill Street Compugraphics, had only lasted a couple of months, then they'd had to let him go. That's the way the industry was.

Today he finished off his part of the project. The boss, Kenny — 'Just call me Kenny!' — gave him the thumbs up, and then while he waited for more work to come through he made a call about getting a new room; there was an agency he used, and they were usually pretty good. In fact, they found one right away. The only drawback was, the people could only let him see it in the afternoons, they didn't do evening appointments. So Alistair took a wander up to Kenny's office to ask if he could leave early the next day.

He took two coffees from the machine with him, just being friendly. There was a blonde woman coming down the corridor from Kenny's office. He didn't pay her much attention because although she was in quite an attractive business suit she was clearly already in her thirties and therefore well outside his sphere of interest. Even if he had been interested in saying hello he wouldn't have had the chance because she walked with her head down. It was only when they were actually passing and he was close enough to see that her hair was dyed and she was probably overdue an appointment at the hairdresser to get her roots done, that he thought she looked familiar — but where from? Had they worked together once? Had they been neighbours? He certainly hadn't followed her, that was for sure.

Alistair knocked on the door and opened it without waiting for a response. That was the way things were around here. Informal. Except Kenny was a bit flustered; his cheeks were pink and there was a bead of sweat on his brow. Alistair wondered whether Kenny had tried something on with the blonde and been rejected. Kenny had plenty of money, and thought that made him attractive to women, but he also looked like a dog's dinner. Or maybe he'd just had sex with her. Maybe that was why she was walking with her head down. Guilt. Shame. Or maybe she was a hooker. Or an upmarket call girl. Although not that upmarket or she'd have had her roots done. Alistair held up the coffee.

'Alistair — thanks,' said Kenny.

'I wanted to ask if you — '

'Look — can you give me ten minutes?' Kenny lifted the phone and pushed some numbers. He held his hand over the receiver. 'No, tell you what — I'll give you a buzz when I'm free.'

Alistair nodded. He put the coffee down. Kenny gestured his thanks.

★ ★ ★

Kenny didn't call. Maybe he forgot. Maybe the blonde was from the bank and was calling in his loans. Maybe the business was going belly-up. The more he thought about that one, the more likely Alistair thought it was. They weren't exactly coming down with work. He'd only been there a short while, but for the work he was actually doing he could have done it part-time.

There was a meeting in the boardroom in the early afternoon; the senior managers, and a couple of people in suits nobody recognised. They were all talking about it at the water cooler, or in the kitchen which doubled as a canteen. One of the girls was already in tears because she was convinced she was going to be made redundant and she'd just taken out a mortgage and what was she to do?

Shortly after the meeting finished Alistair's phone rang and Kenny said, 'Alistair, do you want to pop up now?'

'Sure,' said Alistair. 'Do you fancy another coffee?'

'No — no, thanks.' Something about his tone. Light, but not light. Forced light.

Alistair hurried up to Kenny's office; knocked and entered as usual. Kenny sat behind his desk, still looking flushed, and on either side of him stood the men in suits.

'Come in. Close the door.'

He closed the door, but he knew. His stomach was tight. He felt sick.

'Alistair.' Kenny cleared his throat. 'We're — ahm, we're going to have to let you go.'

Kenny had a file open before him. Closely typed pages. The men in suits were looking coolly at him. Kenny hadn't bothered to introduce them.

'Why?'

One of the suits said, 'I think you know why.'

The other suit had the same steady gaze. Kenny studied the file, but his pupils weren't moving, he wasn't reading.

'Is my work not up to standard?'

'Look,' said Kenny, glancing up. 'Don't make this any harder . . . '

'We've made this up,' said the first suit,

13

pushing an envelope across the desk. 'It's your first month's pay.'

'And the last,' said the other suit.

Alistair looked at the envelope. He could tell by the bulk of it that it was cash, rather than a cheque. Whoever got paid in cash these days? Only people you didn't want on your books, people you didn't want to declare. People you paid with scabby notes yanked out of the petty-cash drawer.

'I haven't done anything wrong,' he said.

'Just take it,' said the first suit.

Alistair stepped forward. Kenny rubbed at his brow.

He left the office without another word. As he closed the door behind him he heard one of the suits mutter, 'Sick bastard,' and for a moment he thought about going back in and saying something.

But he didn't. It wasn't worth it.

He cleared his desk of his few belongings, put on his coat and walked out. He didn't speak to anyone. Nobody spoke to him. They probably all knew already. So what? It didn't matter. In two minutes he was out of there, back out in the city, just another dot in a world of dots.

Alistair sat on a bench in Soho Square while he waited for rush hour. Didn't they know what they were doing? With more time

14

on his hands, he could do more of what he liked best. He spent time in Waterstone's and Virgin and then at 5.25 he made his way down the steps at Oxford Circus station.

His throat was dry; he had the tightness not only in his stomach, but in his groin. Today he would pick out someone and follow her home. There were days when he liked to stalk, and there were days like this when he'd been fucked over by someone when the only way he could get back at them was to fuck over someone himself. And he would do it. And he would feel better. Then he would think about a new job and a new room and a new name and a new history and everything would be fine.

He was standing with crowds on the platform, but he never picked them out here, because the chances were you would lose them in the scramble to get on the train, that they would go in a different door and then get out before he'd had a chance to work up close enough to see if they were up to his usual standard.

He could hear the clatter of the train as it approached. He loved rush hour. There was a train nearly every minute, and every minute there were enough people to pack each train. Pack them up close.

As the train hove into view Alistair thought

15

again about the blonde he'd noticed at the office. Now he remembered where he'd seen her before — here, just a couple of days ago, on the platform, then on the train itself.

He shuffled forward with the rest of them. He could see the driver; the destination of the train. He didn't care what the destination was. It didn't matter.

The blonde — what were the chances of that? First on the train, then at his office. How many millions to one?

He smiled. It was a funny old world.

And then from behind, someone kicked suddenly hard at the back of his legs; they gave way and he tumbled forward. There was nothing to clutch at but thin polluted air. There were screams behind him. He was vaguely aware of them as he hit the tracks with a dull thud.

For some reason, he was still thinking about the blonde when the Tube train cut him in two.

1

Dr Jeffers said it was all about demystifying the profession, having a glass-fronted office, rather than just a brass nameplate and a daunting set of stairs. Big, airy, modern, attractive, no more frightening than a hairdresser's, although three times the price.

Susan, his receptionist, wasn't so sure, even after Dr Jeffers assured her that their clients wouldn't actually have to sit where they could be seen through the glass — that would be a step too far.

There was a comfortable waiting room with a TV and a DVD player out of sight and . . . well, she would say out of mind, but it was hardly the place. No, Susan thought a psychiatrist was a psychiatrist was a psychiatrist, and if you went to one people still thought you were mental. *That's the way it is.* She didn't know anyone — apart from Americans — who had reconciled themselves to the idea that going to a psychiatrist was anything other than something dark and secretive. You didn't go to a psychiatrist, as every American TV show seemed to pretend, for a bit of a chat, you went because there was something — well, wrong with your head.

Susan had been in this job with Dr Jeffers for three years now, ever since he had first opened his private practice, and she had every sympathy for the poor creatures who came through their door, but there was no denying that a lot of them were barking. It was just that there were different degrees of barking, the way there were different pedigrees of dogs.

Susan liked her modern office, but she felt like she was on show. People were looking at her all the time. Occasionally drunks would come up to the window and make obscene gestures. Once a junkie with a ghetto-blaster over his shoulder had come in and asked in all seriousness if she sold batteries.

Dr Jeffers might have thought he was demystifying mental illness, he might have thought his patients would just stroll nonchalantly in, have a cup of coffee and a bagel and chat about their problems while reclining on a soft leather chair, but you only had to take a look out of the window at the poor chap walking up and down outside to know that at least as far as the average Londoner was concerned, the stigma of going to a psychiatrist, no matter what dire strait you were in, remained as strong and widespread as ever. She saw it every day. The pacing. The watch-glancing. The smoking. The move towards the office, the move away. The waiting for pedestrians to pass by, the concern that even a complete stranger would see you entering a psychiatrist's office — the unspoken fear that that same stranger would then wait outside for you to emerge, then laugh in your face and call you a mental case.

Susan sipped her coffee, tried to concentrate on her computer screen, but her eyes kept being drawn back to the man pacing outside. He was of average height, his hair slightly receding, but cut short as well, he had on a combat jacket over black jeans, his face was heavy with stubble and he was chewing gum with a nervous rapidity that couldn't have been good for his fillings — Susan had spent five years as a dentist's receptionist and knew about these things. The man had a newspaper under his arm — then it wasn't under his arm and he was studying an inside page — then it was folded away — then he chewed some more and paced this way and that — then he had the paper out again and apparently opened to the same page. When he held it up Susan recognised the banner: it was the *Ham and High*, the *Hampstead and Highgate Express* — the local weekly. The new one had come out this morning and she already had a copy on her desk, but there was a different headline on the paper the man was examining, so he wasn't even reading this week's edition.

Susan checked her appointments book. Mr Marinelli was in with the doctor now, then they'd close for lunch, and Mr Simms was due at two on the dot. And it certainly wasn't Mr Simms outside. The latter was fat and fifty and this guy was . . . well, he was quite attractive, or might be if he took a little better care of himself.

Right, here he comes. Spitting his chewing gum out on the pavement, the dirty devil. Putting in a fresh stick.

Susan busied herself at her keyboard as the door opened and the man entered. She could hear his gum being worked hard before he spoke. She looked up. He was nervous all right. The newspaper was now rolled up and held tight in his fist, as if he was going to swat a wasp. Susan smiled professionally.

'Good morning. How can I — ?'

'Dr Jeffers — is this Dr Jeffers — yes, of course it is . . . the sign, I mean, I wanted to make an — well, make an enquiry. No — no, I need to see him. Look, I can't sleep, I can't eat . . . I just *can't* — do you understand?'

'Sir, if you'll just — '

'I need to talk to him. He's good, isn't he? He can sort me out, can't he? Can't he?'

'I'm sorry, Mr . . . ?'

'Murphy. Martin Murphy. Is he here, can I see him?'

'Mr Murphy, you don't have an appointment?' Which was, of course, a rhetorical question.

'No, I . . . Look, I'm here now.'

'The doctor is with a client, Mr Murphy. You don't have a referral?'

'A what?'

'A referral from your GP. Usually we expect — '

'No — no! Look, I don't have anything like that, but a guy at work recommended him, said he was the bee's knees. I wasn't going to come but I haven't been sleeping, I haven't been eating. It's making me mental!'

'Mr Murphy, I'm sorry, but even with a referral, we don't have any appointments for at least — '

Susan jumped back as Murphy slapped his hand down hard on her desk. 'Please,' he said. It wasn't threatening, exactly. But she'd had enough.

'Perhaps if you leave your number I can get Dr Jeffers to phone you.'

'Do I look like I can wait that long?'

'I can't really tell.'

It was cold and dismissive and slightly demeaning, and she regretted the words as soon as she said them. He looked hurt. He straightened. He had cool blue eyes and they suddenly didn't look as mental as the rest of him.

'Why not?' he said bluntly.

'Why not what?'

'Why can't you tell?'

'Because I'm not a psychiatrist.'

'But you're his representative here on earth. You should be able to tell. A nurse isn't a doctor, but if someone hobbles into Casualty with his leg pointing north and his foot pointing east she can tell that he's probably broken his ankle. You're the border guard, you're the Maginot Line, you have to have some fucking idea of what's wrong with someone when they come through that door, or else what's the fucking point in you sitting there?'

Susan's mouth had dropped open about halfway through this tirade, and was still gaping like a vandalised drawbridge when the door behind her opened and a tall, bespectacled man in a plain grey suit emerged. Murphy immediately pivoted towards him, extending his hand. The man looked surprised and somewhat reluctantly extended his own hand.

'Dr Jeffers, please, you have to — ' Murphy began.

'I'm not Dr Jeffers,' said Mr Marinelli, his face flushing rapidly.

'Do I hear my name?' Dr Jeffers called jovially from his consulting room behind Marinelli.

Murphy held on to Marinelli's hand. 'There's two of you,' he said. 'You're twins. Like that movie with Jeremy Irons.'

Then Jeffers himself appeared in the doorway, and Murphy shook his head and let go of the other man's hand. 'You're not twins,' he said.

Jeffers was a few inches shorter than Marinelli, with dark hair and a sharp aquiline nose; he had the confident smile and eyes of someone perfectly content with himself, his looks and his wardrobe.

Marinelli wiped Murphy's sweat off his hand and sidled past him.

'We'll see you next week, then,' Dr Jeffers called out. Marinelli waved back, but did not look round. He was already halfway out of the door, putting sunglasses on so that London wouldn't recognise him. Jeffers turned his attention to Murphy, who was now extending his hand.

Jeffers didn't take it. 'Now,' he said, over his glasses, 'who are you?'

'I'm sorry, Dr Jeffers . . . ' Susan began.

The doctor held up a pacifying hand.

'That's all right, Susan.' He looked at Murphy again. 'Well?'

'Martin Murphy. I need to see you right now,' Murphy said, 'or I will kill myself on your plush new carpet.'

⋆ ⋆ ⋆

It was both dramatic and intriguing, and it was enough.

'I wouldn't want to spoil the carpet,' said Dr Jeffers, and invited him into his consulting room.

Susan said, 'But Dr Jeffers, your lunch . . . '

'You run on, Susan. I'll get something later.'

'Can I bring you back a sandwich?'

But he just raised an eyebrow and she smiled awkwardly and picked up the keys to lock the front door. Dr Jeffers had his own set, he could let Mr Murphy out. Damned if she was going to sit there through lunchtime while the good doctor wasted time and money on one of his charity cases. She hated herself for thinking that way — Dr Jeffers worked all the hours God sent him. Half his clients he didn't charge. He didn't eat properly, and he still had that haunted look about him. It was awful, what had happened to his wife. That said, he was probably the most attractive man she'd ever met. Doctors always thought they had a certain charisma that women loved, but in her experience few of them actually possessed it. Dr Jeffers did. He had it to spare. She would think long and hard about how sexy he was while she ate her Cornish pasty in the café across the road. Susan was married herself, but she'd take off to Corfu with Dr Jeffers any time, if she had the chance. Or Rhodes.

2

There was a smell in his office, a bit like new leather, but it wasn't coming from the furniture. Jesus, Murphy thought, it's not his aftershave, is it? Expensive aftershave was an acquired taste, like caviar. Maybe it attracted expensive women. Or men.

Dr Jeffers pulled a chair out for him, then went behind his desk. He tidied some papers away into a file and slipped it into a desk drawer.

'Now,' he said, 'what's this nonsense about you killing yourself?'

'It's how I feel. I can't go on like this. It's driving me mental.'

'I'm sure it can't be that bad.'

'It bloody well is.'

'Well.' Jeffers sat back in his chair and clasped his hands. Murphy saw that he had a photograph, presumably of his wife, on the wall behind him. He had expected to see framed certificates proving what a wonderful psychiatrist he was, but apart from a framed film poster of *From Here To Eternity* there was nothing else on the walls. The lighting was subdued, the room was cool but not cold,

26

there was a very, very subtle music playing in the background and Murphy wasn't sure if it was supposed to be part of the ambience or was sneaking in from the dental practice he knew was situated upstairs. 'I'm trying to think — what movie was it?'

'What movie was what?' Murphy asked.

'The one with Jeremy Irons — about the twins.'

'I'm not sure. *Dead Ringers*, was it?'

'*Dead Ringers*. That's it. Curious movie — what did you make of it?'

'Well, it wasn't for the squeamish.'

Jeffers nodded. 'So — it's Murphy. Martin. And you're Irish.'

'Northern Irish.'

'Northern Irish. Which part?'

'Portrush. Then Belfast.'

'But you've been over here for quite a while.'

Murphy nodded.

'It's the accent,' said Jeffers. 'You've held on to it, but there are a few London inflections creeping in.'

'Yeah, I know. I'm trying to fight it, but it's kind of a losing battle. Look, I'm sorry for barging in like this, but . . . '

' . . . I caught something about you being recommended, but not by one of my colleagues. Might I ask who it was?'

27

'Well, I'd prefer not to say, but it was someone at work. I'm a police officer. No — sorry, I *was* a police officer. Special Branch. Until about a week ago.'

Jeffers nodded again. He wasn't making any notes. 'And is this in some way connected to why you want to kill yourself? The fact that you're no longer in that job?'

'No. Yes. No. I don't . . . actually *want* to kill myself. It's just something . . . '

'Something to get you through the door.'

Murphy shrugged.

'But you're plainly very upset about something,' the doctor continued. 'So why don't you tell me what it is, and we'll see if we can do something about it.'

Murphy took a deep breath. 'I've been fired because I shot someone. I shot a man called Gary Walker. I didn't mean to shoot him, but it's been made to look like I did.'

'You think you've been — what would you say — set up? Framed.'

'No, I don't mean like that. I mean — this is all off the record, isn't it?'

'Does it make a difference?'

Murphy thought for a moment, then shook his head. 'Not any more. OK. Walker is a rapist and a murderer. We know that beyond any doubt, we just haven't been able to prove it. We — '

'If you don't mind me saying, if you can't prove it then surely you *don't* know it beyond any reasonable doubt?'

Murphy took another deep breath. 'OK. If you want to be pedantic.'

'It's not pedantic, Mr Murphy.'

'OK, whatever you say.' He was trying his best not to sound irritated. 'Mr Walker was a strong suspect, the *only* suspect. A couple of years ago the evidence we have on him would have been enough to secure a conviction, but the DPP has cocked up so many high-profile cases that they're now reluctant to move anything forward unless it's copper-bottomed, with a lifetime guarantee. Do you know what I mean?' Jeffers nodded. 'On the night I accidentally shot Mr Walker he was following his usual MO — he picked up a hooker, took her to a remote location, forced her out of the car and was about to stab her when we arrived and he took off. I gave chase. I cornered him. Disarmed him. But he had a gun in his coat and he pulled that. I grabbed it, we struggled, he was shot. I should have gotten a medal, but instead I got sacked.'

'Why?'

'Because he nearly bled to death, because when he recovered he claimed I shot an unarmed man, because the fucking experts said the angle he was shot at, it couldn't have happened the way I said, because my disciplinary record hasn't exactly been wonderful, because they're all so fucking politically correct and because they just wanted an excuse to turf me out. That's why.'

Murphy sat nodding to himself. There was sweat on his brow and a fleck of spit in each corner of his mouth.

'They think you're what the Americans would call a loose cannon.'

'It's bollocks,' said Murphy. 'It's all bollocks.'

'How long were you a police officer, Mr Murphy?'

'Twenty years.' Then he smiled and added, 'I started when I was six.' He was still holding the newspaper tight in his hand, but now he unfolded it and pushed it across the desk towards the doctor. 'Twenty years and look what they did to me.' He pointed at a photograph. It was a grainy shot of him taken outside Aldwych police station. He was carrying a cardboard box. The headline said *FIRED!* Then, in smaller letters: *Cop Who Shot Suspect Gets The Boot.*

Jeffers lifted the newspaper and examined the photo. It was a small picture, and the headline wasn't large, and it wasn't on the front page. It was the sort of story papers ran when things were slow.

'They must have set it up,' said Murphy. 'How else would anyone know when I was leaving?'

Jeffers nodded. 'Do you mind if I keep this?'

Murphy shrugged. 'It's really fucked me up. I mean, usually I can sleep like a fish, but since this . . . not so much flash-backs, more like, I don't know, flash-forwards? What Walker might be doing, who he might be after — do you know what I mean?'

Jeffers opened a drawer and slipped the newspaper into it. He sat forward again. 'This man you shot accidentally — Walker — you must have dealt with hundreds like him before. Have you shot other people before — either accidentally or on purpose?' Murphy nodded. 'So why this reaction now, to a man who has apparently made a full recovery?'

'I don't know. Straw that broke the camel's back — that sort of thing, I suppose.'

'Try harder.'

Murphy's brow furrowed. 'Excuse me?'

'Try harder, Mr Murphy. Tell me what you really feel.'

'I am telling you what — '

'Mr Murphy, come on. You've been a cop for twenty years, you've been sacked,

31

tell me how you feel.'

Murphy sighed.

Jeffers said: 'Look, I can't help you unless you talk to me. We haven't yet invented a machine that can go in there and wander down the corridors of your brain, making notes. I can observe, I can question, I can sympathise if you want, but I can't begin to help you until I really know how you feel.'

'OK.' Murphy huffed and puffed for a bit. He started, he stopped; he examined his shoes. He checked out his fingernails.

'Just relax.'

'That's easy for you to say, you — ' But Jeffers gave him a look and he stopped and chewed on his lip and tried to think.

'All right,' he began tentatively. 'I feel . . . I don't know. He's — well, he's still out there, isn't he? And before — before I got sacked — I could have gone after him. I had the resources and the support of my team and I could have nailed him, but now, Christ, he's just out there. It's like he's . . . '

'Emasculated you?'

' . . . cut off my balls and run them through a mangler.'

They both smiled.

Jeffers pushed his chair back and came round so that he was sitting on his desk directly in front of Murphy. Murphy was sitting far enough back so that it wasn't particularly awkward, but it was a little intimidating. Jeffers probably meant it to be, he thought. He was a solid figure of a man, he looked like he worked out. Good-looking, sleek, charming, he was probably a big hit with the ladies.

'I'm not sure if you're aware of it, Mr Murphy, but I specialise in trauma — helping those who survive murder, those who witness it, those who have seen their loved ones destroyed, those who've seen their whole lives destroyed by one random or meticulously planned act of violence. I have heard things that would make even you ... ' Jeffers hesitated, then moved it in a different direction. 'This isn't terribly scientific — you might be surprised to learn that very little psychiatry is — but I see in your eyes what I see in other victims' eyes. I see it in every part of you. There's a sadness, a terrible, terrible sadness'

Murphy nodded slowly — and before he could stop it, tears had formed up in his eyes, which took him completely by surprise. He blinked, trying to keep them in, but this had the reverse effect. He quickly wiped at the top of his cheeks. 'I'm sorry,' he said.

'That's OK' Jeffers gave him a supportive smile, then returned to his side of the desk.

33

As he sat he opened a different drawer and produced a small white pad with lettering on it. He lifted a pen and began to write. 'Two things,' he said, without raising his eyes from the pad. 'One, I'm going to give you a prescription which will help you sleep. Two, I'd like you to make an appointment to come back and see me.' He finished writing the script, tore it off and pushed it across the table towards Murphy, who lifted it and examined the writing, but couldn't make head nor tail of it. 'And also . . . '

'That's three,' said Murphy.

Jeffers nodded, but this time he didn't smile. 'Three — I, well, I run a support group for victims of violence.'

'Support group? I'm not really into groups.'

'No, it's a bit different from your usual group therapy. We call it Confront. It's about *empowerment.*'

Murphy looked completely underwhelmed. He stood up. 'Well, let me know when it's meeting and I'll see what I can do. I, ah — thanks for seeing me at such short notice.' He took several steps back towards the door. 'I'll make that appointment and uh . . . what do I do? Pay the receptionist?'

'No, don't worry about it.'

'You mean . . . ?'

'It's expensive enough to get the script filled. That's plenty.' He was trying to be helpful, but Murphy snapped back: 'I know I've just been sacked, but I'm not a fucking charity case yet.'

'And I'm not a charity.'

'What was I then, just a diverting little lunchtime chat for you?'

'No, Mr Murphy. You're my patient. And instead of paying me in cash, help me by attending the support group. A man of your experience could contribute quite a lot.'

Murphy sucked on his bottom lip, then gave the slightest of nods. 'Sorry,' he said.

★　★　★

When he walked back into reception Susan had returned to her desk. She glanced up at him and he saw that she had crumbs on either side of her mouth. She had hard eyes, he thought, full of condescension. Gatekeeper eyes. A bouncer in the mental ward.

'I'm supposed to make an appointment and not pay anything.'

Susan cleared her throat, and consulted her computer. 'I'll see if I can squeeze you in.'

'I don't want to be squeezed in. I want a proper appointment, with no squeezing.'

She looked sharply up at him. 'It's just an expression.'

She wasn't sure if he was trying to be funny or not, but she was sure that she didn't like him. She made the appointment anyway. At least he wasn't ranting and raving like he had been before. In fact, he looked like he'd been crying. She smiled to herself. Dr Jeffers sure knew how to cut them down to size.

When Murphy was leaving with his appointment card, she said needlessly, 'Have a nice day.'

Murphy hesitated in the doorway. 'You have crumbs all over your bake,' he said, before stepping out onto the footpath.

★　★　★

He walked for a hundred yards down the road, wondering what on earth had possessed him to almost start crying. Then he turned the corner, and saw his car. His partner, Carter, was sitting in the passenger seat. Murphy climbed in and started the engine.

'Well?' Carter asked.

Murphy smiled. 'I'm in,' he said.

3

'And we have to thank a computer for this?'

Carter nodded. He couldn't do much more than nod because of the McDonald's quarter-pounder he was apparently trying to swallow whole. When he'd first joined Murphy's department he'd been into wholegrain rice and sushi. But they'd soon knocked that out of him. Now he ate all the shit of the day, and was still young enough to do that without piling on the pounds. Of course, he still played rugby when his shifts allowed, and worked out in the gym. And probably went jogging as well.

Murphy ran his fingers over the smooth red surface of the table. He wondered why they didn't have tables like this in their interview rooms. So easy to wipe down. A quick spray and good as new. Clean. Efficient. No ash tray. No burn marks. No graffiti. No sweat. No vomit. No blood. No screams as their subject was tortured with a . . . oh no, wait, that was Iraq. Or Saudi. Or any other country which practised torture. Murphy wasn't much of a traveller. Maybe he should travel. See the world. Maybe he could become a cop

37

in Australia. Or Canada. He could be a Mountie. He could have a big horse called Muffin.

'I thought you weren't hungry,' Carter said, having finally paused for breath.

'I'm not.'

'Then why do you want an Egg McMuffin?'

'I don't want an Egg McMuffin.'

'Then why did you say it?'

'Why did I say what?'

'McMuffin.'

'I didn't say McMuffin.'

'You said McMuffin.'

'Did I say, 'I want a McMuffin'?'

'No, you said 'McMuffin' — but it's pretty much the same thing.'

'Did I say 'I want an Egg McMuffin'?'

'No, you just said 'McMuffin'. But sometimes you're like that. Most of the time it's hard to shut you up, but if you're concentrating on something you sometimes just make do with one word. You might say, 'Coffee', and I have to deduce from that, that what you actually mean is, 'Carter, any chance of a nice fresh cup of coffee while I crack this case?' So when you said 'McMuffin' . . . '

'I didn't say 'McMuffin'.'

'You did.'

'If I said anything, I said 'Muffin'.'

'There's a difference? I thought you were just being economical.'

Thinking out loud. He would have to knock that on the head. He'd probably come up with the name Muffin for his horse in the Mounties because he'd seen an advert for McMuffins on the way in. It had snuck into his brain. Subliminal. In some ways it was a good thing, because not twenty minutes before he'd been listening to a news item on the radio about the importance of men checking their bits and pieces out regularly as a precaution against testicular cancer. He could just as easily have been sitting with his partner in McDonald's and said: 'Bollocks.'

Carter sucked on his strawberry milkshake and took another bite of his quarter-pounder. Murphy looked around him — there were kids everywhere. A birthday party was in full flow over near the door; they were singing and laughing and clapping. Think what you will about McDonald's, but kids love it. They can go three times a week, but it's still a treat. He was looking at the birthday boy himself: fair hair swept to one side, a red jumper, his cheeks flushed, and he was wondering if that was how Michael would have looked now. His boy. He'd be nine now. He thought about him all the time, and he still carried his photo in his wallet and he looked at it every day, but while he still had the image of him, the *feel* of him was going. Practically gone. The way his hair felt, the way his skin smelled, the pitch of his laughter, the salt of his tears. Sometimes there were little moments when these things came back to him, like here in McDonald's, or when he was driving in the car, and for no reason at all he started singing 'Yellow Submarine' because they'd sung it together. He wondered if Michael would have been into music yet. Murphy hadn't discovered music until he was twelve, but kids were so much more ahead of the game these days. He'd recently heard a six year old waxing lyrical on the new album by The Darkness, and he didn't know which was more depressing, the fact that the six year old even knew who The Darkness were, or the fact that he, pushing forty, had been to see them in concert.

'What were you saying about a computer?' Carter asked.

'I wasn't saying, I was asking.'

'What were you asking?'

'I was asking if this was really flagged up by a computer.'

'You know it was flagged up, because I already told you.'

'OK,' said Murphy. 'It was kind of a

rhetorical question. You told me on the phone it was flagged up by a computer. I was just asking for the sake of asking. Like if we both came out of watching the same football match and I said to you, 'That was a great game, wasn't it.' I already know it was a great game, I'm just having a conversation.'

'You think it's likely we'll ever go to a football match together?'

Murphy gave him a look.

'Yes, Murphy, aren't computers remarkable. Software flagged up that three murder victims were all named by a campaign for victims' rights. Confront by name, Confront by nature. I should point out though that no matter how special that software is, it still took a highly trained Special Branch investigator to switch the computer on in the morning. Without him we'd be sunk.'

Carter reached into his jacket and produced several pages of folded A4. He passed them across. 'This is what you were asking for. Confront's current membership — there's twenty-five. And the last three pages cover the previous members. Seventy-eight in all.'

'How'd you come by these?'

'I'm a detective. I detected them.'

'Let me rephrase that. How did you come by these?'

'They produce an information pack for new members. It has a website address. The website has a membership list. I looked it up. And then I printed it off.'

'You call that detection?'

Carter snorted. Murphy quickly scanned the list. Names, just names. 'Anything stand out? None of them have done time for previous revenge killings? Or been thrown out of the SAS for being mental?'

'Far as I can see, they're all civilians.'

'Well, one of them's not very civil. We have three murders.'

'We have three murders.'

'And can this piece of computer software work out if they really are connected to Confront, or who the killer is?'

Carter lifted his milkshake. 'No, Murphy, that's your job,' he said, and then took a long suck.

* * *

After Carter left, Murphy remained at the table for another ten minutes, ostensibly glancing through the list, but actually continuing to watch the birthday party. It was the noise level that got him, and the way kids could be laughing one minute, crying the next, then laughing again. It was like getting spring-summer-autumn-winter all in one concentrated burst, or like sitting through a Richard Curtis film.

He became aware then that two of the parents — there were half a dozen sitting awkwardly at a satellite table — were looking at him; Murphy gave them a sympathetic half-smile — *yeah, the things we have to do, eh?* — then returned his attention to his paperwork. A couple of minutes later one of the McDonald's staff came up and asked him if he'd finished with his drink. His Diet Coke was flat and warm, but it was only half-done. Murphy said no. The man, with an *Eric Spense, Manager* plastic label stuck to his chest, asked if he would mind moving to another table. 'Just — there have been complaints.'

'Complaints?' Murphy glanced around him, mystified — at least mystified until he saw the same couple at the table with the birthday party look quickly away. And then it dawned on him. 'Good God,' he frowned, then said, 'They think . . . Jesus Christ.'

'I'm sorry, sir, if you wouldn't mind.'

Murphy was aware of all the sicknesses the world had to offer, and had direct experience of many of them. But when a single man couldn't sit in a restaurant without being suspected of . . . well, Christ, things were getting out of hand. He had just been remembering what it felt like to be part of something like that. A family. Jesus. He looked up at the manager and for a brief moment considered saying, 'I'm an undercover police officer. Get out of my sight or I will shoot you in the head.'

Not exactly straight out of the manual, but sometimes you had to adapt to survive. But he didn't say it. What was the point? So he gave him a gruff, 'No problem,' and slipped out of the restaurant.

4

Murphy cycled thirty-two kilometres before breakfast, and all without leaving the privacy of his apartment. He had a Reebok exercise bike which sat in front of the TV. He'd splashed out on it three months previously, concerned about his health. Too many cigarettes, too many Cokes. He'd had what's known as a wake-up call. Usually this means someone has a shortness of breath while running for a bus or heart palpitations after a night on the drink, but for Murphy it had been going to his front door in his T-shirt and boxers and shouting at a gang of kids for causing a racket in the middle of the night, and one of them had shouted back, while in the act of running away, 'Why don't you go and fuck yourself, you fat fucker!'

And it shocked him because in his own head he'd always been more Thin White Duke than Meatloaf, but when he went back inside and looked at himself in the mirror he could see what the little bastard was talking about. There was a stomach. Two, if he was honest. Not so much a six-pack as a selection box. And he was getting a little jowly. And the hair was going backwards. And while you couldn't attribute that to his lifestyle, if he was going slowly bald the least he could do was to have his body in some sort of reasonable shape to counteract the mental anguish which would come with his entrance to the land of the chrome dome.

He needed to pull the reins in a little bit. Not go mental with it, just a little bit of gentle exercise, a few less curries, pints, fags.

There was a gym in work he could go to.

But he was hardly ever in work. When they had a job, they came to him. He preferred it that way. He didn't like crowds of people. He didn't like the uniforms or the taking the piss or the shop talk, he just liked to do what he did and be left alone. He was the closest thing to a freelance the Special Branch had, and that was fine by him. Even Carter, his link to the office, only saw him once every few weeks. He'd been to the apartment exactly once. And that had been pretty awkward, Murphy shifting piles of newspapers and CDs and making excuses for the dust and the fact that the age-thin curtains were hanging off their rails. Carter said he'd make the tea and when he did he found a cobweb on the kettle and the milk turned in the fridge. Part of him wanted to stay and act like everything was perfectly normal, but most of him just wanted out of there. When he suggested they go out for coffee, Murphy quickly agreed.

Murphy tried to think who else had been there since, say, Christmas, but was hard-pressed to think of anyone. He spent too much time alone — he knew that. Him and his guitar — and he didn't even play that as much as he used to. He was slowly losing interest in . . . everything. If he wasn't working, he was lost. *I'm like an actor without a role. Mr Benn without a changing-room.*

Thirty-two kilometres. It had taken an hour. According to the computer screen at the front of the bike, that meant he had lost 750 calories. He had sweated through his yellow Brazil top, and the inners were coming out of his trainers. He played Springsteen on the stereo as he showered, singing along with it at the top of his voice. He definitely felt better for the exercise. Maybe if he kept it up, one day he could win the Tour de France. He laughed to himself in the mirror. Sure. On a PlayStation.

When he was cleaned up and dressed he walked back into the lounge, took off the Springsteen and replaced it with an album by Juliet Turner. She was from his neck of the woods, and sounded like it. No mid-Atlantic accent for her. There was something very soothing about her voice, like she'd been badly hurt by someone but had crawled her way back to life and was happy now, but couldn't help looking back. Whatever. It worked for him.

He took the Confront membership lists from his jacket, then sat in his chair by the window. He could see the road outside, the park across the road. There was a fine rain falling, but not enough to discourage the kids playing football. Part of him felt like running over and joining in. Even if they were the same kids who'd called him a fat fucker, they probably wouldn't recognise him now that he was a lean, mean fighting machine. From the floor he lifted the three files on the murdered men.

The first, Thomas Quinn, had been shot dead on his farm in Kent, two years previously. Quinn was anything but a farmer, and had a string of convictions for armed robbery. What he didn't have a conviction for was a hold-up at an off-licence in Wembley during which the girl behind the counter had been shot dead, and a customer, a Michael Ritchie, was shot in the chest, dying three days later in hospital. Another customer, hiding at the back of the shop, later identified Quinn, and a subsequent search of his home turned up the murder weapon. He was charged and a trial date set — and then cancelled when the witness changed his story and the murder weapon went missing. Quinn was released, and then he won the lottery. Literally. Not the big one — but a quarter of a million, enough to buy a farm in Kent and get himself out of the rat race. Which, as he was one of the leading rats, pleased a lot of people — but not, clearly, whoever was waiting for him when he came home from his local pub, drunk as a skunk. Blew most of his head off. The papers called it a 'gangland slaying'; some of the wilder ones called it a 'professional hit'. Murphy wasn't sure what was professional about splattering someone's head all over a wall, but he was willing to concede that whoever had murdered him wasn't prepared to leave anything to chance.

Murphy flicked to the current membership list, and scanned it for the surname Ritchie. He/she wasn't there, but on the former members' list he found what he was looking for — a Karen Ritchie.

He opened the second file. An Albanian illegal called Malik Ali had been arrested and charged with the rape and murder of one Dominique Savage, a twenty-one-year-old art student. Ali's defence team had turned up the fact that Dominique had once painted a series of S&M pictures as part of her degree course, and used this to illustrate the fact that she was into kinky sex games. Ali maintained that Dominique had died by accident while they were practising rough-house sex, that he had applied pressure to her windpipe at her urging, and had merely been carried away in the frenzy of their coupling. He had not meant to kill her. Murphy had never yet underestimated the stupidity of a jury, and it was no surprise to read that Ali had been convicted of manslaughter and acquitted of rape and murder. He received a three-year prison sentence, but served only eighteen months before being released for good behaviour. He immediately went out and raped and strangled someone else, and was being hunted by police when he was found stabbed to death in the wooden shed he'd been hiding out in on an allotment in Greenwich.

That murder had taken place six months previously. Murphy turned immediately to the former members' list, but there was no mention of anyone called Savage. He flicked back to the current members — and there was a Fred Savage.

The third murder had occurred just three weeks ago. Alistair Scott was the chief suspect in the rape and murder of three young schoolgirls over the past two years, but he was smart and careful and meticulous, and although the police had hauled him in more than half a dozen times and were certain he was responsible, they never quite had enough to take him to court. And in the end, twenty-one days ago, somebody had saved them the trouble. Scott had been sliced in two by a Tube train. It had initially been reported as an accident, but then a witness had come forward to say he'd seen Scott being pushed. He'd not been able to provide much more than a vague description of the man he thought was responsible.

The three girls Scott was suspected of murdering were called Bellingham, Martin, and Watson. There was a Bellingham listed amongst the former members.

Murphy spent another thirty minutes familiarising himself with the details, then put the files and the membership lists away in the small safe in his bedroom. The only other things in there were his gun and his mint condition copy of The Damned's first album. According to *Record Collector* this was now worth three hundred pounds, because it was one of a batch of about a thousand which had been printed with a back cover photo of Eddie and the Hot Rods, rather than The Damned. Murphy had never met anyone who was willing to part with three hundred pounds for it. Indeed, as the years went on, he met increasingly few people who had ever heard of The Damned. They were a dying breed, punks. And he was an expert on dying breeds.

5

'She was seventeen years old. She had everything to live for. She was just the brightest, sweetest . . . and he snuffed her out like she was nothing. Nothing.'

Brian Armstrong was close to tears. He stood, trembling, before the group. Murphy supposed he was in his early sixties. Or maybe he just looked older than he was. Death did that to you.

Dr Jeffers sat front and centre, facing the rest of the group. Murphy counted eighteen members present. They were in a church hall on Laburnum Street in Haggerston, which was E2. The ceilings were high and the floors were wooden, and when the sun made its infrequent visits from behind the clouds, it lit up swirls of dust that danced magically around the hunched shoulders of the depressed and defeated who gathered here once a week to talk the great talk about fighting back. Murphy had been fighting back for twenty years, and he knew it was a fight that could never be truly won. Even the small victories, little more than skirmishes, were increasingly hard to come by.

'Thank you, Brian.'

Jeffers made a note in the file on his lap then smiled at Brian, who sat down. Beside him another man patted his leg sympathetically. Brian nodded his appreciation. Murphy had attended more than a few support groups in his time, both in his official capacity back home before he got into undercover, and then with Lianne, after Michael had died. They were all talking shops, designed to let you wallow in your own misery. Maybe that helped some people, but he didn't want to tell anyone how miserable he was: that was bloody obvious. He just wanted the impossible — his son back. And no amount of talking was going to do that.

Talking.

Praying.

Fighting.

Crusading.

Gone, gone, gone, gone, gone . . .

'Brian, as you will recall at our last meeting, we agreed to keep watch on Michael Caplock's last known address, and the good news is that he did return to the family home and we were able to follow him to his new address which is in . . . ' Jeffers consulted his file again ' . . . Camden Town. We have made his immediate neighbours aware of his recent history, so expect some movement there. We continue to monitor him for evidence of renewed criminal activity, which will of course be forwarded to the police if and when we obtain it. Now . . . ' Jeffers smiled, then nodded across the floor to where Murphy was sitting. 'Some of you may have noticed that we have a new face with us this morning — Martin Murphy, late of the Metropolitan Police.' Murphy nodded around the group. 'Martin, welcome to Confront. Perhaps you would like to . . . ?'

Murphy stood somewhat hesitantly. 'Thank you, Dr Jeffers. I'm a . . . well, yes, I'm a police officer — *former* police officer — and I'm sure I don't have to tell you of all people the kinds of scum I've had to deal with every day — every single day. And it's getting worse.'

There were murmurs of support from the group.

He looked to Dr Jeffers. 'I don't know how much I . . . ?'

'Just tell as much as you want.'

Murphy took a deep breath. 'You may have read in the papers what happened to me. There's a scumbag called Gary Walker. He murdered two women — girls — and they didn't die easily. What he did to them . . . ' He let it sit in the air for a moment. 'We knew it was him almost immediately but there was never enough evidence for the DPP; they've had so many cock-ups they're scared stiff of going for it.' Again there were murmurs of agreement around the group. 'Anyway, to cut a long story short, this one night we caught him in the act with this girl — another couple of minutes and she would have been dead. Walker ran off, I caught him, he pulled a gun . . . well, he ended up shot. So guess what happened next? I get the boot, and he gets to walk around free as a bird. Plus he puts in a claim for compensation. Crazy, isn't it?'

There were a few shouts of, 'Ridiculous!' and, 'Bloody scandalous!'

Murphy nodded in appreciation. 'And, well, that's it, really. Ahm, I'm new to all this . . . and thank you for having me.'

He sat down again. There was a small round of applause.

Dr Jeffers raised his hand. 'Thank you, Martin. I think if we're all agreed we'll add Martin's case to the list of those to be pursued.' He looked around the group for approval, which was unanimous. Dr Jeffers made another note, then looked up again. 'Now, Jack McIntosh — where are you?' A squat-looking man in a leather jacket sitting at the back held his hand up. 'Ah, there you are. Jack, I believe you've put together a new surveillance rota?'

Jack stood and held up a clipboard. 'Aye, and I was up half the night doing it, so I don't want any bloody cry-offs.'

Gentle laughter wafted around the group.

* * *

When they broke for coffee twenty minutes later Murphy found himself standing beside Brian Armstrong. Brian spoke in thoughtful, measured tones, and totally without animation. His skin was powdery dry, his thick hair was completely white; although he said he was retired he was of that generation that would go to the grave wearing a shirt and tie and suit.

'Something like this happens, it takes over your whole life,' Brian said. 'It's not like some new hobby, though. It just eats you up.'

'I know what you mean.'

'I spend all my time thinking about new ways of tracing them, or about new ways of finding evidence or exposing them.'

'I'm in the same boat.'

'And you used to be a cop, so you'll be able to help us with that.'

'Whatever I can do.'

A woman with short blonde hair and the kind of slightly too heavy black eyeliner Murphy had always found attractive, said,

'Excuse me,' and reached between them to pick up a biscuit.

'Ah, pilot biscuits,' said Murphy.

She gave him an odd look. 'I'm sorry?'

'Pilot biscuits. What pilots eat. Wee plain ones.'

He smiled. She just looked at him.

'Sorry,' he said. 'Not so sure about the — you know, the appropriateness of small talk.' She contined to look at him. Murphy extended his hand. 'Sorry, I'm Martin, Martin Murphy.'

'I know. I heard.' She shook his hand, very briefly. 'I'm Andrea,' she said.

'Andrea lost her father to a car-jacker,' Brian told him.

'Brian, please . . . ' Andrea began.

'Sorry,' said Murphy.

'That's three apologies in about thirty seconds,' Andrea noted.

Murphy shrugged, said, 'Sorry,' again. Then: 'What happened to your dad?'

Andrea sighed. 'It's all in the paperwork.'

'I don't have any paperwork.'

'You will. One thing you can guarantee about Confront, there's lots of paperwork. It's not the bad guys who'll bring us down, it's the cost of photocopying.'

Murphy smiled, but Brian gave her a look that said, 'How dare you, that's tantamount

58

to treason.' It killed the conversation, so they stood awkwardly for several moments, like three strangers at the funeral of someone nobody liked.

Then Murphy did his best to revive it. 'So, what do you make of Dr Jeffers?'

'What do we make of him?' Brian asked.

Murphy nodded. 'Yeah. What do you think of him?'

'He founded the group,' said Brian.

'He inspires us,' said Andrea. 'Keeps us focused.'

'It makes such a difference, being able to talk to other people,' said Brian. 'To know that you're not alone.'

Murphy nodded from one to the other. 'Yeah, I can see that. Although . . . ' He left it hanging.

Brian's brow furrowed. 'Although?'

'Well . . . ' And he looked kind of pained.

'Well what?' Andrea asked.

They both drew a little closer. Murphy dropped his voice even lower.

'I hear what you're saying — and yes, he did found the group and I'm sure he is great, but you know . . . we're kind of all in it together, we've actually been there . . . but are you sure he's not just a bit of a do-gooder? You know: 'Let's set up a support group, that'll look good on the old CV, drum up some business as . . . ' '

He stopped because they weren't listening any more. Brian straightened as if he'd been slapped in the face. Andrea's cheeks flushed and she lowered her eyes. Murphy turned slightly, and saw that Dr Jeffers was standing directly behind him. Listening. He reached between them and set his coffee cup down on the table. Then he faced Murphy. He didn't blink as he spoke.

'My wife Olivia was murdered four years ago. She disturbed a burglar. He smashed her head in with a poker.'

Murphy looked at him blankly for several long moments, then said weakly, 'Oh. I'm sorry. I didn't know.'

Dr Jeffers nodded slowly. 'They caught him, he confessed, a trial date was set, then they lost the DNA evidence. He retracted his confession and was released. He's still out there. And *that* is why I set up Confront.' He gave one of those thin-lipped smiles that aren't a smile at all, then turned abruptly away.

Murphy stood awkwardly between Brian and Andrea. Behind them, the other group members were beginning to retake their seats. Brian cleared his throat and then turned to join them.

Andrea said, 'I'll just have another . . . pilot

biscuit.' She picked one up off the plate.

'I should have stuck to the small talk,' said Murphy.

Andrea nodded. 'Small talk's fine,' she said. 'You could do with better jokes, though.' She moved away.

Murphy thought she was probably right. In fact, you could apply it to every aspect of his life. It could all do with better jokes.

* * *

After the meeting, when the others had filed out, he approached Jeffers who remained in his chair at the front, making some notes.

'Dr Jeffers?'

He said, 'Mmm-hmm?' without taking his eyes off his paperwork.

'I — ah — didn't mean anything by . . . '

'Don't worry about it. You're quite right to be suspicious.' Then he did glance up. 'I suppose it goes with the territory. You being a cop — sorry, an ex-cop. It's no bad thing that you're suspicious. If you learn one thing with this group, it's not to take everything you hear as the gospel truth.'

'I'm glad you're taking it like that. I'm not suspicious at all, really. I was just enquiring. But it was . . . well, in bad taste.'

'Nonsense. You weren't to know.' Jeffers took a deep breath, clicked his pen off and closed his folder. 'My wife would have been thirty-three last week. I always promised her that I'd take her to Paris before she was forty. It's not going to happen now.'

'No.'

'What gets to so many of us, Martin, are the ifs, the possibilities, the unfulfilled promises and dreams that have been stolen away.'

'I understand.' He stood there awkwardly, then had a bright idea. 'If it's any consolation, I've been to Paris, and if you ask me, it's over-rated.'

'Thank you, Martin — that's no consolation at all.'

But he smiled with it, and Murphy kind of laughed and gave a little shrug of his shoulders. 'Sorry — my mouth sometimes kind of opens before my brain gets in gear. I think it's those pills, they're making me dopey.'

'We must persevere.'

'Do you mind me asking something?'

'No.' But he was mildly irritated now.

'If you've been through this . . . *trauma* . . . yourself, do you go to a psychiatrist, or do you sit at home and counsel yourself? Or write yourself a prescription?'

'That's none of your business, Martin.'

'I know that.' But still he stood there.

Jeffers looked exasperated. '*What?*'

'It's none of my business if I go to see you as a patient. But I thought the group was all about sharing. Sharing's caring.'

'*Sharing's caring?* Isn't that something they teach in nursery school?'

Murphy shrugged.

'Martin — I don't have a psychiatrist, and I don't sit at home and talk to myself. I have come to an accommodation with my situation that I am reasonably happy with. And Confront helps with that.'

Murphy nodded. 'Thank you. So there's light at the end of the tunnel.'

'Yes, there is.'

'That's good to know.' He left it at that. But he didn't leave. He wandered around the church hall looking at notices pinned to the wall. He straightened a pile of hymn books; he stood in the doorway watching the traffic until Jeffers came out and locked the door behind him.

'Still here?' The psychiatrist asked.

'Still here. Just deciding what to do with myself.'

'You need to get yourself another job.'

'I was thinking that.'

'You'll be fine, Martin. It just takes time.'

63

Jeffers nodded goodbye, then walked off with his briefcase swinging by his side.

★ ★ ★

Murphy found a bar a few hundred yards up the road. He sat in the corner with a pint of Guinness and read a *Sun* someone had left behind. He focused on the entertainment gossip and the sport. It wasn't exactly the newspaper for hard news, but he wanted to avoid whatever there was. He had had enough misery for one day. He was aware of the old warning about mixing business and pleasure, but he wondered if anyone had ever philosophised about the dangers of mixing business and misery.

'Cheer up, mate, you look like you've been to a funeral,' the barman said when he brought him his third pint.

'I just have,' said Murphy.

6

They all gave what time they could. For some, juggling jobs and kids, it was a couple of hours twice a week; for others, like Brian Armstrong, it was four days and four nights. His wife had died the previous year — her heart broken, he said — and he'd retired from his managerial position with an insurance company shortly afterwards, so he could afford the time. Not that it was a case of *affording* the time, as he quickly corrected himself. He was *giving* the time wholeheartedly. In fact, Dr Jeffers thought he was doing too much for the group and had persuaded him to cut back. Now he sat at home waiting to donate his time, which he thought was kind of a waste when he had so much to offer. There was a lot of talk about time, but that tended to happen when you were out on surveillance.

That's what it was. Surveillance. After a fashion.

Murphy had spent more than enough time in cold, stinking cars to know that it rarely aspired to the American movie version of surveillance, all coffee, doughnuts and

65

wisecracks. Especially if you were stuck with someone like Brian Armstrong, sipping lukewarm vegetable soup from a tartan flask while trying to get decent reception for *The Archers*.

'Do you know, I haven't missed more than half a dozen episodes of *The Archers* in twenty-five years?'

'Twenty-five? Wow,' said Murphy.

'It's very relaxing,' Brian said. 'I almost feel like one of the cast.'

'Well, at least you know it *is* a cast. There's some people are convinced *Coronation Street* is real. Whenever they have a villain, and the actor goes out for a drink after work, he always gets women beating him up. I read that in the *Sun*. Our newspaper of record.'

'I can't be having *Coronation Street*,' said Brian.

Murphy nodded.

'Give me Ambridge every day.'

Murphy nodded some more.

'They have their problems, but they're nice problems, mostly. I could live in Ambridge.'

The theme music started, and they settled back to listen and watch Gary Walker's house. Watching Gary Walker's house was like watching paint dry, but enduring *The Archers* was like listening to it dry. Brian tutted and smiled and once he even chuckled.

When Murphy went to light a cigarette Brian gave him a look. Murphy felt like saying, 'It's my fucking car.' But didn't. He also felt like blasting out 'Too Drunk To Fuck' by The Dead Kennedys. But didn't.

The surveillance rota worked in such a way that you could be watching anyone, in any location, with any partner. You always had a partner, that was a rule; it was about mutual support, and it also acted as a deterrent in case you were tempted to take the law into your own hands. However, if you were a new member, and naturally fired up with enthusiasm, you were allowed to spend your first few surveillance sessions concentrating on your own particular Nemesis, mostly to get it out of your system. The only stipulation was that your partner had to be one of the more experienced members of the group who could keep a responsible eye on you. Brian, Murphy acknowledged, had not one but two responsible eyes, he had a responsible nose and mouth, responsible legs and arms and torso; he was, all in all, a thoroughly responsible guy. He bored the pants off Murphy, so it was a relief when on the third night of watching Gary Walker's house Brian went off to brighten someone else's life with the plot machinations of *The Archers* and Murphy got a pleasant young Nigerian called Stephen whose brother had been beaten to death by a gang of skinheads who'd been thrown out of Combat 88 for dragging down its good name. Stephen had been in Confront for three years and was more or less resigned to the fact that he'd never have enough evidence to put any members of the gang away, but he absolutely believed in what Confront stood for and swore he would be a member until his dying day. Or something like that.

* * *

Fred Savage was the only one who had chosen to remain a member of Confront after his personal demon, Malik Ali, was murdered. He ran a newsagent's shop opposite a Thistle hotel off Piccadilly. It was small and cramped and closed at 8 p.m. every night. Murphy wondered if there was much profit in it. Instead of wandering in and buying a paper, Murphy allowed Savage to find him. He stood outside with an *A-Z*, looking extremely puzzled.

'It's Martin, isn't it?'

Savage was standing in his shop doorway. Murphy gave him a confused look. 'I'm sorry?'

'Martin from the meeting — Confront?'

'Yes, but how did you know me?'

'I was at the back. Those first meetings are always confusing — so many new faces to take in. You look like you're lost.'

'I am. I've a job interview — security thing. I phoned this number in the *Standard* and they gave me this street, but now I'm here I can't find it anywhere. I've been up and down half a dozen times. Number 310. I'm starting to think they're taking the piss.' Murphy showed Savage a piece of paper on which he'd earlier written an address.

The other man examined it, and then smiled. 'It's just down there. This road is cut in two by that road, but it continues on the other side. No, I know it doesn't look like it continues, but it does. Honestly.'

Murphy looked doubtful, but said, 'Right, fair enough, if you say so.'

'Do you have time for a cup of coffee?'

Murphy glanced at his watch. 'Well, if it's only over there, sure.' He followed Savage into his shop. It smelled of fresh pastry and tobacco. Savage saw Murphy eyeing the croissants behind the counter, and asked him if he wanted one.

'Nah, I'm on a diet.'

Savage tried to talk him out of it, but Murphy remained resolute. He had turned his life around. He was on the straight and narrow — well, not exactly narrow, or

69

particularly straight, but he had to make a stand somewhere. Draw a line in the sand.

So he sipped his strong black coffee and said, 'Confront is a great idea, isn't it?'

Savage nodded. 'Saved my life,' he said.

'Saved it?'

'In more ways than one.'

'How do you mean?'

'Well, after Dominique died — you know about Dominique?'

Murphy nodded. 'I read about her in the paperwork. Terrible.'

'Thank you. She was the first in our whole family to go to university. She was my pride and joy, you know. Anyway, I was in a really bad state afterwards, really down. My wife — nobody could get me out of it. Then I read about Confront in the paper, just a little mention in one of those *Guardian* articles about the state of the justice system, and I thought I'd go along, just with the tiniest hope that it wasn't the usual bullshit. And it wasn't. It was — well, you know what it was. Is. And it saved me, turned me around. It gave me a goal.'

Savage broke off to serve a customer. When his back was turned Murphy lifted an iced finger from the pastry tray and took a bite from it. He was still chewing when Savage turned back.

'Lead us not into temptation,' said Murphy, holding up what was left of the finger, and wiping crumbs from his lip. 'Sorry, couldn't resist.'

'Don't worry — can't say I blame you. I've to stand beside them all day and I don't always resist. What does the good Lord say? Lead us not into temptation — deliver us from evil. For Thine is the Kingdom, the power and the glory. Amen.' Then he smiled. 'And in case you're wondering, that's the other way I got saved. By the Lord.'

Murphy raised an eyebrow. 'Really?'

'It's not so strange. I saw the light, or was shown how to see the light.'

'Really? Who by?'

'By Dominique, of course.'

'Dom . . . '

'I have a psychic healer. Dominique spoke to me through her. She directed me back to the Lord.'

'Right — I see. Well, each unto their own. I suppose I can kind of see how it fits in with Confront. It's that old eye for an eye, tooth for a tooth thing, isn't it?'

Savage laughed. 'I hadn't really thought of it like that, but I see how you could make that assumption. But no, I'm not into the hell and brimfire stuff, Martin. I believe in forgiveness.'

'So you pursue these people through Confront to *forgive* them?'

'Of course I do. I forgive them, but I also try to make sure that they are brought to justice. That they receive whatever punishment society deems suitable.'

'Is that not a contradiction?'

'I don't believe so.'

'And that's what you'd do if you ever found who killed your daughter? You'd make sure he got sent to jail, but you'd forgive him as well?'

Savage nodded. 'Before I was saved I was a very angry, miserable man. But with the Lord in my life it's just different, you know? Anyway, it's not going to happen. The man who killed my daughter — his name was Malik Ali. Unfortunately, he himself was murdered.'

'Unfortunately? Didn't you jump up and down and cheer?'

'No, Martin. I felt bad for his family. It is a dreadful thing to lose a child.'

Murphy took another sip of his coffee. 'I don't know how this Malik died, but if you'd had the chance, would you really not have done it yourself?'

Savage shook his head. 'Of course not. As the Big Man says, let he who is without sin cast the first stone.'

Murphy nodded at the newsagent over the

rim of his coffee cup. 'Yeah, I take your point. The problem is that there must be a hell of a lot of people out there without sin, because the stones are hailing down like nobody's business.'

'You're right there,' said Savage, with a resigned sigh. 'You're definitely right there.'

And then he offered Murphy another iced finger.

7

On his fifth night on patrol for Confront, and the last on which he would be allowed to practise surveillance on 'his' case, Murphy picked up Andrea from her house, and drove to Gary Walker's. She looked slightly tearful when she got into the car, but he didn't say anything; she'd tell him all about it in her own time. Except she didn't and it was a couple of miles down the road before he ventured, 'You all right, love?'

'I'm fine, and I'm not your love.'

Murphy shrugged and drove on. They parked about a hundred yards from Walker's house. Andrea took a notebook from her bag, opened it to a blank page and wrote the date, the time and the location.

'Don't forget to mention me,' Murphy said.

She didn't write his name. He thought she might later, if anything dramatic happened. Like maybe a light going on in Walker's house. Or his gate swinging in the wind. That's how exciting it had been all week.

'Do you want me to tell you about his MO?' Murphy asked. 'That's *modus* — '

'I know what it is.'

'Well?'

'If you insist.'

'It's not a matter of me insisting, it's about whether you want to know.'

'Why don't you just tell me?'

'Whatever you say.' He made a show of clearing his throat. 'All right, take a note Miss Jones.' But she only scowled at him. He said, 'Did you ever think of lightening up?'

'I'm perfectly *light*.' She raised her pen, just in case he hadn't noticed it. 'Now if you don't mind?'

Murphy smiled to himself, then launched into it. 'It's hookers he goes for. Not your sophisticated call-girl type who take credit cards and fly to the South of France for gigs, but more your tart on the corner with the crack habit. Anyway, he picks them up in his car, drives to some remote location — he says he likes to do it out in the open, so he won't get blood on his seats, you see — and so she asks for extra money. He agrees — he agrees to anything she wants because she's never going to get to keep it. They go somewhere dark and he knifes her. He doesn't screw her first. Or later, for that matter. If he did, we'd probably get some decent DNA on him. DNA stands for — '

'I know what DNA stands for.' She kept

her eyes on the page as she wrote. Murphy strained to see the words, but could make head nor tail of what appeared to be some variety of shorthand.

'Brian and one of the other guys called on the neighbours yesterday, told them who Walker was, what he was up to. They didn't seem unduly concerned. He doesn't have a job as such, so there's nobody to tip off there.'

'Has there been a regular interval between his attacks on these women?'

'You mean is he working to some sort of a timetable?' She nodded. 'Like every time there's a full moon?'

'Don't be facetious,' she snapped.

'I'm not. Some of them really do do it that way. The moon really does affect them like that. It's probably how the old werewolf stories came about. Psychos who feel the pull of the moon. You're not writing any of *this* down.'

She rolled her eyes. After that they sat in silence for another twenty minutes. Murphy turned this way and that in his seat. She sat perfectly still, her eyes focused on Walker's house.

She didn't object when he played 'Too Drunk to Fuck'.

She didn't say anything when he tuned into

a radio documentary on the tribesmen of the Kalahari.

She didn't blink when he flicked halfway through it to the live commentary on Manchester United v Barcelona in the Champions League.

Eventually he said, 'So who do you support?'

A pained expression and: 'Sorry?'

'Which football team?'

She shrugged.

'I support Man U. That's Manchester U — '

'I know what it is.'

He let it sit for another couple of minutes, then he asked: 'Have I done something wrong?'

'Wrong?'

'Wrong. I was just wondering. The cold shoulder and all.'

'You'd know if I was giving you the cold shoulder.' She tore her eyes away from Walker's house. 'Look, I'm here for the same reason you are.'

'What, to meet new women?' He gave her a smile, but she didn't return it. 'You know that movie with Hugh Grant where he joins support groups just to — '

'Look, just stop it, OK?' She turned in her seat. 'Let's just get on with what we're here

77

for, all right? I'm not here to make friends.'

'OK.' He raised his hands in mock surrender. 'I understand.' He drummed his fingers on the steering wheel. He checked his reflection in the mirror. He tried to get the overflowing ash tray out to empty it, but it wouldn't budge. He had been on dozens, maybe hundreds of surveillance ops over the years and never felt this antsy.

'So,' he said. 'Your old man giving you a rough time over this?'

Andrea sighed.

'You know,' he said, 'if you frown like that for much longer you're going to end up with lines on your forehead. Like a ploughed field.'

'I'm not frowning.'

'You mean you always look like that?'

She stopped herself from saying something. She put her pen down and dug her hands into her pockets.

'Do you want me to put the heater on?'

'Yes.'

'Well, I can't. That would mean the engine going on and that would mean lights and exhaust and it's a million to one chance, but he might notice and we don't want that.'

'Then why did you ask?'

'I really don't know. Politeness. Concern for your wellbeing. The usual stuff.'

She blew air out of her cheeks and sighed.

They sat for another fifteen minutes. Another light went on, and then off, in Walker's house.

Murphy walked to a shop on the corner and bought a can of Diet Coke and a Twix. He'd asked her, but she didn't want anything. When he got back he offered her a slurp and she said, 'No, thank you.' Then he offered her a stick of the Twix and she shook her head.

'Are you sure?'

'Yes.'

'You're not just being polite?'

'No.'

'Maybe you would have preferred a Mars bar?'

'No.'

'Or a Turkish Delight? Turkish Delights are ninety-nine per cent fat free. It says so on the wrapper. Or it might be ninety-five.'

She cleared her throat.

Murphy said: 'I say that because I'm on a diet. I'm not insinuating that you need to lose any weight or anything. Because you don't.'

She shifted in her seat. They both watched the house for another while. Murphy said: 'There's Polo mints in the glove compartment.'

Andrea continued to stare straight ahead.

'I'd reach across to get them, but you can't do that these days, can you? Not with a complete stranger. I mean, you're not a complete stranger, not completely. But you know what I mean.'

She waited another minute and then said, 'Do you want me to get you them?'

'If it's not too much trouble.'

She gave him a look and reached forward to open the glove compartment. When she opened it the Polos fell out, together with a photograph. Murphy cursed inwardly. Andrea handed him the sweets. The photo was face up. She only looked at it for a moment before replacing it and closing the compartment.

After another short while she said, 'Is that your son?'

Murphy nodded.

'He looks like you.'

'Balding and overweight?'

'No.'

Murphy shrugged. He offered her a Polo and she surprised him by taking one. She surprised him even further by initiating a conversation. She said: 'If this man Walker had died, would you have been charged with murder?'

'No, I don't think so. Manslaughter maybe.' He smiled to himself. 'Manslaughter — cut it in two and you have man's laughter. I'm sure there's a philosophical point to be made about that, but luckily I have the IQ of a Lambeg drum.'

'A what?'

'A Lambeg drum — you've never heard of a Lambeg drum?'

'I've never heard of a Lambeg drum.'

'Well, it's a huge big drum the Orangemen whack to death on the Twelfth.'

'The Twelfth?'

Murphy looked at her. 'You must know about the Twelfth.'

Andrea shook her head. Then she gave him the smallest smile and said, 'Perhaps ignorance is bliss.'

Either he was growing on her, or the Polo mint was pretty damn sensational.

They sat for another few moments, then he said, 'I kind of put my foot in it with Dr Jeffers the other day.'

'You kind of did.'

'You might have warned me.'

'I might have.'

Murphy smiled. 'I'm seeing him — you know, as a patient. Is that how you started out?'

'In the beginning, yeah.'

'You don't see him any more?'

'Only in group.'

'So he sorted you out?'

'Sorted me?' She gave a short, dismissive

laugh. 'You don't get better from this.'

'I know. I didn't mean . . . I meant, you went as far with him as you could. The group took over. I can see how therapeutic it is, meeting like that; doing this, you get to take your anger out on someone who ruined your life. You get to ruin his, one way or another.'

'Something like that.'

'It was your father, wasn't it?'

Andrea nodded slowly.

'Do you want to talk about it?'

This time she shook her head. So they sat in the dark for another ten minutes, watching the house and listening to the football commentary. But then she surprised him again by starting to talk, her voice low, not much above a whisper; she looked down at her notebook and made nonsense drawings as she spoke. 'He was out Christmas shopping, and he came back to find someone trying to steal his car. He tried to stop them, but they drove straight at him, then dragged him for half a mile. They wouldn't let us see the body for three days. Which is about as long as the driver got.'

'So now you pursue him to the ends of the earth.'

She looked up now, and met his eyes for almost the first time that night. 'Oh no, he's dead.' But before he could respond Andrea stiffened suddenly in her seat and pointed down the street. 'Look,' she hissed. '*Look!*'

For the briefest moment Murphy found it difficult to take his eyes off her. But then he followed her gaze and saw that Gary Walker had emerged from his house and was now backing his car out of his driveway.

'Alrighty,' said Murphy, straightening in his seat and turning the key.

8

Walker drove a blue BMW with the speed and care of someone who's had a few too many drinks, but doesn't want to get pulled over by the cops. Slow, careful, indicating well in advance, the only man in London adhering to the thirty miles an hour speed limit. Tailing him was wee buns to Murphy, but he could almost feel the excitement coming off Andrea. Not that it was manifesting itself by making her jump up and down in her seat and screaming, 'Get him! Get him!' It was an understated kind of excitement: her cheeks were a little flushed, her tongue darted in and out, wetting her lips, she turned her pen over and over in her hands. She crunched that Polo mint, and said things like, 'He's turning,' and 'Not too fast,' when it was obvious he was turning and what sort of an eejit did she think he was? Did she think he was going to draw level with him and peer in to see if he was up to no good? Or honk his horn and tell Walker to get a move on?

Relax.

Take it easy.

Two things he would have said to her

under normal circumstances. Normal as in, she's my girlfriend and we're late for a concert or she's my wife and she's about to give birth, but this wasn't normal, and she wasn't his girlfriend or wife, and he didn't know why he was even thinking that she was, or could be.

'Where do you think he's going?' Andrea asked.

'I don't know.'

'Are you close enough to him?'

'Yes.'

'What if we get stuck at lights?'

'We'll catch him.'

It was late, and the traffic was light enough, so he was pretty sure they would catch him. Certain, in fact.

'Maybe he's going for a Chinese,' he said.

'It's a long way to go for a Chinese.'

'Maybe it's a good Chinese.'

'He's by himself, he's not going for a Chinese.'

'What's wrong with going for a Chinese by yourself? I do it all the time.' She didn't respond, but he was sure that she was thinking: *I'm sure you do.* 'Besides, he could be meeting someone.'

'You mean like a date?'

'Why not?'

'Well, that's not his . . . *modus operandi.*

And not this late.'

Murphy smiled and said, 'It could just be a date, date. He doesn't have to kill her. He may be a murdering bastard, but it doesn't mean every time he pops down to the shops he feels the need to kill someone. He'd never get his shopping done.'

'I don't think he's going for a Chinese,' said Andrea.

She based this on the fact that there weren't any more shops to be seen; they'd entered a solidly industrial area, or what had once been a solidly industrial area. Most of the factories and warehouses were dark and disused; many were fenced off and there were big signs that said *Beware of the Dog* and *Security Patrolled* and *24-Hour Security*, but who was going to spend money guarding a falling-down warehouse or roofless factories? They were just signs to deter the easily deterred. It was a wasteland and the only living things in it came out at night: rats, prostitutes and the men who came for sex.

Walker's car was one of many. Murphy knew the area reasonably well: it was the closest thing this part of London had to a red-light district. There were no neighbours to complain about it, so the cops mostly turned a blind eye. On a good night, or a bad night, depending on your point of view, you could get as many as a hundred hookers plying their trade, which made for a lot of through-traffic. So it wasn't difficult to keep tabs on Walker. He cruised through once, twice, slowing each time, waiting for a girl to approach the car, taking a quick look, but then driving on.

'He knows what he's looking for,' said Murphy.

'What do you mean?' asked Andrea.

'The other girls he killed, they were both Oriental.'

'Oriental?'

Murphy nodded.

Andrea said, 'That's sick.'

'Of course it's sick. Killing anyone is sick.'

'I don't mean that. I mean you and your 'maybe he's going for a Chinese'. *That's* sick.'

Murphy shrugged.

'You shouldn't make jokes about it.'

'I know, you're right. I'm sorry.'

'You don't even mean that, do you?'

'Yes, I do. Kind of.'

Walker turned in the gateway of another disused factory, then headed back out of the industrial zones. 'Mustn't have found what he was looking for.'

'Not what, *who*,' Andrea corrected. 'These are real people.'

She glanced at her watch. Murphy checked

the clock on the dash. It was after eleven.

'What time do you have to be home by?' he asked.

'I don't have to be home by any time.'

'Does your husband lock the door if you're not back by curfew?'

She gave him a look.

Up ahead, Walker turned his car again and began to drive back towards hooker central.

'Ah,' said Murphy, 'he couldn't resist. One last look.'

This time as he cruised through, a small Oriental girl in a white shirt, school tie and tartan miniskirt, tapped on his window.

'Don't do it, don't do it, don't do it,' Andrea said over and over as the girl conducted her negotiations. But evidently satisfied with her fee, she climbed in.

'Shit,' said Andrea, her pitch beginning to rise a little. 'Now what do we do?'

'What are you supposed to do, according to Dr Jeffers and the group?'

'We're supposed to watch, and call the police if there's any evidence of criminal activity.'

'Is there any evidence of criminal activity?'

They were about two hundred yards behind him now; he was slowing as he passed each factory entrance, looking for somewhere they wouldn't be disturbed.

'He has a prostitute in his car, he murders prostitutes.'

'But technically he's not committing any serious offence until he actually murders her.'

'Well, we can't wait for that!'

'No — but neither can we call it in. He hasn't *done* anything.'

'I know, I know.'

Walker had turned into a single-storey warehouse with its gates open and roof mostly caved in. There was an expansive car park surrounding it, and two other exits, which were also lying open. A wreck of a car squatted to the left; on the other side was another vehicle with its headlights off but a faint green glow coming from its dash. Walker drove past this car and out of sight behind the warehouse.

Murphy looked at Andrea. 'What now?'

She opened her handbag and pulled out her mobile. 'We call the police. I don't care about the fucking technicalities.'

Murphy drove through the entrance.

'What are you doing?'

'What does it look like I'm doing?'

'We're not allowed . . . we observe . . . '

'You think I'm going to sit here and let him kill someone else?'

'No, but we can't just — '

'Yes, we can.'

89

She looked at her phone. 'But what about . . . ?'

'We wait for them, they'll just be coming to pick up a body. Very least we can do is put him off. Chase him so he can live to murder another day.'

Murphy turned the headlights off. The moon was out, the stars were bright, there was more than enough light to navigate the grounds of the warehouse without them. They moved forward quietly, slowly, the engine dulled so that they could hear their tyres crunching over the gravel. The building was several hundred metres long. There were a number of gaps in the wall where the brickwork had collapsed, but there was little to see inside, apart from more decay. As they rolled along, an odd shaft of moonlight reflected off a puddle or lingered on broken glass.

Murphy eased the car up to the corner, then inched it forward. About a hundred metres away, along the back wall of the warehouse, they saw Walker's car. The lights were off.

'What do we do?' Andrea whispered. 'Just use your horn, scare them off?'

Murphy shook his head. 'He's not in the car.'

'How can you tell?'

'I can tell.'

'What makes you so bloody sure?'

He rolled their car right up beside Walker's, and he could feel Andrea tense beside him.

'Martin, don't . . . please!'

'It's OK.'

The car was empty.

'I told you he likes to do it al fresco.'

'Martin, please, just use the horn. Wherever he is it'll frighten him off.'

Murphy shook his head. The car moved forward again. Behind the main warehouse there were a dozen long Nissen-style huts with curved corrugated iron roofs; some of them bore trade signs, as if the failing industrial park had rented them out to small businesses in a last-ditch attempt to claw back some money, but these too had failed and were now lying just as vacant.

'Christ, Martin, he could be up behind any of those. Just use your fucking horn, OK?'

But he kept driving.

Andrea suddenly reached forward, intent on blasting the horn herself, but he caught her by the wrist, and squeezed hard.

'My car,' he hissed. 'You keep off the fucking horn!'

She looked stunned. He let go of her wrist, but pushed her arm back away from the steering wheel.

'Martin? You can't just let him — '

'I don't intend to.'

Her mouth dropped open slightly. 'What are you going to do?'

'What do you *think* I'm going to do?'

'Martin, please. You're scaring me.'

'Just be quiet, will you?' As he piloted the car along the narrow strip he peered into the alleys between the huts, searching for some telltale sign.

'He could be anywhere, Martin. Please don't do this!'

'I know what I'm doing.'

Then, four huts along, he caught the merest glimpse of the prostitute's shirt, brilliant white, caught in a security light set to pick up any movement within a certain radius but which blinked on from the fenced-off property behind the huts. Murphy turned into the gap between the huts, which was just wide enough to take his car, then cut the engine. He reached into the back seat, shifted a couple of newspapers and curled his fingers around the claw hammer he'd put there earlier.

When she saw it, Andrea's hands went to her face. 'Murphy — no.'

'There's no other way. Just wait here. Lock the doors.' He climbed out of the car.

'Murphy . . . '

He closed the door as gently as he could, then began to walk up the alley; he heard the soft click of the car doors behind him as Andrea locked herself in. He was wearing Reebok sneakers. He walked silently *and* comfortably. He got to the end of the first hut, then stopped dead and listened: faraway sounds of traffic, an aircraft, the distant hum of a generator. Then a man's voice — gruff, commanding, close at hand but still difficult to pinpoint. He stood, listening, trying to get the direction. Then the girl's voice. Negotiating, she was still negotiating. She laughed. Murphy turned to his left and hurried forward. This alley was both narrower and more thickly overgrown, but the tramped-down grass showed him exactly where Walker and the girl had gone.

There.

Barely a dozen metres away.

The door to the hut was off its hinges and lay flat and moss-covered in the grass. He could hear their voices. He crept closer, closer . . . and then froze as a car horn was suddenly blasted from somewhere behind him.

But not just *somewhere*. Andrea.

It sounded again and again and again.

Then there was a figure in the doorway and curses coming from the hooker. The figure darted out, turned in Murphy's direction and then stopped suddenly.

'Evening all,' Murphy said.

It was Walker all right. For the briefest moment they stared at each other, and then Walker twisted on his heels and took off at speed in the opposite direction.

Murphy hesitated for just a moment, shouting into the doorway: 'Are you all right, love?'

'Fuck off!'

And then he gave chase.

9

Andrea was still blasting the horn when the prostitute came stumbling out of the darkness, her sudden appearance enough of a shock to freeze her hand over the horn. Wild thoughts rushed through her mind. *Christ, he's killed Murphy and he's chasing her! What have I done! She's leading him right to me! He'll kill us both!* She lunged across to make sure that her door really was locked, completely aware of what a pathetic gesture it was.

He'll smash the windows in!

But she had to do something. She looked at her ballpoint pen. Her only weapon. Her only defence!

What am I doing here? What the fuck am I doing here!

But then she saw that the prostitute wasn't stumbling because she was being chased or was hurt, but because she was missing one of her shoes. She stopped at the end of the alley and looked at the car, which she clearly realised hadn't been there a few minutes ago. She slipped off her other shoe and moved, evenly balanced now, towards it.

Andrea cautiously unlocked her door and stepped out of the vehicle. 'Are you OK?' she called.

'No, I'm not fucking OK,' the prostitute snarled. 'Fucker made me lose my shoe.'

Braver now, Andrea, hurried up, full of concern. 'But he didn't hurt you?'

'No, and he didn't *fuck* me either and I left the soddin' money in his car.'

Even in the poor light Andrea could see that she was a lot older than she dressed, her skin was pock-marked and distressed, her hair tangled and matted. Murphy was right. It wasn't the high end of the market Walker went for.

Not that it matters.

'Get into the car,' said Andrea. 'We'll take you to the police.'

The prostitute looked surprised. 'You're not the police?'

Andrea shook her head. 'We're just here to help.'

'Help?' The woman looked incredulous. 'You fucking chased him off, you fucking moron.' She began to walk in her brown school stockings past Andrea. 'He's fucking run off because of your fucking horn.'

As she brushed past, Andrea instinctively reached out to her. 'I need you to make a statement. It'll help, believe me. You've no idea who he is.'

'And I don't give a fuck.' She punched Andrea hard, full on the mouth, with her free hand, splitting her lip. Andrea released her arm and stumbled away, her hands going to her face. The prostitute rubbed at her own knuckles, cursed some more and then disappeared back into the darkness.

* * *

Walker had the head start, but it wasn't as if there was any doubt about where he was running to. He wasn't going to leave his car out here in the middle of nowhere for the cops to pick up or for someone to steal or for kids to vandalise, so whatever circuitous route he took, it was pretty clear where he was going to end up. And he'd started off in the wrong direction. So Murphy jogged easily back the way he'd come, and was standing with his arms folded, resting against the bonnet of the blue BMW when Walker came puffing out of the darkness towards it a couple of minutes later.

Murphy didn't move.

Walker approached the back of the vehicle, breathing hard, and put his hands on the boot to steady himself.

'So this is how it ends,' he said.

'This isn't the end, it's not even the beginning of the end.'

'Somebody should be writing this down,' said Walker. Then he smiled, came forward and extended his hand. Murphy grasped it, and they shook.

'Everything all right?' Murphy asked.

'Great — fine — thought I'd lost you for a moment in there.'

'Howse Jeanie?'

'She's a great little actress. She should go on the stage.'

'Better pay, that's for sure.'

'I never see you down the office, Murphy.'

'Ah, you know me, I'm always away working somewhere.'

'Don't know how you stick it.'

'Ah, you get used to it.'

Walker was still breathing hard. 'Christ,' he said, 'I'm not getting any younger.'

'You should join a gym. Or get an exercise bike, that's what I have. I did twenty-five kilometres this morning, and I didn't knock my ash tray over once.'

Walker straightened, took another deep breath. 'Talking of exercise, do you have a fag on you?'

Murphy shook his head. He pushed himself off the bonnet. 'How's the wife?'

'She's great. She's going back to college.

Doing a Psychology course. Haven't a fucking clue what she's talking about half the time.'

'Well, tell her I was asking for her.'

'You should come to dinner.'

'Yeah, I will.'

'You always say that.'

'Yeah, I know.' He smiled. Walker smiled. Murphy raised his chin. 'Well, make it good.'

Walker squared up in front of him. He bunched a fist and said, 'This is going to hurt me a lot more than you.'

'Aye, bollocks,' said Murphy. 'Just try and — '

Walker smacked him, hard.

Murphy reeled away, clutching his nose. 'Jesus fuck!' he groaned.

'Are you OK?'

'No, I'm not fucking OK! My chin, my fucking chin!' Murphy examined his hands; they were full of blood. He wiped them on the sleeve of his jacket and pinched the broken knot on his nose. 'You were meant to do my chin.'

'You moved!'

'I didn't move! I wasn't ready!'

'Well, what's the difference — your chin, your nose . . . ?'

'The difference is my chin would have recovered, my nose could be fucking bent out of shape.'

'Have you considered that it might be an improvement?'

'Oh, fuck off.'

'Here.' Walker came forward with a tissue. Murphy took it. 'I better get going.'

'OK. Say hello to Jackie.'

'Will do.'

'And thanks for this.'

'Forget it. I can do with the overtime.'

Walker climbed into his car, reversed, and then made a point of squealing the tyres as he drove off.

★ ★ ★

Andrea, crying and hugging herself, let out an involuntary yell as the figure loomed out of the darkness. As it tried the door she squeezed herself down as small as she could — and then it was Murphy's face looking in at her and she breathed a sigh of relief, although even that hurt, the warm air on her split lip. She reached across and pulled the button up and he tumbled, cursing to himself, into the driver's seat.

'Oh thank God, oh thank God!' she said. 'Are you all right? I was scared to death!' He just nodded at first, and she thought he was just sweating from pursuing or fighting or even killing Walker, but now she could see

100

that it was blood dripping onto the seat, squeezing out from between the fingers of the cupped hand he held to his nose.

'Jesus, Murphy, what have you done?'

'What have *I* done?' Murphy spat, incredulous. 'What has *he* fucking done?'

'Is he . . . ? Did you kill him?'

Murphy shook his head. 'No. We had a bit of a fight, he got my fucking hammer off me, but he took off and I lost him.' He sighed and looked down at his own fingers, sticking together. 'Maybe if we're lucky I've given him enough of a fright to . . . ' He looked at her for the first time, and realised that she too was bleeding. 'Christ,' he said, reaching out to her and raising her chin gently. 'What happened?'

'The girl, the prostitute . . . well, she wasn't very appreciative.'

'Jesus, you shouldn't have tried to interfere.'

Andrea abruptly burst into tears. He went to give her a hug but she raised her hands to ward him off; then she couldn't stop herself from crying even harder and when he tried to hug her again she didn't resist. She shook against him, great shudders. 'I was so frightened,' she blubbered. 'I shouldn't have used the horn.'

'It's OK.' He rubbed her back.

After a while it became awkward, and she

pushed herself away. She opened her handbag and gave him a fresh tissue and kept one for herself. He took his tissue and dabbed carefully at her lip. She took her tissue and wiped carefully at his nose.

'Christ,' he said. 'This is like *Casualty* on a really low budget.'

She smiled, but that hurt, and he laughed as she winced, which made her laugh, and wince, some more.

$$\star \quad \star \quad \star$$

A mile away, Walker stopped and picked up the hooker. Her stockings were torn and he was the third car to stop for her in ten minutes.

'Well, thank Christ for that,' she said, pulling off her wig.

'I was going to say 'Well done, you're a pro,' but you know what I mean.'

She lit a cigarette and said, 'There's got to be better ways to earn a living.'

'I know. And now all we have to do is type up a report.'

'Thanks for that. The final nail in the coffin.' But she smiled and said, 'Everything OK?'

His knuckles were slightly bruised and there was a splash of blood on his shirt, but yes, everything was OK.

10

Lawrence Sinclair was out in the back garden, refreshing the dogs' water, when he heard the car pull into the driveway. A few moments later, the front door slammed. Great, he thought, wake the neighbours. Although the barking of the greyhounds was probably doing that anyway, this didn't occur to Lawrence. He wasn't a happy man. He glanced at his watch — a quarter past midnight. She was getting later.

It had crossed his mind on more than one occasion that Andrea might not be going out on patrol with Confront at all, but having an affair. Or going out on patrol *and* having an affair. It stood to reason. Sitting in a car for hours at a time. Bored watching a house. You'd get talking about things. Your life. Your problems. Maybe she would start crying — she seemed to be crying all the time these days. So perhaps there'd be a sympathetic hug and then a kiss. Or they would just joke together the way strangers can, the way married couples have forgotten to, because they know each other inside out. So maybe they'd discover a shared sense of humour and, of course, a shared trauma. She would say, 'I love my husband, but . . . ' and then rhyme off what was going wrong. And he would say, 'You shouldn't live like that if you're not happy.' And then he'd tell her about his unsatisfactory life, how his wife was always complaining or nagging or what she wouldn't or couldn't do for him or what he couldn't or wouldn't provide and how it had all gone wrong since their father or brother or mother or daughter had been murdered. And she would say, 'I know, I *know*.'

Lawrence had imagined a thousand ways in which it might happen. And at least part of the reason things were so frosty in the house was that he suspected her of infidelity but had not confronted her; and she hadn't a clue that he thought that way. He spent longer looking after the dogs — they needed a lot of walking anyway, but when he wasn't doing that he had them at the stadium or he went to the bar down there and had a drink with his mates, anything to get away from the atmosphere in the house. And yet — as soon as he was gone, he missed her. And sometimes he raced home to try to catch her out with her lover.

But he never caught her.

He looked for evidence, but there was none. No tousled, sweaty hair, no whiff of aftershave, no guilty looks or blushing at inopportune moments. Not even a semi-naked lover in the wardrobe, like in one of those ridiculous *Confessions* films he'd sneaked into as a teenager.

Lawrence was having the kind of thoughts a man with a beautiful wife has when he hasn't had sex with her in a long time.

He lingered over the dogs. People who didn't know greyhounds thought they were snappy creatures, but Lawrence loved them and he'd never been bitten once. Other owners thought he doted on them too much — 'That's why they don't win, Lawrence. Treat 'em mean, keep 'em keen.' And he was so paranoid he thought maybe they were referring to his wife as well.

Lawrence glanced back up at the house. Normally she came straight in and put the kettle on, but the kitchen light was still off. Lawrence had entered the garden through the garage, leaving that light on so that it was bright enough to sort out the dogs. Maybe she'd gone straight to bed, hammered up those stairs in a fury the way she did sometimes. He waited for another couple of minutes to see if the bathroom or bedroom lights went on, but no. And then he realised that she hadn't taken their car, that one of the group had picked her up — and now they were back and the car must still be there because he hadn't heard it drive off. So she'd brought him in.

He knew it was a *him*. She'd told him about the new guy over dinner — no detail, *just some new guy* in her bored voice.

And now he's inside, Lawrence thought. Maybe she thinks I'm out at the stadium. She's inviting him in to . . . But no — he'd told her he wasn't going out. There was football on, he was planning to watch that.

But still. Lawrence gave the dogs a final petting, then hurried across to the garage. He switched off the light and locked up, then stepped back into the hall. He could hear their voices now — they were in the lounge. Andrea's voice and someone with a bit of a brogue, Irish or Scottish, he wasn't quite sure. The door was half-closed.

Right.

Lawrence strode up to the door and pushed it open. They were sitting together on the sofa, facing each other. She already had a bottle of whisky out and had poured drinks which sat by their feet.

'What the hell do you think you're doing?'

Andrea didn't spring back, like she was caught out or embarrassed; she merely bent around the man, and looked at Lawrence. So did the man. He'd a short leather jacket on, and was kind of stocky — but Lawrence only really had eyes for Andrea, dark, accusing eyes — but then he saw that there was blood on her chin and her lip was bulging.

'Andrea?' He hurried forward. The man sat back. 'Oh, my God.'

'Don't panic, Lawrence. It's not as bad as it looks.'

'What happened?' He knelt beside her and looked closer. He reached up to touch but she flinched.

'Don't . . . now look what you've done.' He'd knocked over her drink.

'Sorry, sorry. For fuck sake, Andrea, forget the drink! What the hell is going on?'

The other man picked up the glass. 'I'll get you another,' he said, and he walked over to the sideboard and started to pour her one. Then he said, 'Do you want one?' to Lawrence, like he owned the fucking house.

'No! I don't fucking want one!' Andrea was looking away again, but he pulled her back and said firmly, 'Tell me what happened.'

His wife glanced beyond him at the guy pouring the drinks, then back to Lawrence before saying: 'We were following one of the — you know, bad guys — and he picked up this prostitute and he was going to kill her so we had to do something. I pressed the hooter to scare him off and Martin went after him.

He got his nose half-broken.'

'What happened to *you*, Andrea?'

'I'm telling you, it's nothing. The *hooker* didn't realise what danger she was in: she thought we were just losing her business. So she slapped me. It's *all right*, Lawrence.'

'It's *not* all right, it's not all right at all.' He turned to this Martin guy, who was now holding two drinks. 'What do you think you're playing at, putting her in danger like that? She could have been killed!'

'Lawrence!'

'No, no,' Martin said. 'He's right — you're right, it *was* stupid.' He came forward, handed one of the drinks to Lawrence, even though he'd made it clear he didn't want one. 'I don't know what I was thinking. Lawrence . . . is it all right if I call you that?' He didn't wait for a response. 'I used to be a cop, you see. It was just my natural instinct to go after him. I shouldn't have left Andrea alone. It won't happen again.'

'Too fucking right it won't.' He was up on his feet now, glaring at Murphy.

'Lawrence — just stop it!' Andrea was up and off the sofa; she pushed him back. She took the other drink off Murphy and knocked it back in one, wincing as the glass touched her lip and then coughing as the whisky hit the back of her throat. 'Look,' she said, 'you just need to *calm down*.'

Her husband continued to glare.

Murphy said: 'Maybe I should go home.'

Lawrence looked from one to the other. *What was the point? What was the fucking point? She never listened to a word he said.*

'Fuck it,' he said. 'I'm putting the kettle on.'

He walked out of the room and into the kitchen, where he filled the kettle. While he waited for it to boil he looked out of the kitchen window but saw his own reflection. He raised his hands, which were bunched into fists, and examined the white knuckles. Then he punched the white Formica counter top once, hard.

★ ★ ★

'I should go.'

'No, stay.'

'You've things to talk about.'

'I know, and I don't want to.'

'You should explain to him.'

'I don't have to explain anything, not when he's in that kind of mood.'

'His wife's just come home beat up, and with another man.'

'I'm not with another man. I'm with you.'

'Thanks.'

She smiled. 'I mean, it's business — he knows it's business. He knows how committed I am; he's no right to get worked up like that. I'm sorry.'

'Not your fault. Not his, either. I really should go home now.'

'Just get me another drink, would you? Then sit down. He's going to be huffing out there all night.'

'Maybe I should go and speak to him.'

'Just leave him.'

'But what if he — '

'Leave him. Christ, it's been bad enough tonight without him throwing a wobbler.'

'He's worried about you.'

'He's got a funny way of showing it.'

Murphy fetched the drink. He could hear Lawrence banging about the kitchen. Cupboard doors slammed. Then, after a while, it went quiet.

'Put some music on,' said Andrea. Her voice was slightly slurred already.

'I'm not putting music on. Be like a red rag to a bull.'

'He's not a bull.'

'You know what I mean.'

'He's a big child.' Then she shouted: 'Do you hear that, Lawrence? You're a big child!'

But there was no response.

Andrea drank four glasses of whisky in the

next hour, and they weren't small ones. She talked and talked and talked about what had happened and how scared she'd been, she analysed and debated and scolded herself, and then Murphy, getting drunker and drunker all the time. Why had he left her? Why had he put his life at risk? What had it felt like to be face to face with Walker? What were they going to tell Confront? What would Jeffers say? A hundred slurred questions. Then she fell asleep on the sofa.

Murphy found a rug to put over her, then walked through the house, looking for Lawrence. It was a nice house, extremely neat and tidy. There were a few framed photos of the pair of them sitting about, clearly taken on holiday together, but they looked a lot younger. There was no evidence of children. The kitchen was spacious and smelled mildly of dog food and strongly of air freshener. Murphy, with his glass re-filled and still in his hand, spotted Lawrence in the back garden, leaning over some kind of wire-mesh enclosure. He saw movement within it, but it wasn't until he stepped down onto the grass that he saw they were greyhounds. Three of them, snarling, yapping. But not at Lawrence. Lawrence looked round and saw him, then returned his attention to the dogs.

'She's sleeping,' Murphy said.

Lawrence nodded, but continued to focus his attention on the dogs.

'I never had a greyhound,' said Murphy, coming up close to the fence. 'Jack Russell for a long time.' Still no reaction. 'I often wondered about greyhounds. You know that old stereotype thing about black guys, how they're all really well hung and that, and I don't know, maybe it's true, but they can't all be . . . do you know what I mean? There's some black guys must have really small . . . '

Lawrence was looking at him now, all right. 'Why are you talking about black cocks?' he asked.

'I'm not. What I mean is, is it the same with greyhounds?'

'That they have big cocks?'

'No. I mean, everyone says, about humans or anything that goes fast, that *he runs like a greyhound*. I was just wondering you know, if . . . as a breed they're pretty fast, but there must be lots of greyhounds that are slow as well, that aren't anything special. That get puffed out when they run more than a few yards, overtaken and sneered at by poodles.'

Lawrence nodded slowly — and then abruptly burst into laughter. 'I have never heard so much shit talk in all my life. How many drinks have you had?'

Murphy laughed as well then and drained his glass. 'Too many,' he said.

Lawrence shook his head. He nuzzled one of the greyhounds through the mesh. 'I'm . . . ' he began, then stopped, thought about it for another few moments, then continued. 'I'm sorry for losing my rag. I just worry about her. That was a brave thing you did, going after him like that.'

'It wasn't brave. It was stupid. He was armed — I just had an old hammer. It was just autopilot. And you're right — I shouldn't have done it with Andrea there. If he'd killed me he could have killed her as well. It won't happen again.'

Lawrence moved along the cage, making little kissing sounds to the dogs. Murphy followed.

'You don't approve of her going to Confront, do you?'

Lawrence hesitated for a moment, then glanced back at Murphy. 'You're new, aren't you? What do you make of it?' he asked.

Murphy shrugged. 'Don't know. Early days yet. Only really been to one meeting.'

'Yeah. Well. One's enough.'

'You didn't take to it?'

Lawrence shook his head. 'Each unto their

own, but if you ask me, it's just a glorified talking shop, isn't it? You can call it Confront and you can go and ask for people's signatures on a bloody petition, you can cause these guys to lose their jobs, but you're not actually confronting, are you? What you did tonight . . . *that's* confronting.'

'Well, it's something. Basically you're saying you don't object to me doing it, but you'd rather I didn't do it while your wife was around.'

Lawrence answered slowly. 'Something like that.' He tutted. 'It's just — well, you know about her dad, don't you?' Murphy nodded. 'When the guy died, the guy what done it, I thought she'd stop going. But no, she's still out there every night, her own personal bloody crusade.' He straightened from the cages and winced at a twinge from his back.

'What happened to the guy?' Murphy asked.

'He got knocked down, didn't he?'

'Ironic, that.'

'Yeah, well, I'm a great believer in what goes around comes around. Anyway, I'm not complaining.' Lawrence rubbed at his back, then turned and started to walk back towards the house. Murphy stood there awkwardly while the dogs snarled at the wire. Then Lawrence turned from the doorway. 'Do you want a refill or not?' he asked.

'OK,' said Murphy.

★ ★ ★

'You're too drunk to drive,' said Lawrence.

'I'm too drunk to *walk*,' corrected Murphy. Nevertheless, the car was there in the driveway and he had his keys in his hand. 'I will go by back roads and minor roads, and some footpaths and gardens. The police will never catch me.'

'Leave it here and get a taxi.'

'No, I'm fine, honestly.'

'You've had the best part of a bottle of whisky.'

'Every part is the best part. And so have you.'

'But I'm just going upstairs to bed.'

'And so am I. Albeit in my own house. I'll be fine. Go to bed. And don't forget to take your wife.'

'I'll try not to.'

Murphy staggered down the driveway, fumbled with his keys, and eventually got into the car. Lawrence leaned against the driver's door and said, 'You're mad.'

'I'll be fine. Just point me in the right direction.'

'Well . . . ' He stood, and raised his hand.

'If you go down here and turn . . . '

'Got it,' said Murphy. 'I'll just follow the road until it stops. Follow the yellow brick road.' And then he began to sing, 'Follow, follow . . . we will follow Rangers.' Then he laughed. 'You a Rangers or a Celtic man, Lawrence?'

'Not really bothered.'

'That's good. That's good. I'm a Celtic man. Celtic through and through.'

He winked and drove off at a snail's pace. When he got to the corner he gunned the engine for a joke, then waved back at Lawrence, still standing in his drive. Then he drove on, out of sight, out of his mind.

11

Murphy ate breakfast in McDonald's, first one in the restaurant, still drunk, then went home and sat on his exercise bike for an hour. More accurately, he fell asleep on his exercise bike, facing the TV. The last thing he was vaguely aware of was his legs becoming heavier and heavier, and Kylie Minogue's 'Can't Get You Out of My Head' seeming to last for a very long time on VH1. He had previously placed his exercise bike in front of the TV, and side-on to the CD player. He had also taped a Velcro strip to the handlebars and attached the remote controls for both so he could alternate between them. Or, as he seemed to recall, waking stiff, his neck aching, slumped over the handlebars and drooling on the carpet, he'd actually been listening to The Undertones' greatest hits but watching Kylie on the screen, which seemed like a fair compromise drunk or sober.

When he checked his watch, with the sun penetrating the curtains, it was nearly ten. He crawled into bed for some proper lie-down sleep. But it wouldn't come. He tossed and turned for a couple of hours, then got up and shaved and showered and dressed, then picked up his acoustic guitar and tried to write something, but there was nothing there. Once there had hardly been a day that went past without him composing something — lyrics, a tune, a pop song, a rock anthem, a torch song, a country weepy. There wasn't much he hadn't turned his hand to — apart from rap; he was too old and too white for that. He'd even had a stab at a rock opera about Jack the Ripper — spent two weeks between cases closeted away, really getting excited about what he was doing, then he'd popped down to the shops one lunchtime and picked up a paper and there in the Arts Section was a review of a new West End show called *Rip Her To Shreds* which was all about Jack the Ripper. The review said the show was on a hiding to nothing because the same territory had been covered first, and better, by something called *Sweeney Todd, The Demon Barber of Fleet Street*. What hope was there then for a third take on it? It didn't exactly break his heart, but it really pissed him off and he hadn't written anything of substance since. Or ever, as he reminded himself.

Murphy put his guitar back in the wardrobe in his bedroom.

He spent an hour going over the files on

Confront, but didn't really focus. He found himself thinking about Andrea and how she was quite hard work, but there was something about her he found intriguing. And then he laughed to himself. *Yeah, intriguing — like that's what I go for in someone: I fancy a bit of* intrigue *tonight.* No, what he liked about her was that she was attractive without being intimidatingly so. That she seemed to wear her emotions on her sleeve. That she seemed to be her own boss. He wondered how she'd ever ended up with someone like Lawrence. They were probably childhood sweethearts. He was the tough on the block, big balls and big dreams, she was a few years younger, easily impressed, easily moulded. Married within a year. Marry in haste, repent at leisure. They probably didn't have sex any more. Or once a month. On a Saturday night after the pub. She would probably give him all the gory details in the coming days and weeks as McIntosh's rota threw them together.

He wondered what he would tell her about himself. That was how it worked, wasn't it? An exchange of information. Shared confidences. She would bare her soul, and he would make shit up.

That was his job. Or his game? He was never quite sure.

Usually his life depended on everything in his background being absolutely verifiable, and he had a back-up team to make sure it was. But within the definite facts he allowed himself a licence to bullshit, because you had to, you had to adapt to any given situation. With Lawrence, for example, he could have said he was really into greyhounds and then instructed Carter to turn up everything he could on the bloody dogs: history of, profile of English and Irish greyhound stadiums, the top dogs, the betting, and useful bits of trivia like the fact that greyhounds have been around for thousands of years, they were even mentioned in the Bible (Proverbs xxx verses 29 and 31) — that was one of Lawrence's gems. But it was a lot of trouble to go to, and it might be for no reason at all. Lawrence wasn't even in Confront, and Andrea didn't seem the type to pick up a gun and wreak havoc. So he'd merely said he used to have a Jack Russell, which made him a dog-guy, and he'd shown enough interest in the skinny snidey little savages in Lawrence's cages for the other man to invite him down to the races because greyhound fancying was a dying art and Murphy guessed he was the type to jump on anyone who showed the remotest interest. So he'd said, 'Yeah, that would be great, Lawrence. Maybe I'll end up buying a couple,' and Lawrence had said: 'Maybe I'll end up selling you a couple.'

'Maybe I'll see how they run first.'

'They'll be more expensive if they win.'

'And cheaper if they lose.'

'Tell you what, we'll split the difference.'

'You'd really sell your dogs?'

'Sell and buy better ones.'

'So they're not really that good.'

'Didn't say that. But there's always better ones. Like if I owned Spurs, and I love Spurs, and they're in the Premier League and all, but if I had the money to buy Arsenal, I'd buy them because they're going to win things. Who do you support, Martin?'

And if he'd been telling either the truth or been trying to get in with Lawrence he would have said, 'Oh yeah, I'm a Spurs man too,' but he said, 'When I moved over here first I ended up in Charlton. So Charlton.'

Lawrence had laughed, and taken the piss, so now they were football buddies as well.

It was easy, making friends, Murphy thought. Easy when you were paid to do it and you were on a case, but he could count his real friends on the thumbs of one hand.

McBride. *Father* McBride.

Once, a long time before, they'd been in a punk band in Belfast together. The

Co-ordinates. One became a cop, the other a priest, and they lost touch. Then they'd hooked up twenty years later in London. The priest had lost a lot of hair, his stomach was hanging over his belt, and he was struggling with celibacy. We might be mirror images of each other, Murphy thought.

Christ, he really was on a bit of a downer.

He tried to think of the last time he'd spoken to his best friend. At least three months ago.

How many messages had McBride left for him? At least a dozen.

He lifted the phone and called him. He wasn't in; he tried his mobile.

The priest answered on the second ring with a pained, 'Yes?'

'Father, top of the morning to you.'

'Who is this?'

'Me. Murphy.'

'I can't talk right now.'

'Can't talk or won't talk?'

'What?'

'You're huffing, aren't you, because you left messages and I never got back to you. I've been away on a job. I couldn't call. It was very hush hush.'

'I'm not huffing, Murphy.'

'Well, what's the big fucking problem then? Why the brush-off?'

'It's not the brush-off, Murphy, I'm just busy.'

'Oh yeah? What's so fucking important?'

'I'm giving someone the last rites.'

'Oh.'

'I'll call you later.'

'OK.'

'Murphy?'

'What?'

'Sucker.'

McBride cut the line. Murphy cursed. He tried calling him back, but his mobile was now switched off. 'Bastard,' Murphy said to himself, but then laughed. He went back to bed, he set the alarm for 7 p.m., and this time he got over. He dreamed about the usual stuff and woke in a sweat, with what was left of his hair dank against his head. He watched the alarm tick up to bingo then hit it on the first ring.

After his shower he went to the wardrobe and picked out the flashiest suit he had. He supposed it was quite out of fashion now, but when he'd bought it three years ago it had been the coolest thing on the block. He knew this because the man who designed it told him so, and also gave him a couple of hundred off it. He would have given it to him free as a thank you for the undercover work he'd been doing in their West End shop, but cops weren't allowed to accept gifts, not officially anyway. So instead he'd popped in a few weeks later and been fitted for the suit and enquired about discount for cash. 'Would fifty per cent be all right, sir?'

'It certainly would.'

His wife had often begged him to buy a nice suit but he had resisted because of the expense. She'd said, 'A nice suit pays for itself.'

He hadn't understood what she meant then, but he did now. A good suit, cut right, covered up a multitude of sins and now, looking at himself in the mirror in the bedroom, he appreciated that at least he didn't look like as much of a fat bastard as he felt.

He winked at himself. All dressed up like a dog's dinner.

Which was apt. Not for the first time in his life, Murphy was going to the dogs.

12

Murphy spotted Lawrence early on in the evening, but stayed well clear. Instead he placed a series of losing bets through the Tote and drank a couple of pints in Laurie Panthers — named after the Derby winner's owner, don't you know? — the busiest of Romford Greyhound Stadium's bars. Although it had clearly had a make-over in recent years and was a bit too clinical for his liking, the same couldn't be said of the clientèle. They were rough and ready, what some might call the salt of the earth, but to Murphy they looked more like *Crimewatch*'s greatest hits. This was probably laying it on a bit thick, but there were at least five faces he recognised, all from the lower end of the criminal food chain. For once it didn't matter if they recognised him either — he was an ex-cop now. Wouldn't stop him getting a hiding, mind.

As the punters drifted outside for the fourth of the evening's six races, Murphy kept an eye on Lawrence. One of his dogs was entered in the final race — name of Aladdin Slane — but he clearly had money riding on this one as well. He seemed to be a different man here — louder, friendlier; he did a lot of hugging and cheek-pinching. He laughed uproariously at his friends' jokes, he punched arms and bought rounds of drinks. Lawrence was a man of the people, in the midst of his people. Perfectly at home. He shouted encouragement at the top of his voice right from the start of the race, and if the volume couldn't get any higher, the pitch could. He jumped, he roared, he clapped and eventually he groaned and cursed, flamboyantly tearing up his betting slip and throwing the pieces into the air. Then he laughed along with his friends and turned back into the bar. They ordered a fresh round and started analysing the race in a raucous take-the-piss manner. Murphy stood with his drink at the other end of the counter, with his back to Lawrence, but was still able to keep an eye on him in the bar mirror.

He was half-watching Lawrence, half-trying to catch the barman's attention, when a six foot plus black guy with close-cropped hair pushed in beside him. Murphy nodded but the guy just stared at him. So Murphy ignored him and held a finger up in a failed attempt to attract a drink. He thought he had him when the barman came down towards him, but he ignored Murphy and

126

looked at the black guy.

'Same again,' the black guy said. While the barman got him a pint, the black guy stared down at Murphy. Murphy kept his eyes on the barman, but he could feel the eyes burning into him. Did he know him from somewhere? Had he put him away once? Was he going to have to get into a scrap here in the bar? Maybe he should — maybe that would impress Lawrence. Wasn't that what he was doing, after all, getting close?

Then the black guy said, 'I hear you're into big black cocks.'

Murphy turned slowly. He looked up. The man's face was set like basalt. He could have given Frank Bruno lessons in deportment.

Murphy said: 'They don't have to be big.'

The guy moved a little closer, bent down so that his face was on the same level. Murphy's fingers tightened around his glass. He wasn't exactly a master of unarmed combat, but he could handle himself better than most. However, he was worried that if he smacked *this* guy in the jaw he would probably break his hand. But a pint glass would do nicely. You couldn't argue with a pint glass. Well you could, but you'd lose.

The black guy was close enough for Murphy to smell his breath, and he wondered what sort of a man sucked breath fresheners and drank beer at the same time.

The same sort of a man who smiled suddenly and said: 'Look at your face.' He winked and nodded across the bar where Lawrence was now standing looking at him. Lawrence raised a pint and laughed; his mates, standing around him, laughed too. The black guy punched Murphy lightly on the shoulder and said: 'Lawrence wants to buy you a drink.'

Murphy finally relaxed his grip on the glass and tilted it towards the bar. 'Another pint of this would do rightly,' he said.

The guy said, 'Love your theory about the greyhounds and the cocks. And yes, there are slow greyhounds. But we're *all* well hung,' he winked, then hailed the barman, and again got served first time.

★ ★ ★

Aladdin Slane was just out of trap three, hurtling around the course at 4/1, with Lawrence and his friends screaming their support, when Murphy felt a slight pull on his arm. He turned to find Andrea standing beside him.

She smiled and said, 'What're you doing here? Didn't have you down as a greyhound man.'

'I'm not. I'm cheering for the rabbit.'

'It's not a rabbit.'

'Oh. Well, don't tell the dogs, they'll be inconsolable.'

'C'mon, you *bastard*!' Lawrence screamed.

Andrea smiled indulgently. Aladdin Slane was in the lead.

'He invited me the other night,' said Murphy, his eyes on the dogs. 'Well, I mean, it wasn't like a formal invite. He said if I was doing nothing I should pop my head in, say hello. Didn't think I'd see you though.'

'Well, you wouldn't ordinarily. I've a night off Confront, and Lawrence fancied a few pints because Aladdin was running and I don't want him driving with drink on him so I said I'd come down and pick him and the dog up.'

Murphy nodded. He kept his eyes on the race.

She said, 'You're not on the rota either tonight?'

'Nah. Time off for good behaviour.'

Lawrence was bouncing up and down now; his friends were half-screaming at the dogs, half-laughing at Lawrence getting carried away.

'Did you tell Jeffers about me going after Walker?' Murphy asked.

'No.'

'Thank you.'

'That's OK. As long as you don't do it again.'

'Lesson learned.'

And then there was an exaggerated groan from Lawrence as the dogs flashed across the line.

Andrea raised her eyebrows at Murphy and they laughed together. Lawrence slipped quickly down to the side of the track to speak to one of the stewards. They couldn't hear what he was saying, but he was complaining about something.

Andrea said: 'Chelsea.'

Murphy's brow furrowed. 'Chelsea what?'

'I support Chelsea. And my favourite sweets are Opal Fruits. And my breakfast cereal is Frosties.'

Murphy smiled, remembering the conversation now. 'Chelsea? Living proof that money can't buy beauty. And they haven't called them Opal Fruits for donkeys. You'll be talking about Starburst. But I'm right with you there on the Frosties.'

She smiled up at him, nodded slightly, then slipped forward to join Lawrence as he came back from giving off steam to the steward. She snaked her arm through his and said, 'Don't worry, pet, didn't he come in third?'

Lawrence shook his head. 'Third isn't first.

Third out of twenty is good, third out of six — he isn't trying.' He sighed, accepted the commiserations of his friends, then turned and nodded at the bar again.

'Right,' he said, 'let's drown our sorrows.'

Andrea said, 'What about Aladdin?'

'He can get his own fucking drink.' Lawrence cackled and began to lead his mates back into the bar. But then he stopped and told them to go on. He put his arm around Andrea and gave her a hug and said, 'Come on, we'll go and sort him out.' He winked back at Murphy and led his wife away.

Murphy was still watching them when his mobile rang and Carter said, 'Walker's been shot.'

13

'Well,' said Carter, 'he was doing something *you'd* never think of doing.'

'Oh yeah?'

'Oh yeah. Wearing body armour. He took one to the chest and two in the back. His ribs are a bit busted up, but he'll live.'

'And the body armour — how would that have helped him if he'd been shot in the head?'

'You really are a glass is half-empty kind of a guy, aren't you?'

'Wait till you get to my age, Carter. The glass isn't only half-empty, but then some hellion grabs it and smashes it in your face. Just for fun.'

They were in a Subway fast food restaurant in the West End, opposite to where *Rip Her To Shreds* was playing to, as far as Murphy could determine from the small groups of people emerging from the theatre, less than packed houses. It was a little after 11 p.m. and theatreland was winding down. Murphy was partaking of a sub, cookie and Coke deal. Carter had a bottle of still water.

'I thought we had someone keeping an eye

on him,' Murphy said, biting into his tuna and onion sub. The tuna and onion was a nod to his new healthy living regime. The cookie was a yearning from the dark side.

'We had — Thompson and Blemmings. But they were in a car outside. Walker arrives back from the twenty-four-hour Tesco's, lets himself in and *blam blam*! The shooter was inside waiting for him.'

'And we couldn't have seen that coming?'

'You know what our budget is, Murphy. If we'd had someone inside we'd have had to keep him there all day, no matter where Walker was. And that's expensive and we haven't the manpower and — '

'OK, all right. Point taken. I'm sure Walker appreciates it.'

Carter took a drink of his water. He was ten years younger than Murphy, he was slim, he had all his own hair. He used to really annoy Murphy, when he started out, just down from some swanky university and full of the joys of spring, but Carter had eventually kind of grown on him. He didn't talk quite so posh any more and although he was far from being as world-weary and cynical as the rest of them, he was beginning to show signs that he might be heading that way. Little things, like not always reading them their rights, like turning up for work pissed from the night before, like not always having a fresh shirt; and arrogance, little flashes of arrogance. Murphy always thought of arrogance when he thought of cops; more so back home, because they carried guns and that kind of power allows a man to walk taller, but the same applied here — it was just a little more subtle. Not so much of a *don't fuck with me* attitude, more of an understated swagger, a confidence. Carter had that now, although sometimes the old, fresh-faced him still shone through: once, when they had had to arrest someone and there was a bit of rough stuff involved, Murphy had caught Carter saying, 'Sorry,' each time he punched the crim. It was a reflex response, but somehow quite endearing.

'Anyway,' said Carter, 'at least we're on the right track.'

'How do you work that out?'

'Well, as Walker doesn't actually exist, if his criminal past is our total fabrication, and that fabrication was only revealed by you to the meeting of Confront, then it stands to reason that the shooter has to be a member of Confront.'

'Didn't we know that already? Isn't that why I'm undercover?'

'We *guessed* that was it. Now we *know* that was it.'

'But now Walker's shot and we have no witnesses, and I'll bet you're about to tell me we've no weapon and the lab's bugger all use to us.'

Carter shrugged. 'It's still good to have it confirmed.'

Murphy ate some more of his sub. He was thinking that he had no idea what a sub actually was. No — he knew what it was, because he was eating it, but where the word came from. America, he presumed, like most things — including, he seemed to recall Lawrence telling him, greyhound racing — but it had to be short for something. Substitute? Substitute for something better to eat. Submarine? Because of its shape, or its capacity to sink diets. He wondered if there were branches in Germany, and whether they served U-boats rather than subs.

Carter said, 'What are you smiling at?'

'Nothing,' said Murphy. 'Is the boss putting out the press release?'

Carter nodded. 'Just a couple of paragraphs — police investigating a shooting death, name of deceased, that he had a previous record, some drug convictions. Enough for anyone to think it was just a dealer, and enough for Confront to confirm that they got their man.'

Murphy put what was left of his sub down.

'You don't think it was too quick?'

'The press release? It won't be out until tomorrow.'

'No. Walker getting shot. I joined the group — what, a week ago? — and suddenly my man's dead. There must be others who've been there for months, years maybe, and nothing as wonderful has happened to them.'

Carter thought about it. 'Maybe the shooter's trying to impress you. Maybe he thinks an ex-cop will benefit the group. This is his way of getting you to stick around. Or maybe word got out that Walker had a go at you. Maybe the shooter doesn't take kindly to someone having a go at one of his colleagues. Maybe it's the girl — she got hurt, didn't she? Is her husband the type of — '

'I was with her husband when Walker was shot.'

'Oh, right. Doing what?'

'Watching greyhound racing.'

'Sounds like fun.'

'You know, sarcasm is the lowest form of wit.'

'Yeah — right.'

Murphy sat back. 'What about Walker's wife?'

'She's spitting nails.'

'She wasn't there?'

'Out at the theatre, came back to find the

whole roadshow at her house.'

'I'd like to go and see her.'

'You can't do that.'

'Maybe I could phone?'

Carter shook his head, then drank some more water.

Murphy said, 'How much of that do you get through a day?'

Carter examined the bottle for a moment. 'Five or six bottles.'

'You should take it easy.'

'I should take water easy?'

'What do you call the one that was in *Brideshead Revisited* but wasn't Jeremy Irons?'

'You've lost me.'

'You've heard of *Brideshead Revisited*?'

'I studied it at — '

'The TV series.'

'There was a TV series?'

'How old are you, Carter?'

'Was it a silent TV series, back in your day?'

Murphy sighed. 'My point is, the other actor in *Brideshead*, he was appearing in some West End show and it was hot on stage so he would drink a lot of water during the day to keep himself hydrated, but he drank so much he actually poisoned himself and nearly died.'

'He poisoned himself, with water?'

'He nearly killed himself.'

'By drinking water?'

'By drinking water.'

'That's bullshit, Murphy.'

'It was in the paper. Honest to God.'

'Well, if it was in the *paper* . . . '

'There were photos 'n' all. 'How I nearly killed myself with water' by whoever starred in *Brideshead Revisited* on the TV who wasn't Jeremy Irons.'

Carter took another drink. 'Well,' he said, wiping the back of his hand across his mouth, 'I'd better watch out.'

'You better had.'

They sat in silence for a couple of minutes. Murphy took a bite out of his cookie. It was lovely. Perhaps he should just reconcile himself to being fat and bald.

Carter put the top on his water. 'I should go,' he said.

'Aye,' said Murphy. 'A world to put to rights.'

'Well, I was thinking of bed.'

'Aye,' said Murphy, 'that too.'

★ ★ ★

Bed? Murphy walked the streets. There was a light rain falling. He found a bar close to the

Garrick Theatre and drank until closing time. He got talking to a large American tourist who'd been to see *Rip Her To Shreds*. 'Best show I've seen this year — those god-damn critics don't know what the hell they're talking about.' The tourist was in his fifties, he wore a trenchcoat and smoked a cigar; his wife looked younger, or maybe she'd just had some work done. She had sparkling teeth and when she turned he could see scarring behind her ears. Their hotel was just around the corner, and they invited him back to the guests' bar.

After three more whiskeys and a lot of talk about old Ireland, the man said he was going to the bathroom; the woman moved onto his bar stool and draped her arm around Murphy. He could feel her bones through his jacket, brittle, sparrow-thin. 'Do you ever do any foolin' around, Martin?'

'Foolin' around?'

'You know . . . a little swinging.'

'Well, this is Swinging London.'

'So why don't you come upstairs with Hank and me?'

'Sounds good to me,' said Murphy.

Hank came back from the toilets and looked immediately to his wife. She nodded; he smiled. 'Shall we go up?' Hank said.

Murphy raised his glass and said, 'You two

go on up. I've a call to make and I'll just finish this. Room . . . ?'

'Three-oh-nine.'

'Three-oh-nine it is then.'

He winked. The woman kissed his cheek. Hank squeezed his shoulder. They held hands as they walked to the lift in their good theatre clothes.

Murphy finished his drink, pulled up his collar and ventured back out into the rain. Life, he thought, was generally all about getting your hopes up, and then having them dashed. It was about the chase, and the capture was generally a disappointment. He staggered outside, held himself up against a railing, and then was sick over a bicycle locked up behind it.

His head was spinning; he was sick again.

When he had recovered sufficiently he pushed himself off the railing and walked away. There were a thousand miserable thoughts fighting for his attention, but they were beaten off by the one positive thing he could take out of the night's events. He had managed to pull a fat American bi-sexual and his spindly wife. See? Despite evidence to the contrary, he hadn't really lost his touch.

Murphy laughed off into the darkness.

14

Carter rarely did much of the undercover stuff. He was more of a behind-the-scenes man, a facilitator, an organiser, the steady rock to Murphy's jumping frog. Or something like that. But when they were short of manpower, or he just took the notion, he did his bit. Nothing major. Not impersonating an astronaut, not pretending to be a hitman or a designer of bridges, something small, something that required a certain level of performance, but nothing Shakespearean. More like rep, or at his very worst, panto.

This time, he was checking out the former members of Confront who had left after their relatives' murderers had themselves been murdered. Murphy had already spoken to Fred Savage. Alex Bellingham, brother of one of the three girls Alistair Scott had killed, had moved to America some weeks before Scott had fallen under a Tube train and been cut to bits. He might have known it was coming, and gotten offside, or he might equally have been totally innocent. Whatever way it was, Carter wasn't going to be able to find out in the near future. Bellingham had gone first of

141

all to New York, and then, in his father's words, he'd 'gone on the road, and he's just not the type to stay in touch.' Carter, pretending to be an old friend from boarding-school organising a reunion, responded with a 'Don't I know it,' improvising like a pro.

That left Karen Ritchie, whose adopted brother Michael had been shot dead in the off-licence by Thomas Quinn. Carter was more or less level with her, standing just a few plots along in the graveyard. Her white coat was belted against the strong breeze, which was also making it difficult for her to tidy the series of small potted plants which had once lined the grave of her brother but which had long since spilled their contents and were now being blown back and forth amongst the gravestones.

As Karen scrambled after them, Carter caught two up as they rolled past and she said, 'Thank you, thank you,' as she hurried after another pair.

Carter crouched down with the two he'd rescued, and partially buried them in the rectangular expanse of polished white pebbles which stretched out before Michael Ritchie's headstone. As he finished making them secure Karen knelt down beside him and said, 'Thank you so much. That wind . . . '

'I know. It just seems to funnel into this

part of the cemetery — it's like this nearly every time I'm here.' He stood then, and nodded behind him. 'I'm here with my mum,' he said. She followed his gaze, but couldn't decide which grave he was looking at. Then he glanced down at Michael Ritchie's black marble headstone. 'Your husband?'

'Brother.'

'Oh.' He was looking at the dates. He tutted. 'He was young,' he said.

'Twenty-two.'

'It doesn't say *died*. It says *killed*.' Karen nodded. 'Do you mind me asking, what happened?'

'He was shot dead. During a robbery.'

'God.'

'Your mum?'

'Heart.'

'Sorry.'

'S'OK, smoked like a trooper.' He managed a smile, then began to turn away. But then he stopped and said, 'Are you all right?'

Karen nodded, but then she hugged herself and said, 'I hate coming here, but I can't stop.'

Carter smiled sympathetically. 'I hate coming here too. But I have to. My dad sends me to make sure she's dead.'

She laughed out loud at that. He came forward and offered her a cigarette. She took it, he lit it for her, she said, 'It didn't put you off then?'

'I'm giving up next week.'

She smiled. She looked glassy-eyed. Then she knelt down to the plants again. After a moment Carter joined her.

'You don't have to,' she said.

'I know. It's the Good Samaritan in me.'

So he helped her for half an hour, and they chatted, and then they walked back to the car park. He steered the conversation once more to her brother's murder, and she was happy to talk about it. He learned that she'd been depressed since Michael's death, that her doctor had put her in touch with a support group called Confront; she told him what the group did and he made the right noises; she said she'd found it therapeutic but hadn't been able to devote as much time to it as she would have liked, especially since she'd started her training recently.

'What are you training for?' he asked.

She looked a little bashful. 'I'm at the police training college at Hendon.'

'My car tax is up to date,' Carter said quickly.

She smiled again. 'I was worried there might be a — you know, conflict of interest.'

'Why? Does this group do anything . . . dodgy?'

'No, nothing like that, they're great. But they do a lot of surveillance stuff, and they really hound all the bad guys and . . . well, I've got to learn to do it another way, haven't I? By the book.'

Carter nodded. 'Yeah, I suppose.'

'Anyway, the guy that killed Michael, he got killed himself a couple of months ago. I know it's selfish, but I just kind of thought, Well, that's that chapter over, get on with your life. I didn't want to be involved with all that misery any more, do you know what I mean? So I had two reasons to leave.'

They were approaching their cars now — Carter's obviously unmarked, and hers one of the new Minis, a lovely shade of yellow.

'Nice car,' he said.

'It's my little darling and my best friend.'

Carter laughed. 'You need to get out more.'

He unlocked his own car. She unlocked hers, opened the door, and then hesitated. She smiled over at him and said, 'It was really nice talking to you.'

'Likewise.'

'I . . . ah, I don't suppose you'd fancy going out for a drink sometime?'

Carter smiled back, nodding at the same time. 'Love to.'

'Does it seem awful, asking someone out in

a cemetery? No — don't answer that. Here . . . I'll give you my number.' She took a pen and an old envelope out of the side pocket on the driver's side, and quickly jotted down her name and number. She stepped over to Carter and handed it to him. 'So the ball's in your court.'

Then she jumped back into her vehicle, started the engine and roared away, waving at him as she went.

She's very pretty, Carter thought, even as he was tearing up the number.

15

Murphy was waiting for a gap in the traffic to cross to Jeffers's office when he saw a motorcycle pulling in directly opposite. *That's a pretty damn fine machine.* The biker, climbing off and guiding his charge up onto the footpath, was in an equally fine set of leathers. He had the figure to wear them as well. Murphy had spent a lot of time on bikes as a kid and had dreamed of one day getting something other than the rackety old scrambler he'd had, something fast and hard and sexy, with red leathers to go with it, but of course he never had. Now here he was pushing forty, and even if he still had the inclination to buy a flash bike or deck himself out in cool leathers, he would fight it because he knew how ridiculous he'd look. *Desperately trying to hang on to something I never had.*

As he finally found a gap in the traffic and skipped across the road, he consoled himself with the knowledge that while Mr Sleek might have the perfect bike and the leathers to go with it, and enough money to support both and probably a fantastic wife as well, he was evidently not completely flawless. He was visiting the head doctor as well.

We're all the same. Fine on the outside, mental within.

But then Murphy saw that it wasn't a fellow patient after all. Nor even an up-market courier. As Mr Sleek opened the door, he also removed his helmet to reveal: Dr Jeffers.

Well, fair play to you.

Murphy hadn't thought much about the good doctor's extra-curricular activities, but if he'd been pushed he probably would have pictured him driving a golf-cart rather than a top-of-the-range Honda Goldstar. Pringle sweaters rather than leathers.

Jeffers was being handed post by his receptionist when Murphy came through the door.

'Hey, hey,' he said. 'It's Evel Knievel!'

Susan gave him a frosty look and started to say something, but Jeffers gently cut her off. 'It's all right, Susan — Martin, come on through.'

Jeffers led the way. Murphy winked at Susan as he went past. He had an appointment, but he was fifteen minutes early, and she didn't like it one bit.

★ ★ ★

Jeffers was getting changed in a file-room at the back of his office. He called out, 'Take a seat, Martin, I'll just be a minute.'

'No hurry! I know I'm early.' Murphy sat. He could hear the slight creak of distressed leather, and he could smell it too. That's what it was — not aftershave. 'Like your outfit,' he said. 'And nice bike. I used to have one, gave the wife bloody nightmares on the back, up the road near Portrush where they do the North West . . . you know, the road race?' No response. 'You should go if you get the chance. Used to be I'd never miss them. Remember Joey Dunlop? King of the roads, he was. Magic.' He laughed. 'Aye, me and the wife. I was a bit *Easy Rider*, she was more *George and Mildred*.'

Jeffers finally reappeared, now wearing a smart black suit with a thin red tie and a white shirt. He smiled at Murphy as he took his seat and said, 'Sorry about that, but I don't get out that often.'

'Oh aye?' said Murphy. 'The wind in your hair, and all that? If you *have* hair — and fortunately you have.'

Jeffers smiled and said: 'You seem to be in good form.'

'Of course I am!' Murphy exclaimed happily. 'Walker's dead. Shot in the back like the dog he is. Was. Fucking brilliant. Excuse

149

me.' He rubbed his hands together with glee, like he'd just gotten a bet up at the horses — or the dogs. 'Seriously though, Doc — what a result, a bloody marvellous result . . . '

Jeffers clasped his own hands together and gave Murphy a quizzical look. 'Martin, you weren't . . . well, you weren't involved in any way, were you?'

Murphy edged forward in his seat, his face flushed with excitement. 'Me? Christ, no. I mean — if only! But it doesn't matter, he's wiped out! I only had to mention it a couple of times at Confront and he was gone.'

Jeffers unclasped his hands and rested them on the arms of his swivel chair. He gave Murphy a cool look and said: 'Martin, I want to make this absolutely clear. I — we — at Confront do not condone violence of any kind. It flies in the face of everything we're trying to achieve. These are damaged people, they want closure, and that is not achieved through violence. If Mr Walker has been shot, then we cannot — '

'Aw, come on, Doc,' Murphy cut in. 'I used to be a peeler in Belfast. I know what goes on — a nod or a wink in the right direction, someone gets removed.' Jeffers began to shake his head, but before he could respond further Murphy waded back in. 'Dr Jeffers, give me some credit. I don't just walk into this kind of set-up blind. I checked youse out and by my reckoning three, now four of the guys Confront's been tracking are tatie bread. What's that? A coincidence? I don't know who's pulling the trigger, but if you ever find out, you tell him from me, well done mate and I owe you a pint. Or ten.'

Jeffers sighed. He put his head back against his chair and looked for several moments up at the ceiling. Then he fixed his eyes on Murphy and spoke with the calm authority of a schoolteacher trying to put the class clown in his place. 'Martin, just listen to me on this, try to understand: in the past few years we have tracked around sixty cases. We have had some notable successes, we have had quite a few failures. And yes, indeed, a small number of those we have investigated have died, but please, you were a police officer, try and appreciate these facts: first of all, they're murderers and rapists and psychopaths, so *of course* a certain number of them are going to come to a sticky end — that's the world they move in. Frankly, I'm surprised a lot more of them haven't been murdered. Six of our subjects have also died from natural causes — three from cancer, two from heart attacks, one was an epileptic and choked to death. A dozen of them have simply disappeared, or perhaps that's overly dramatic — we've merely lost track of them. We're a small group, Martin. We make life difficult for these people where we can, but mostly we just campaign against the leniency of a judicial system that allows them to walk free amongst us, able to commit further horrific crimes.'

He let that sit in the air for several moments, then eased his chair back and turned to his filing cabinet.

Murphy nodded to himself. 'Well,' he said, after due contemplation, 'you're hardly going to advertise if youse *are* bumping people off, are you?'

And this time Jeffers laughed. He turned with Murphy's file in his hand and said, 'You're like a dog with a bone!'

Murphy shrugged.

'Right then,' Jeffers continued. 'How is this medication working out?'

16

The managing director of Hillside Turbo Tan was one of the palest people Murphy had ever met. Which said a lot. His name was Terence Blacker, but he very quickly told them to call him Terry. He got them coffee and offered them buns. He said it was his birthday and that the staff had clubbed together to buy him a cake and buns because they knew he had a sweet tooth. He patted his stomach and said, 'It's a constant battle,' and Murphy nodded, because it was. That morning Murphy had bought a set of scales for the bathroom. He intended to weigh himself every morning. He would keep a record. He'd bought a notebook as well in which to chart the decrease in his weight. He was going to be a lean, mean fighting machine, and then he was going to get someone to do something about his hair — cut it in such a fashion that it would disguise his encroaching baldness without looking like a Bobby Charlton comb-over. Murphy was aware that he was becoming obsessed about the deterioration of his body, but he couldn't help himself. Even as he ate one of Blacker's birthday buns, he was thinking about the fat content and the calories. And then he was thinking: *Am I a little bit gay or something?*

And then he was thinking, *Did I say that out loud? Why are they looking at me?*

So he said, 'Sorry, what?'

Brian Armstrong, sitting beside him, repeated his question. 'I said, do you want to start?'

Murphy nodded, then swallowed his mouthful of bun. 'Yes, of course,' he said. 'I'm sure you're wondering what this is all about.'

Blacker smiled and nodded. They had been vague on the phone, something about a group, and could they meet for a chat. Blacker, who had a chain of five tanning salons, didn't get much in the form of corporate action, but there was a first time for everything. Corporate, he was sure, would be very lucrative. Hence the buns.

'You mentioned a group?' Blacker ventured.

'Yes, we represent a group called Confront. Perhaps you've heard of us?'

'I . . . I think perhaps I have. You're an insurance . . . ?' He had no idea at all.

'We are a support group for the relatives of victims of violence.'

'Oh yes — of course.' He hoped he didn't sound too disappointed. So they weren't

154

exactly from BP. Still. 'And you're interested in some sort of group rate? That won't be a problem. I think it's a fantastic way of helping your members. Tanning is so . . . *uplifting*.'

Murphy glanced at Armstrong, who nodded. Murphy opened the folder on his lap and removed the two photographs. He set them on the table and pushed them across to Blacker, who smiled quizzically and looked down at them.

His brow furrowed. 'Is this some sort of sick joke?' He was looking at colour photographs of two bent and broken corpses: two teenage skateboarders who'd been beaten to death. 'I'm sorry, I don't understand. What on earth is this all about?' He looked paler than ever.

'We're not interested in group rates for tanning. Mr Blacker,' said Armstrong heavily.

'These two lads were beaten to death eight months ago,' said Murphy, leaning now on the edge of the desk and pointing at the first photo. 'Simon Marwood, aged fifteen, and Peter Jennings, aged seventeen. They were cousins, lifelong pals, spent every hour of the day looking for fresh and challenging places to skateboard. Found a disused swimming pool in the back garden of a house in Chiswick, thought it would be perfect; hadn't been there more than a few minutes when

155

they heard screams coming from inside the house . . . '

'I'm sorry, I don't know what this — '

'Well, listen, and you'll find out.' It was the first time his tone had been anything but friendly, and it stopped Blacker instantly. 'You see, Terry, like any public-spirited citizens, Simon and Peter went to see if they could help, and for their trouble, they were beaten to death. Like this,' he jabbed his finger at the first photo again, 'and like this.' He hit the second.

There was more colour in Blacker's cheeks now. He stared at the one who'd introduced himself as Martin Murphy, and for the first time began to feel genuinely uncomfortable; there was an intangible air of threat about this one, something about the dark look in his eyes and the way he sat slightly hunched forward as if he was prepared to spring for him at any moment. The other one, Armstrong, was still sitting back, but not watching him, watching Murphy. It seemed like he was in charge. But in charge of what?

Relax. *Relax.*

Blacker forced himself to sit back. He clasped his hands and said, 'Gentlemen, this is a very sad story indeed, but I have to admit I'm rather perplexed. Is it some sort of donation you're looking for?'

'No, no donation,' said Armstrong.

'Action,' said Murphy. 'A *response*.'

'A . . . ?'

'These boys were killed by three men who'd stolen the safe from a Bond Street jewellers. They'd also kidnapped the manager and were torturing him to reveal the access codes. These boys didn't realise what they'd stumbled into until too late. The jewel thieves caught them and killed them, along with the manager. They got the safe open and helped themselves to over three hundred pounds' worth of necklaces.'

'Three *hundred* pounds?' Blacker looked confused.

'Exactly. They got nothing. They picked a bad day. A week later, one of them tried to fence one of the necklaces to an undercover cop. He got arrested, he squealed on the other two and the DPP worked a deal which saw him done for the robbery but not for the murders. He spent *eight months* in prison. That's not a lot of time for being involved in the murder of three people, is it?'

'No, but — '

'The point is, Mr Blacker, that murderer is working downstairs in your tanning salon. He's your branch manager.'

'What? Young Andy?'

'Andrew Cameron. Now, what are you going to do about it?'

★ ★ ★

They walked to the car. It was parked on a meter about a hundred yards down from the tanning shop. Murphy said, 'How did I do?'

'Great, son, great.'

'I thought maybe I was a bit overbearing. It's the police thing in me.'

'No, not at all. Just right. Implying what we could do to his business without actually spelling it out.'

They climbed into the car.

'So what do we do now? Hang about to see what happens?'

Armstrong shook his head. 'We press home our advantage.' He checked the small notebook in his lap. 'Cameron lives . . . not far from here at all. Let's tell his new girlfriend what he's been up to. Let's tell his neighbours. Let's tell anyone who can mess up his life.'

Murphy settled into the passenger seat. 'I could get used to this,' he said. 'There's something very satisfying about it.' Armstrong smiled and started the engine. 'Maybe we could turn professional. Harass people for a living. *Intimidation Is Us*. What do you think?

We could make it a franchise operation. We could open Intimidations all over the country. America. We could be billionaires, what do you think?'

'I think we should have some lunch.'

'I think you could be right. There's a McDon —'

'I have some soup in the flask. Scotch Broth.'

'Lovely,' said Murphy.

★　★　★

He spent three of the next seven nights out on surveillance. Different partners, same tragic story. On the third night Murphy went out with Peter Marinelli, whom he'd met briefly on that first approach to Jeffers in his office. Marinelli worked by day as a wedding photographer, but at night he put his skills to use, surreptitiously snapping baddies up to no good. This night they were waiting for a rapist called Mahood to turn up outside the house where one of his victims had lived. She was fourteen, and had committed suicide after his attack. The victim's sister was the only witness to the rape. Mahood had taken to waiting outside her house in an attempt to intimidate her out of giving evidence. It was a condition of his bail that he kept away from her, but the police were too stretched to make sure he kept to it. So Marinelli was going to photograph and videotape him when he arrived and hope that it would be considered evidence enough that he was in breach of his bail and he could then be put back inside.

Marinelli was a talking box with a passion for the movies. Murphy liked his movies as well, but didn't keep a constantly evolving chart of his top one hundred like Marinelli did. He told Murphy he had kept his chart since he was thirteen, and talked extensively about its ebbs and flows. This was fascinating, although only to Marinelli.

His current top five favourite movies of all time, in reverse order, were: 5, *Battle of Algiers*; 4, *To Kill A Mockingbird*; 3, *The Seven Samurai*; 2, *Rollerball* (the original 1970s version, not the crap remake); and 1, *Once Upon a Time in America*. It was, as Marinelli said himself, an eclectic list. He then asked Murphy for his top five. He decided it would be too obvious to include *Death Wish*, even though he had fond memories of it as a teenager. It wasn't so much the fact that Charles Bronson was a one-man army of vengeance, but that he had a face like a bagful of spiders, so there was hope for a spotty, skinny Murphy that he too could be a movie star one day.

How times have changed.

Skinny!

So he ummed and aahed and eventually came up with *Titanic* and *The Great Escape* and *The Eagle Has Landed* and *Zulu* and finally *The Magnificent Seven* and at that point Marinelli excitedly pointed out that *The Magnificent Seven* was actually a re-make of *The Seven Samurai* and Murphy said, 'Oh really?' Then Marinelli said there was another fascintating twist to the tale, because the director of *Samurai* had originally been inspired by the Westerns of John Ford, so it was a case of American culture inspiring Japanese culture which was in turn influenced by . . .

Murphy, who was rapidly losing the will to live, was saved by his mobile ringing.

A familiar voice said, 'Hello, chum.'

Murphy held up his hand to Marinelli and mouthed, 'Later.' Marinelli raised his camera and scanned with his night-vision lens for Mahood. Murphy said, 'Hello, chum,' back to his friend the priest. 'It's been a long time.'

'I've been busy burying the dead.'

'Same here,' said Murphy.

★ ★ ★

They met the next day in a small park close to Murphy's apartment. The sun was out,

161

there were children trawling for fish or frogs in a small pond, there was a wino asleep on a bench, there was glass on the path and the ching-ching beat of reggae coming from the apartments that backed onto the park.

McBride was surprised that they were meeting in a bright park at all, rather than say, a dark boozer. He said so.

'I'm not just a one-trick pony,' said Murphy. 'I like the finer things in life as well. Park. Air. Ducks.'

'I see no ducks,' said McBride.

'There used to be ducks, but they were carried off by poor folk and eaten.'

'That's a sad indictment of our society.'

''Tis, 'tis.' They sat quietly for several moments. Murphy glanced at him. McBride looked away. 'I'm sorry I haven't been in touch,' Murphy said. 'You left all those messages.'

'Forget about it.'

'You made the effort.'

'You've been busy.'

'Not that busy.'

McBride finally looked back at him. He punched his arm playfully. 'Hey, mate, we all go through periods of being anti-social.'

'I'm getting lazy. It sometimes feels like too much of an effort.'

'To meet me?'

'To meet anyone. To *do* anything.'

'Did you ever consider getting out of your line of work?'

'And do what? I don't know anything else. I can't *do* anything else.'

'What about the music? You used to go busking.'

'I'm sick of busking. It's just like banging your head against a brick wall. Hours of abuse and a handful of foreign coins and bottle tops. I want to write songs, but I can't. I'm too lazy. And even when I do they're maudlin shite. I have no interest in anything.'

'Well, you know I'm always here to answer your pastoral needs. Or to get pissed with.'

'I know that. I appreciate that.'

'Did you ever consider that you might be depressed?'

'Of course I'm *fucking* depressed.'

'I mean depressed enough to need treatment. A good psychiatrist.'

'I'm seeing one.'

'Well. That's good. Is he helping?'

Murphy lifted a stone from the path and skimmed it across the pond. It bounced three times and then clattered off the rocks on the far side. 'It's difficult to tell,' he said. He forced a smile onto his face. 'I think we've re-bonded sufficiently now. And enough fresh air, let's hit the pub.'

'OK,' said McBride.

163

17

Murphy was five minutes late for the next meeting of Confront because of a raging hangover and the knock-on effect of a breakdown on the Circle Line; he arrived looking somewhat flustered and out of breath. He took a seat at the back, nodding his apologies forward to Dr Jeffers who didn't acknowledge him, and then smiling across at Andrea, who returned it, but only fleetingly. Someone had set up a small TV and video, and they were studying the videotape Marinelli had made of Mahood outside the house of the rape victim's sister. Murphy hadn't been on the rota the night Marinelli had captured the footage. And it wasn't great.

'I know it's him,' Jeffers was saying, 'but it's not clear on the tape.'

'I couldn't get any closer,' said Marinelli, 'not without tipping him off.'

'I appreciate that you've done your best. I'm just not sure the court would consider it sufficient to . . .'

'Point of order?' It was one of the men to whom Murphy hadn't yet been able to match a name. He had his hand raised.

'William?' said Jeffers.

'Dr Jeffers, why are we worried about tipping him off? If we got closer, got a good quality tape, then wouldn't that be enough to put him back inside? Just seems like we might be wasting an opportunity by keeping our distance.'

They discussed it round and about for another ten minutes. Murphy tried to catch Andrea's eye again, but without success. Armstrong reported on the visit to the tanning studio and revealed that Mr Blacker had made Cameron redundant. He had also been given notice to quit his apartment and had left within forty-eight hours, although not before providing his landlord with a forwarding address for his mail, which the landlord had happily passed on to Confront. This received a round of applause from the Group.

Jeffers thanked him for his report, then lifted a new file from a small pile at his feet and flicked it open. He examined it briefly then nodded slowly around the semi-circle of chairs. 'Now we turn to Mr Murphy and the death of Gary Walker, which I presume you have now all heard about?' They all had. 'Good. I don't think there will be many mourning Mr Walker.' There was a ripple of agreement. Someone behind Murphy gave

165

him a supportive pat on the back. 'Every time a case is closed,' Jeffers continued, 'we also face the loss of a valued member of our group — although of course many choose to stay on. Mr Murphy has only been with us a few weeks, but he has already proved himself a valuable and enthusiastic member.' Murphy nodded bashfully. 'However, I would venture that with Martin, we have hardly even scratched the surface.'

Murphy felt his cheeks colour slightly. He was aware of the others looking at him.

'Martin? Is there anything you wish to share with us?'

He gave a little laugh the way surprised and embarrassed people often do. 'Nothing immediately springs to mind,' he said. Then he added quickly, 'Beyond that I'm happy to keep coming along, you know, to do my bit. I ah, I was, as you know, a police officer and I'm sure I can help — you know, really help with some . . . you know, maybe improving your surveillance techniques, or maybe we could look into getting hold of some equip — '

Jeffers cut in: 'It's a question of denial. It's a question of guilt.' His voice sounded somehow deeper, harder.

'I'm sorry? What is?'

'You haven't been honest with us, Martin.'

All eyes were upon him, but his own were caught in Jeffers's intense gaze.

Christ. I've given myself away. How? HOW?

No, he can't know. Not for sure. Perhaps he suspects. The cover story — it had been too simple, going in as an ex-cop. But I've been careful, so careful . . .

Get through it, get through it.

Murphy managed a hesitant smile. 'Sorry, I'm not quite with you.'

'We have no secrets here, Martin. If you tell one person something, you tell us all.'

'Secrets? I'm not sure I foll — '

'Tell us about your son, Martin.'

And that shocked him, really rocked him. He felt it in his blood, in his heart, in his stomach, in the back of his neck, as if someone was plunging an ice-pick between his shoulder-blades.

'This isn't about my son,' he managed to say. 'It's about Walker.'

'Tell us about your son, murdered by Irish Republican terrorists.'

'I'm telling you,' and he could hear his own voice, magnified, tremulous, 'it's about — '

'Tell us, Martin!'

'It's got nothing to do with you, it's private.'

'Private! Here? Martin, you have watched

167

these people bare their souls, you've listened to them dredge up their worst memories and fears. Why should you come amongst us and not do the same?'

Murphy glanced around the group and saw conflicting emotions on their faces — confusion, sympathy, shock, surprise, and on Andrea's, looking away, guilt.

The photo in the car. She'd only seen it for a moment, but a moment was all it took. Confront exists to collect information, and they've collected me quickly and efficiently.

The bloody photo.

Jeffers had him, and he wasn't letting go. 'Martin, we demand honesty. Every one of us has a personal stake in what we do. We have lost wives and fathers, mothers, daughters, sons . . . what have *you* lost? Your job? No, Martin, that's not why you're here. Perhaps you haven't even admitted it to yourself, but we can see it, Martin, do you understand?'

Murphy didn't nod or shake his head; he just sat there, stunned.

'So are you going to tell them, or am I?'

There was a tightness across his chest. He wanted to get up and run *now*, go back to the office and say, *I've been compromised, it's all over.*

But he couldn't move.

Because he knew he'd gotten himself into

this position. Some part of him had been aware of the stupidity of carrying the photo around with him. Some part of him had left it where it could so easily be found. Some tiny part of him had planted it there as a safety device, something he could grasp for if his cover really was blown. He could exploit the horror of his own life in order to expose the killer in Confront. That's what he told himself. That's what he was saying over and over and over in his head. And at least half of him believed it.

★　★　★

'I . . . I haven't deliberately misled you,' he began, his voice ragged.

Just give them the absolute minimum. Don't get into it.

Don't get into it.

'Walker was the scum of the earth, but you're right — it wasn't personal, it was just . . . anger.' He took a deep breath; he glanced around. Andrea was looking at him now; she even gave him a supportive smile. 'My son . . . my son died a long time ago. *And it was my fault.*' It sat for a moment. 'I worked in Special Branch — you know, in Belfast. I did a lot of undercover work — paramilitaries, both sides. It was addictive, but I suppose all

169

addictions are dangerous.'

Stop now. You don't have to tell them this. Lie. Fabricate. Distort. It's what you do best.

But he could not stop himself.

'It's also a single man's game, not suitable when you have . . . ' He sighed deeply. He couldn't meet their eyes; stared at the floor instead. 'One day I came home and they were waiting in my house. They had my wife and son and I knew that I was going to die.'

Murphy paused for a moment as he desperately tried to find a coherent way through the jumble of thoughts and images cascading within his mind.

'They . . . they . . . '

'It's all right, Martin,' Jeffers said softly. Murphy forced his eyes up. Jeffers was looking intently at him, but both his demeanour and his words were suffused with sympathy. Murphy gave him a thankful nod and steeled himself to continue exploring his tragedy.

'They weren't content with just killing me. They wanted to twist the knife. You have to understand, the war, the 'Troubles', were drawing to a close; those that were still fighting were either gangsters fighting over territory or extremists determined to destroy the coming peace at any cost. What they wanted me to do . . . they wanted me to drive a bomb into an army barracks and detonate it. They said: 'Do that or we kill your wife and child as well'.'

There were tuts and groans from his audience.

'So I took the bomb and I drove to the barracks, but when I came to the gates, I couldn't do it. There were two hundred people inside. I just . . . couldn't do it.' He was aware that his voice was breaking now, and there was a dampness on his cheeks. 'When I got home they had cut my son's throat. He was handsome and cheeky and he bled to death before anyone could help him.'

Murphy let out a sigh that came from a thousand miles away, then slumped forward. His shoulders sagged and vibrated. The tears would not stop. They allowed him time. A minute, nearly two. Then Jeffers said quietly, 'What about your wife?'

Murphy dragged a sleeve across his face. 'I'm sorry, I don't usually . . . ' He trailed off, lost in memory. Then gradually he became aware of the question again. 'My wife? They tied her up and they made her watch.'

'Christ.' Someone at the back.

'The bastards.' Behind him.

'Fuck.' The first time he'd heard any of the others curse at a meeting.

He looked around them then, at their

gaunt, drawn faces — people who had experienced every trauma life could throw at them, but who still found fresh horror in what he had gone through.

'And do you know something?' he asked. 'You were right. It *is* about denial, it *is* about guilt. There isn't a minute of any day which passes without me asking myself why I made that decision. Why did I save two hundred strangers, but sacrifice my son? And worse than that, was I even saving those strangers, or was I just saving myself? Was I just saving my own life?'

It was a question he had never uttered in public before, but a billion times in private. He had never, ever, dared to answer it, because he feared and loathed what that answer had to be. What the truth must be.

'If I could only bring him back,' he said, his voice barely above a whisper, 'just for five minutes.'

Jeffers gave him a few moments, then said softly: 'It's not your fault.'

There were nods of agreement all around the group.

Of course it's my fault.

I destroyed my own son.

'Martin — do you hear me? It's not your fault!' Dr Jeffers looked around the group. 'It is not any of our faults. This is what we all face. This is why we Confront.'

They burst into applause.

Murphy shook his head; he held up his hand and the applause died. 'No, look . . . I understand what you're saying, and I support entirely what you do, but it's different for you, for all of you. You can do something about it, but I can't. I can't confront these people . . . They were never caught. Don't you think if I knew . . . '

But this time it was Jeffers's turn to hold up his hand. 'Martin.'

' . . . don't you think I'd go to the ends of — '

'*Martin.*'

He stopped. He wiped at his face. 'Sorry . . . sorry. You're in charge.'

'Martin. Listen to me. I have told you that people appreciate what we do. Sometimes when we ask for information, no matter how private or privileged, it is forthcoming.'

'What are you saying?'

Jeffers glanced down at his file. 'I am saying that three years after you were transferred over here, a drug dealer looking for a way out volunteered the names of two men he said were involved in the murder of your son.'

His heart was ready to burst through his chest. If he hadn't been sitting, he would have fallen. As it was he had to struggle to stay upright. 'That's not possible.'

'Their names were Michael Riley and Matthew O'Hagan. They were arrested, and under questioning Riley made a partial confession, but said that O'Hagan carried out the murder. However, the confession was retracted and no charges were brought.'

Murphy was shaking his head. 'I would know about this.'

But Jeffers wasn't finished. In fact, he was saving the best for last.

'Michael Riley died last year, Martin. Matthew O'Hagan is currently living here in London.'

And this time he did pitch forward, his head swimming, his heart hammering, aware through the racing darkness of only two things: that the man who had killed his son was living in this very city, and that he was fainting like a girl.

18

They were all very nice to him, but he didn't need *nice*. He needed . . . but he couldn't concentrate on one subject for long enough to decide what he needed. *Out of here. Away from these clucking hens.* They had offered him warm tapwater and kitchen roll to soak up the sweat that rolled off his brow. They offered him a lift home or to get him a taxi. Jeffers made him promise to come into his office the next day to discuss it all. He was genuinely concerned about him. He said he'd debated long and hard whether to reveal what he knew at the meeting or in private, and had decided on the meeting only because of the tremendous support the group could offer him. He said they'd been like distant cousins before, now they were his brothers and sisters.

Murphy didn't want to hear any of this *shite* talk.

He wanted *out*.

He made vague wavy promises to them and thanked them and said yes, he'd be fine, it was just a bit of a shock and he needed to get his shit together and not to worry about him and he'd see them next week or on the rota, then he hurried away. He stood outside trying to catch his breath. He looked at the traffic and the buildings and thought about his son's killer being out there. In that building. Or in the back of that cab. Or drinking in that pub.

He went to the pub. He ordered a Bush and a pint of Carlsberg. It was a little after 3 p.m. He counted a dozen other customers. It was, nominally, an Irish pub. There were harps on the wall along with faux ancient maps of Ireland. But the staff sounded like Essex boys. He wondered if Matthew O'Hagan drank in Irish pubs. Or even *this* Irish pub. Maybe that was him, by the cigarette machine. Or there, reading the *Daily Mirror*. Or that woman with her shopping bags around her feet, asking for an ash tray — maybe that was his wife, or daughter or mother.

Then Andrea was standing beside him at the bar, looking concerned. She said, 'I followed you,' and put a hand on his arm.

'It's all that surveillance work paying off,' said Murphy. It came out more sarcastically than he intended, but she ignored it.

'I was going to say let's go for a drink when we were over there, but I . . . well, you know how it is.'

'I know how it is.'

'I'm sorry. I don't think he should have told you like that.'

Murphy shrugged. 'You tipped him off.'

'I know. Look — I really am sorry. I just thought there must be more to you than . . . well, and then I saw the photo and I mentioned it to Dr Jeffers and he thought it was worth looking into. But we'd no idea what we'd find. It was a real shock.'

'You're telling me.' He took another drink. 'Listen, you really don't want to be around me just now, all right? I'm not going to be much company.'

'I don't expect good company. I just want to make sure you're OK.'

'Yes, I'm fine and dandy, can't you tell?' Then he apologised again. He sighed and said, 'All right, if you insist. What are you having?'

'Just a Diet Coke.'

'How can you support me in my time of need if you're having a Diet Coke?'

'I have the car. I have to feed the dogs.' He looked at her. 'OK, I'll have a glass of white wine.'

Murphy ordered the drink. He forced a laugh out of himself. 'That was a bit embarrassing,' he said, 'keeling over like that.'

'It's perfectly understandable.'

He shook his head. 'It was just like getting

177

punched in the head.'

'Exactly.' Andrea sipped at her wine. 'I was worried about you.'

'That I might have concussion? Or a grazed knee?'

'No, about what you might do.'

'Dr Jeffers sent you to stop me turning into Charles Bronson?'

'No. No, he didn't. *I* came to stop you turning into Charles Bronson.'

Murphy shook his head. 'Why would you even care?'

'Because I do.'

'Well, you don't have to worry. Right now I'm more like the Charles Bronson in *The Great Escape* than the Charles Bronson in *Death Wish*.'

She was smiling. 'You've been spending too much time with Peter Marinelli. Him and his bloody movies.'

Murphy laughed then and said, 'Yeah, I'm turning into a bloody anorak like him. What I meant was — '

'I know what you meant. Charles Bronson, the tunnel king or whatever, he gets scared of the dark.'

'I'm impressed.'

'And I'm married. Doesn't every man have a copy of *The Great Escape*? And doesn't every man endlessly watch Steve McQueen on his motorbike and imagine doing the same thing?'

Murphy held up his hands. '*Hände-hoche*,' he said.

★ ★ ★

Andrea was on her fourth glass of wine, there was a heavy flush to her cheeks and her words were somewhat slurred. But even though she was talking, he could tell that she was distracted, and eventually she broke off mid-sentence, mid-*rant* about how snappy greyhounds were and how much time Lawrence wasted on them, to open her bag and take out a folded sheet of paper.

'I thought you might want this,' she said and held it out.

He looked at it suspiciously. 'What is it?'

'Look and see.'

So he took it and unfolded it and there was an address written in capital letters. 'This is where he lives?' She nodded. 'Does Dr Jeffers know about this?'

She looked slightly sheepish. 'He knows about the address. He's put it on the list of cases we're going to investigate. But there's a bit of a waiting list. I copied it.'

'What do you think I'll do with it?'

'Well, I'm hoping you won't do anything

stupid, and you'll work with us. But I knew you'd want to at least take a look. See where he lives, what he looks like. It's only natural, isn't it?'

Murphy nodded. 'Thank you.'

'You won't, will you? Do anything stupid?'

'No. I learned my lesson with Walker. This is one for the group.' He was saying it, but he wasn't thinking it. He was working out the fastest way to O'Hagan's house, and how he would kill him.

But then Andrea threw him by saying, 'When this happened to your son, how long was it before you made love to your wife again?'

Murphy took a quick drink, set the glass down, then said: 'Jesus, what tangent did that fly in on.'

'I'm just . . . I would just like to know. Compare.'

'Well if you must know, I'm still waiting.'

'How long after it happened did you split up?'

'About a year.'

'Lawrence and I haven't made love in eighteen months.' Then she added quickly, 'Sorry, is that too much information?'

'No. Yes. No. It's whatever you're comfortable with telling me.'

'Eighteen months. What about you?'

'I haven't made love with Lawrence at all.'

She giggled and took another drink.

Murphy shrugged. 'It's been a long time. Although of course I keep in practise at home.'

She spat out a mouthful of drink, then wiped at her mouth. 'That *is* too much information.'

★   ★   ★

It was dark outside, he could see that through the window. Andrea was drunk, and so was he. The bar was packed now. The Chieftains were on the jukebox. Twice her mobile rang and she ignored it. The third time it rang she switched it off.

Murphy said, 'The dogs will be starving.'

She said, '*This* dog is starving.'

'You're no dog,' said Murphy.

'Is that some sort of a compliment?'

He smiled and said, 'We should get something to eat.'

'And be seen with you in a restaurant? People might talk.'

'You're being seen with me in a bar, and we're being ignored.'

'We're just having a drink. A restaurant is much more . . . suggestive.'

'Suggestive of what?'

'That there's something going on. Soft lights, romantic music.'

'I was thinking of McDonald's.'

'I was thinking of your place.'

'Were you?'

She nodded and said, 'We could order a Chinese.'

'My place is a real mess.'

'Eighteen months,' she said.

'I'm not exactly Mr Houseproud.'

'Eighteen months.'

'My wife kept the Hoover.'

'Eighteen months.'

'I'll order a taxi.'

'You do that.'

He did that. He took her home. She held his hand in the taxi. The driver heard his accent and started talking about the Troubles and how he used to be a soldier but was never posted over there and he was glad because he had no fight with the Irish, although he very nearly had a fight with Murphy because they were drunk, but not so drunk that they didn't think he'd gone the long way round and was charging them a fiver extra. Andrea calmed him down and paid for the taxi herself. She said to the driver, 'He's just upset, he's had some bad news.'

'That's all right, missus, no harm done,' and then he looked down at the money she'd given him and said, 'That's exactly right,' in a disappointed voice.

Andrea said, 'Oh, I forgot the tip.' She leaned back into the cab and said, 'Don't sleep in the fucking subway. There's a tip.'

The driver sped off, hurling curses back at them.

They kissed then, in the middle of the road, until another car beeped its horn and Murphy drunkenly gave it the fingers.

He led her upstairs and into the bedroom and they collapsed on it, fully clothed, although not for long. They made drunk love and it was great. But in the very instant after orgasm, his and hers, he was thinking about O'Hagan.

★　★　★

Pounding heads and dry throats.

They lay in the messed bed, sweated, drank water, made love again. Murphy waited for Andrea to mention Lawrence and eventually she said, 'He'll think I'm out on surveillance. I'll say my mobile was switched off. We had a row before I went out anyway. It'll be OK. I still love him.'

'That's good.'

She lay in his arms for a while longer, then rolled over and fell asleep. Murphy lay staring at the ceiling, willing his head to go but not having the wherewithal to get up for painkillers. Eventually he drifted off. When he woke a couple of hours later he could not remember if he had dreamed of a dead boy and masked men, as he usually did when sober, and that was a relief. Andrea was already sitting up, with the covers crumpled across her chest, and when she saw that he was awake she switched on the bedside light and looked at her watch; she ran her fingers through her damp hair and noticed the photo of his son he kept on top of the locker.

'Do you mind?' she said. He shook his head. She lifted the photo and angled it to get a proper look. 'He would have been a good-looking young man,' she said.

'Aye.'

'No pictures of your wife. You're not still holding a flame for her?'

'Nah.'

'What happened?'

'Well, she blamed me for everything, and I agreed. Nowhere for us to go really, after that.'

'It must have been hard.'

'It's still hard.' He pulled the blankets back to show that it was still hard. She laughed. She put the photo back, face down, and then cuddled down beside him. She stroked it and said, 'It's funny, sex, isn't it? As you get older you don't really miss it at all.'

'Speak for yourself.'

'I mean, you don't really miss it and then suddenly something sets you off and you can't get enough of it.'

'I am a fortunate man.'

'And maybe I'll go home tonight and make love with Lawrence and find that we're all better now. I just needed to do a dry run.'

'I'm a test pilot. A stuntman.'

'You're not taking me seriously.'

'You're holding my cock, I can't.'

She sighed jovially, and put it in her mouth.

★ ★ ★

Later she said, 'It was my father who died, but Lawrence, his parents died really young and so my dad became like a father to him as well. More than that even, they were like best friends as well. They did the dogs together — three, four nights a week they were down there. So once my dad died, Lawrence — you know, he looks the same, he talks the same, but he's just *not* the same.'

'Like living with a stranger.'

'Yes, but also no. I mean, he's clearly not a stranger, and so much of him is the same, it

185

just drives me mad. If he could give me one-tenth of the attention he gives those fucking dogs, well . . . ' She sighed. 'Does this make any sense?'

'Total sense. In fact, I'm going to get myself a dog. They're clearly the solution to everything.'

She shook her head. 'But I do love him, and we will work it out.'

'I know you do. And I'm sure you will.'

'As soon as I leave here, that's the end of it. You do understand?'

Murphy nodded. 'When do you leave?'

She shrugged. 'Couple of hours?'

Then she moved towards him and they kissed again.

19

The man emerging from the Shoreditch terrace appeared to be in his late forties; he was squat and looked like he worked out. He wore a short black leather button-up jacket, black jeans and brown suede shoes. There was a gold stud in his right ear and his grey hair was cropped short. Pug nose and small eyes. The eyes of a killer? Murphy didn't know. Had he seen those eyes before? He should remember, he should remember every single tiny detail about the moment he walked into the house and found his wife and son being held hostage. But he didn't. It was a blur. Worse than that, a fading blur. He remembered men in balaclavas and the calmness of his wife. He remembered her eyes all right, because they were pleading with him to save them. And he had failed. But everything else was going, going, gone. Because you couldn't live with that kind of a scene in your head. Couldn't live and expect to continue living. You'd put a gun to your head. And he nearly had.

It was the right address, nice but nondescript house, nice but nondescript area.

There was nothing to say that this really was O'Hagan. He could be a relative, a tenant, a friend, they might be having dress-down Fridays in the Mormons — but then the front door opened behind him and a woman in a blue dressing-gown with a towel wrapped around her head shouted after him: 'Matthew!' and the man stopped and turned and saw that she was holding a plastic HMV bag. He hurried back and took it off her. He paused to kiss her, and then she pushed him away and said, 'You'd forget your head if it wasn't screwed on.'

Matthew. What were the chances of someone emerging from the home address of Matthew O'Hagan and answering to the name of Matthew, and not being Matthew O'Hagan?

Many billions to one, he thought.

You are my man.

I feel it.

Right here.

Murphy got out of his car and followed. He stayed about a hundred yards behind him. It was 11.15 a.m. and the sun was bright enough to wear sunglasses, but he left them off. The ones he had in his jacket pocket had small, circular lenses, like John Lennon's; he thought they were pretty cool, but for this job they were too distinctive. He wasn't worried about being recognised: he was aware of how much he'd changed physically in the past few years. But the chances were that O'Hagan kept a fairly good eye on his surroundings, because once you were a killer you always had a killer's fear of being caught. So the idea was not to stand out. Nevertheless, as he walked, Murphy found himself getting closer and closer. Several times he had to make himself slow down. His stomach felt like there was a ton weight in it; his muscles ached from the tension of just watching O'Hagan and not crushing his head in a vice.

O'Hagan looked in an estate agent's window. Murphy stayed clear of the reflection.

O'Hagan entered a bookie's; Murphy bought a cup of coffee in a café across the road and sipped it for twenty minutes until O'Hagan emerged. When he stood up Murphy took off his jacket, turned it inside out to expose the blue lining within, then walked with it over his shoulder; he stayed on the other side of the road until he saw O'Hagan enter HMV. He waited outside for five minutes, then entered himself.

He spotted O'Hagan in the DVD section. They had a special offer advertised, three DVDs for twenty quid, and O'Hagan already had two in his hand. Murphy recognised one of the covers as *Forrest Gump*. He wondered if O'Hagan got teary-eyed near the end of the movie where Forrest discovers he's a father. This man who had slit the throat of his son.

O'Hagan made his third selection: *Spartacus*.

Murphy tried not to draw moral parallels between O'Hagan's purchases and the facts of his violent life.

Just do what you do. Follow. Don't speculate on what O'Hagan's final choice might mean. It doesn't matter whether it's The Last Temptation of Christ *or* On the Buses.

Do not judge the man by his clothes, or his DVDs. Judge him by how he has lived his life.

Oh God. What was that from, the Bible or a movie?

O'Hagan approached the counter with his DVDs, but then opened the HMV bag he already had and produced another disc Murphy couldn't see. Murphy lifted a DVD at random and stepped into the queue behind O'Hagan; there were two people in front of him.

O'Hagan was saying, 'The receipt's there. Just I got it home and my wife had already bought it. It hasn't been played.'

Northern Irish accent.

Good. Another nail in his coffin.

The teenager behind the counter just nodded and took the disc back. The customer is always right.

'Sir?'

Two other tills had opened up, and the two people in front of Murphy turned out to be together, so they went to the first one, and another teenager in a red top and square glasses was calling him over.

Murphy approached the counter and put the DVD down. He was now standing right beside O'Hagan. Close enough to touch. To leap upon. To crush.

'That's a great movie,' said the boy. 'Have you seen it?'

Murphy looked down at the box. Gene Hackman in Francis Ford Coppola's *The Conversation*.

Murphy shook his head. The boy looked at him, clearly psyched up from his customer care course, determined to be smiley and chatty and create a bond between them. Murphy on the other hand wasn't about to unleash his own Northern Ireland accent. Because when two Northerners hear each other's accent abroad, they inevitably start a conversation. At home they invariably ignore, or shoot at each other, but abroad, they're the best of friends. They start reminiscing about the 1982 World Cup or Tayto Cheese and Onion crisps.

'If you ask me,' the boy said, 'it's much better than *The Godfather*.' O'Hagan turned with his bag of DVDs and headed for the door. 'I'd put it on a par with *Godfather II*.'

O'Hagan went through the doors.

Murphy lifted his own bag and said, 'I'm sorry, you're confusing me with someone who gives a fuck.'

He went after O'Hagan.

★ ★ ★

'How many days?'

'Three.'

'And what have you got to show for it?'

'Sore feet. Blisters. He does a lot of walking. He goes shopping quite a lot, but not for anything substantial. He doesn't appear to have a job. Maybe he's retired, although I'm not sure if the IRA have a pension scheme. Maybe his wife supports him. She goes out most days at lunchtime and doesn't come back till quite late in the evening. I saw a uniform — I think she's a nurse. It wasn't like your regular NHS uniform, it was a lot more modern-looking. I don't know. She could be a beautician. If I lose him or he doesn't go out one day, maybe I'll follow her instead. And I see by the glazed look in your eyes that this is boring you. OK, I don't have anything huge and earth-shattering to show for following him about for a few days, but then I was never expecting to have anything huge or earth-shattering. I'm just building a picture. I'm just — following.'

They were in a bar just around the corner from Murphy's apartment. The priest was wearing a baseball jacket and blue jeans. And his dog collar. He might have qualified as a trendy vicar, but there had never been anything remotely trendy about McBride. When they had been in a band together in the spiky-haired days of the late 1970s, McBride, despite his best efforts, had still managed to look like a hippy. And he was prone to embarrassed flushes. The years had added weight and jowls, but had not reduced his awkwardness in social situations. His musical ability hadn't moved on much either. When they'd first reunited in London Murphy had persuaded him to help out with one of his musicals. *Jesus Christ Superstar* was having one of its occasional revivals in the West End, and Murphy was toying with the idea of doing something with the David and Goliath story; he thought he might bounce ideas off McBride, and McBride could keep him on the straight and narrow as far as all the

God-stuff was concerned. But it hadn't worked. Because (a) Murphy was a creative loner (b) McBride didn't have a creative idea in his body and (c) it was a crap idea.

Murphy said, 'Do you remember that *David and Goliath, the Musical*?'

'Jesus, man, one moment you're on O'Hagan, the next you're on musicals.'

'Sorry.'

'Yes, of course I remember it. What were we thinking of?'

'I had another bash at a musical a few months back. Jack the Ripper.'

'Yeah, I remember you mentioned it.'

'But then I found out there was already one on in the West End.'

'Yeah, I remember thinking that at the time.'

'You knew already? Well why the fuck didn't you say?'

'There's already a billion love songs out there, doesn't stop you writing a better one. Or a worse one.'

'That's different. Love is universal, this was a particular story.'

'Well, I didn't like to say. You get so enthusiastic about things.'

Murphy sighed.

McBride said, 'You're not just following, are you?'

'No, I'm not just following.'

'It's more than just painting a picture.'

'It's more than just painting a picture. Right you are.'

'But to what end?'

'I don't know about what end. That's the thing about ends. They come at the end.'

'Your bosses don't know you're doing this?' Murphy shook his head. 'And this group thing you're involved with, they don't know either?'

Murphy shrugged. 'They gave me the info. They kind of expect that you'll check it out yourself. But he's way down their list. It doesn't matter anyway. I'm not *doing* anything.'

'Apart from spending every hour God sends you following this guy.'

'I'm not. I keep an eye on him — when I have the time. Look at me now. I'm enjoying a pint with an old mate. Perfectly relaxed. Although that reminds me, I must go and relieve the other guy I'm paying to keep a watch on O'Hagan.'

'You're joking.'

'I'm joking. Relax. It's all in hand.'

'Yeah. Right.' McBride sipped his pint then put it down. He looked around the bar. The carpet was threadbare, the curtains were yellow with nicotine. The barman told everyone who came in and looked remotely foreign that Jack 'The Hat' Mc-something had once killed someone in here during the Kray Twins' era in the 1960s. He had told McBride the same story three times, once for each of his visits. Which was three times more than Jack 'The Hat' Mc-something had probably been there.

'I'm just worried about you,' McBride said, still not looking at him.

'I know that. You shouldn't.'

'Yeah, but if that's him and he did what he did, then you'll want to do something about it, and I don't mean getting him done for double parking.'

'An eye for an eye, a tooth for a tooth.'

'I knew you'd say that.'

'Well, it's in the Bible.'

'There are a lot of things in the Bible, and they're not all written in stone — although, obviously, some of them are. What I'm saying is that a lot of it is more like guidelines. You have to adapt them for the times you live in.'

'Why?'

McBride finally looked back at his friend. 'Come on, Murphy — that's so Old Testament. Times change. We have electricity. We don't lop people's heads off. You're a police officer, you don't take the law into your own hands. That's just anarchy.'

'We used to be into anarchy. Punk's not dead, you know.'

'Yes, it is. We grew up, mate, and we put childish things and anarchy away.'

'So he can just sit there, he can watch the telly and buy chips, while my son's dead.'

McBride's shoulders sagged as he sat back in his chair. 'You know what I mean. Maybe this group — Confront? — have the right idea. Maybe they can collect evidence against him, hound him out, whatever it is they do. But not you, Marty, not you.'

'Why not?'

'Because you're barkin' at the best of times. You don't need this.'

Murphy blew air out of his cheeks. 'I know. I know what you're saying, but the thing is, the genie's out of the bottle and it won't go back in.'

'So what are you going to do?'

'I don't know.'

'I could suggest prayer.'

'You could.'

'But I sense I'd be on a hiding to nothing.'

'Right you are.'

'But the good thing is, you've done nothing wrong. Not yet. So there's hope for you.'

'Hope for *me*?'

'You know what I mean.'

'I'm not sure that I do.'

'I mean, at the moment it's just . . . you know, curiosity. But . . . '

'Curiosity killed the cat.'

'Exactly.'

'So, am I the cat, or is he the cat, or are we both cats?'

'I'm not sure.'

'I thought that.'

After that, they drank their pints and talked about football, which was fine. There were no grey areas in football. Game of two halves. Twenty-two men and a ball.

20

Murphy was on the Gatwick Express when Carter phoned. Forensics hadn't found anything useful from the Walker shooting, and nothing out of the ordinary had been turned up by an exhaustive trawl through Confront's membership files.

'What about the Baker killing?'

'Baker? Which one was that?'

Murphy reminded him. 'Eddie Baker, the car jacker, killed Andrea Sinclair's father then died in an ironic car accident.'

'An ironic car accident? Do they have sarcastic ones as well?'

'You know what I mean.'

'Baker, Baker . . . ' Murphy could hear him flicking through files. 'Here we are — Eddie Baker, your basic hit and run. Eight months ago now, nobody charged, no witnesses, so it could have been an accident. Or murder most foul. What's that noise?'

'What noise?'

'The chugguda-choo, chugguda-choo.'

'That would be a train.'

'Where are you off to?'

'I'm off to Gatwick. Do you want to do

your airplane impression as well?'

'Why are you going to Gatwick?'

'Because that's where the planes land.'

'And where do you think you're flying to?'

'Belfast.'

'Belfast?'

'Belfast.'

'Are you allowed to do that?'

'Allowed?'

'I thought there were all kinds of dangerous people in Belfast who wanted to kill you.'

'There are. But I doubt they'll recognise me. My hair has receded and I've put on weight and I'm not going to hang out with gangsters and I might wear sunglasses and a big hat.'

'Is this business or pleasure, Murphy?'

'Belfast is always a pleasure.'

'Murphy?'

'A bit of both.'

'Connected to this investigation?'

'I don't know yet.'

'Do you want to tell me more?'

'Not really, no.'

'Have you got clearance for this from upstairs?'

'You mean God?'

'I mean the boss.'

'No, of course not.'

'Might I ask why, then?'

'You may ask whatever you wish.'

'Murphy . . . '

'I just need to check something out. It's strictly on a need-to-know basis, and you don't need to know.'

There was a pause then. Just the chuggada-choo of the train and the gabble of half a dozen people around him who were also on their mobile phones.

'You don't want me to tell the boss, do you?'

'I didn't say a word.'

'But you don't.'

'It's entirely up to you.'

'I don't think it's wise, you going there.'

'You're entitled to your opinion.'

'Do you want me to come with you?' Carter asked.

'That's exactly what I need. You sticking out like a sore thumb.'

'I can blend in.'

'With that accent?'

'Murphy are you sure you — '

'I'm sure. Just relax. I'll be in and out in no time.'

'So you'll be back tonight?'

'I wouldn't bank on it.'

When Murphy cut the line he took a bottle of water out of his travelling bag, and swallowed down four of the eight paracetamol he'd brought with him. He had gotten very drunk with the priest and his head was still banging. He rested his head against the window. There was something soothing about the steady rhythm of the train. He thought briefly about Andrea. She had been true to her word. She hadn't called. Or dropped him a note. Or sent him flowers. It was better that way. Of course it was. Really.

The train was still some way short of Gatwick when he had a slight moment of panic. He checked his bag quickly — then found his old address book. He breathed a sigh of relief, then checked the pages he'd marked that morning once again. OK.

He was going home, and it filled him with dread and happiness.

★ ★ ★

He was glad the police at the gate didn't pick on him. If they'd said, 'Excuse me, sir, what is the purpose of your trip today?' like they occasionally did with shifty-looking Belfast passengers, he didn't know how he would have replied. *Business or pleasure, sir?* What they really meant was *Are you any kind of a terrorist intent on causing murder and mayhem?* He wondered if anyone had ever said, 'Yes.'

The flight was fifty-five minutes long and it was a budget airline which provided neither peanuts nor drinks without you having to pay through the nose for them. It was no bad thing. He didn't need another drink. In fact, he was never drinking again. He had weighed himself before leaving. He was exactly the same weight as he had been before he'd started his fitness regime. He had probably ridden two hundred kilometres on his exercise bike in the past week; he had tramped the streets of London following O'Hagan. And yet not an ounce of a difference.

'It's not about the exercise bike,' McBride had told him, drunk *and* hungover, lying on his couch, his belly thrusting out from his jeans and with curry stains on his clerical collar, 'it's about a complete lifestyle change.'

'And what would you know about it, you fat fuck?'

'A lot more than you think. My church — we play host to all kinds of groups, Weight Watchers, yoga, all that stuff . . . I pick things up, y'know. Just I don't always put them into practise. But these things I do know: it's about balance, it's about attacking every problem, not just one, drawing up a strategy, setting achievable goals. I'd draw you a pie chart, but you'd probably eat it.'

'Har bloody har.'

'I'm serious. I mean, there's no use in exercising and doing the pies and pints. They just cancel each other out.'

'I'm not bloody stupid,' Murphy had said.

'Well, there's two schools of opinion on that.'

★ ★ ★

They landed at the City airport, sweeping in from the sea and then twisting across the old Harland & Wolff shipyard. Its massive yellow cranes stood neglected, but with the sun bouncing off them they looked as if they were glaring down on the massive hive of activity at their feet: but it wasn't ships that were being built any more. The yard which had built the *Titanic* was now becoming the Titanic Quarter, one of the largest building projects in Europe, reclaiming industrial wasteland and turning it into suburban wasteland.

Murphy hurried out of the airport. He decided against hiring a car. It was only five minutes in a cab to the city centre and another ten beyond that to Kincaid's house in Malone Park. He was going to let the cab go and just walk back into town, but the moment he saw the house, he decided to hold onto it. Kincaid had clearly moved on:

somehow he doubted that the former head of Special Branch was deeply into garden gnomes. Not that type of a man at all. He knocked on the door and a suspicious-looking woman with grey hair tied up in a bun confirmed that the last occupants had moved two years previously. He asked where and she said she wasn't sure, but she thought maybe somewhere down the Ards Peninsula.

That figured.

Somewhere safe, out in the Protestant heartlands. Rather that than stay in the city and take the risk of running into one of the bastards you'd put away for life.

Life.

Life, Jim, but not as we know it.

Murphy took the cab back into town, paid the cabbie then found a pub. It was lunchtime and he was hungry and he had to decide what to do next. It wasn't like Kincaid was going to be in the phone book. There were ex-colleagues he could call to check if he still had that place down the coast, but not without tipping them off that he was home, and that might leak out and get him into difficulties. And then what if they wanted to know about all his personal stuff? He didn't want to get into that any more than he had to. Besides, he hoped to save that for Kincaid himself.

He sat over a Diet Coke. A waitress came up and asked him if he was having lunch and he said he would have the Prawn Open. They were fresh Norwegian prawns, she said. He wondered what had happened to the fresh Portavogie prawns that used to come as standard. Perhaps there were none left. Or they'd moved to Norway. He ordered the sandwich and when he'd finished she came over to take his plate and ask about dessert. He said no.

She said, 'There's fresh strawberry cheese-cake.'

'I'm on a diet.'

'Or there's banoffee.'

'I'll have that.'

He'd always been a sucker for banoffee. Well, not always. He'd only discovered what it was in his late twenties. Previously he'd thought it was some kind of obscure gaelic dish. Then when he discovered it was merely a combination of bananas and toffee he'd quickly become a convert. Plus, there were only ten thousand calories per slice. Unless you had fresh cream with it. That added on a few.

He was on holiday, kind of, and you couldn't diet on holiday, so his diet would start properly when he got home. Murphy checked his address book again, found the number he was looking for, keyed it in, then hesitated before pushing the button.

Hesitated for ages.

How long had it been? Too long. Whose fault was it? Exactly.

He pressed and then it was answered on the third ring.

'Hello?'

'Kate?'

'Yeah. Who's this?'

'It's me.'

There was a pause, and then a hesitant: 'Martin?'

'No other.'

'You bastard.'

'Him as well.'

'You complete fucking bastard.'

'Now you're going too far.'

She sighed. Five years of hurt in a digital sigh. 'You bastard,' she said again, but softer.

'Can I come home?'

She sighed again. 'Yes, of course you can.'

He said, 'You were always my favourite sister.'

And for a third time. 'No, Martin, I was always your *only* sister.'

'Same thing, isn't it?'

She put down the phone.

21

Kathleen, Kate, Katie lived in a semi-detached overlooking Stormont. Two Stormonts, really — the sweeping drive up to the impressive old parliament building, seat of government, discussion, dispute and walk-out, and the Stormont Hotel, a few hundred metres away and not nearly as impressive but probably a lot more profitable.

Jesus, the Stormont Hotel. He'd gone to dances there as a teenager. Dances? Discos? All the local spidermen with their flares and moustaches, he and McBride and a handful of others in their punk gear, just waiting for the punk song that never came, and the hiding that always did. The good old days.

Kate's husband Ken had been a civil servant, although not in Stormont, and a part-time member of the Ulster Defence Regiment. He was a Protestant, she was a Catholic, love across the sectarian divide, etc. etc. And true to form, he'd been shot by the IRA for his trouble. It was a long time ago. She had two kids, who were now in their early twenties. She had not remarried. When Murphy had been in the depths of despair over the death of his son she had tried to snap him out of it by saying, 'You know, you don't hold the copyright on grief.' It had snapped him out of it all right. Snapped him all the way to London, and he hadn't spoken to her since.

So when he rang the doorbell at number 126 he didn't quite know what to expect. A slap in the chops, quite possibly. From a prematurely grey woman, weighed down by the torments of living and dying in Belfast.

But then the door opened and he said, 'Is your mother in?'

She looked at him for quite a while, during which his smile threatened to crack and dissolve, then she said, 'You're funny.'

She came forward nevertheless and they hugged. She held him for a full minute. Then again, but this time at arm's length. She examined him. 'You've changed,' she said.

'I know. So have you.'

'We're getting older.'

'You're not. Look at you — you look younger than when I left.'

'Away with you.'

'You do, seriously. Your hair, your figure . . . my God, I never realised I'd a regular wee honey for a sister.'

'Oh, stop talking bollocks and come in.'

She led him into the house. Down the hall

and into the kitchen. He sat on a stool while she poured a cup of tea. He said, 'Howse the kids?'

'They're not kids any more and they have names.'

'I know that. Patrick and Stephen.'

'Patrick's fine. He's in the civil service, like his dad. Stephen's at Queens, he's studying Law. And Jamie's at the childminder's.'

'Jamie?'

She looked at him.

'Oh God,' he said. 'I'm sorry. I didn't know.'

'Well, that's what happens when you huff off.'

'I didn't huff off.'

'Whatever you did, once you'd stopped huffing you should have given us a bell. You knew where we were, we didn't know where you were. The ball was in your court.'

'I would have, but my bosses said I couldn't have any contact with — '

'Oh bollocks.'

He nodded. 'Aye. Bollocks.' He lifted his tea. He put it down again. 'I've just been . . . you know.' He sighed.

'Even your wife has been in touch more than you.'

'Ex-wife.'

She rolled her eyes. 'Jamie is three years

old. He was a bit of a surprise.'

'Who . . .'

'His father will be home from work shortly. He's a solicitor.'

Murphy nodded. 'That's nice. And he's got his foot in the door as well.'

'He hasn't got his foot in the door, Martin, he lives here. We live together. We'll probably get married.'

'Has he been married before?'

'Yes, he has.'

'What went wrong?'

'Martin.'

'Did he have an affair or is he gay?'

Kate shook her head, then turned to the cupboard and took out a tin of biscuits. When she took the lid off he could see Penguins and single bar Twixes and Breakaways. He took two Penguins. She said, 'You always did have a sweet tooth.'

'I still have. Although just the one nowadays.'

She smiled and said, 'This is a bolt from the blue.'

'I know. I'm sorry.'

'Don't apologise. You've just . . . missed so much.'

'I know that.'

'Sometimes I really needed you and you weren't here.'

'I know. I wanted to be. I just had . . . things. You know what I'm saying.'

She nodded. They stared at their tea. He ate a Penguin.

'So why are you here?'

'Cheaper than a hotel. And I want to borrow your car.'

She burst out laughing. 'You never change. You never *fucking* change.' And she came round and gave him another hug.

* * *

He had never liked Kate's choice in men — not her early boyfriends, not even her husband, all that much, so his inclination was to dislike the big, cuddly kind of guy who came through the back door with his hand already extended and booming a warm, 'So you must be Marty.'

Indeed, his inclination was to respond with, 'And you must be the fat bastard who got my sister pregnant.' But he resisted this inclination, partly because he was in no position to call anyone fat, and said, 'That's me.'

They shook hands. 'Brian,' said Brian. 'Maybe I should go back out and buy chips, give youse a chance to get reacquainted.'

'We are reacquainted,' Kate said, a little too quickly. She covered it with a laugh. 'I mean,

Christ, we know each other inside out. Nothing's changed.'

Brian went to the kitchen door and said, 'I'll get this suit off.' Then he hesitated for a moment and glanced towards Murphy. 'If it's any consolation, Katie huffs as well.' Then he winked and scarpered off upstairs with Kate shouting after him what a bastard he was.

When she came back into the kitchen she said, 'I have some of your stuff upstairs.'

'Stuff? What kind of stuff?'

'Stuff that used to be yours and that your wife — '

'Ex-wife.'

'Didn't want. There's a lot of books, records, old photos. Stuff.'

'I'm not really bothered. Maybe another time.'

'Marty, we need the space. I've kept it long enough, either go through it or I'll dump it.'

'So dump it.'

'I can't dump it, it's your stuff.'

'All right, I'll take a look later.'

'Promise?'

'Promise.'

Later she said, 'Jamie'll be home in five minutes. Are you OK with this?'

'Why wouldn't I be OK with it?' She shrugged. 'I'm fine now. Honest.'

Then her son came home and Kate could see the tears in her brother's eyes. It wasn't that Jamie was the spitting image of his own boy, he was really quite different. But there was something. Murphy played with him over his teatime, and then into the early evening, Jamie laughing and yelping and climbing all over him. Then he helped to put him to bed and read him a story, and kept reading, long after the exhausted child had fallen asleep.

When he came downstairs Kate said, 'Thanks for doing that.'

He nodded and said, 'Any time.'

'Don't you think he looks like his daddy?'

'He does. Mr Potato Head.' But before she could say anything he raised his hands and said, 'Only raking. He's lovely. The boy, I mean. And Brian's all right.'

'He's more than all right.'

'The boy's smart. I'd forgotten how smart they could be.'

She put her hand on his arm and squeezed gently. He nodded, and forced up a smile.

★　★　★

Kate made dinner and the three of them sat in the kitchen eating it. Neither of the older boys was due home.

'They'll be sorry to have missed you,' she said.

'Am I going somewhere?' said Murphy, but then followed it with a smile.

'You can have Stephen's room,' said Kate. 'It's the least messy.'

He thanked her, though he wasn't quite sure if that was her way of saying, 'Time for bed.' It was only a little after eleven. He'd drunk a bottle of red wine, almost by himself. There was another bottle open on the table, and one on stand-by.

'So,' Murphy said, 'are you two getting married?'

Kate laughed and said, 'Right to the point, as ever. There's no rush, is there, love?'

'No rush at all.' Brian lifted the first of the dishes and set them in the sink. Then he glanced at his watch and said, 'I've a couple of phone calls to make.'

He squeezed Kate's shoulder and went upstairs. Kate made sure the door was closed behind him, then topped up her glass and removed a packet of cigarettes and a lighter from a cupboard. As she lit up Murphy said, 'That's a bit sneaky.'

'I'll blame it on you.'

'I'll deny it.'

'His first wife died of cancer.'

'Ah.'

215

'I'm a real three a day girl. I'll be a hundred and twenty years old before it kills me.'

Kate had lit a candle at the beginning of the meal, but it was a tiny, party effort, not built to last, and it had burned right down to the point where its light was weak and now its shadows weren't so much thrown as limply hanging, like an airport windsock in a negligent breeze. But it suited them, a kind of conspiratorial campfire-embers darkness, their voices low, the faint drone of Brian on the phone upstairs, the occasional but persistent drip from the cold tap.

'Do you ever hear from her?' Kate asked.

'Who, the former Mrs Murphy?' Kate nodded. 'No.'

'Why not? Do you ever try to make contact?'

'No. She's taken off for parts unknown with her new man. A wanker of the highest order.'

'She went for the same type, then.'

Murphy smiled. 'Can't blame her. She takes all this my-life's-in-danger-but-now-I've-got-a-new-identity stuff quite seriously.'

'Is there any need? I thought maybe since all the war ended . . . '

'I think she could quite easily waltz down the Falls in Union Jack panties and nobody would bother her. I also think she likes that she no longer has to deal with all the old shit. New life, new friends, new lover.'

'Do you still love her?'

'What sort of a question is that?'

'The obvious one.'

Murphy shrugged. 'Too much water under the bridge now. Be different if she just lived down the road, but she made the break and she's gone. So I've moved on to pastures new.'

'Have you?'

'Well, the pastures are kind of overgrown and untended, but yes I have. All I really need is to meet the right . . . cow.'

Kate took a sip of her wine. She tilted the glass, looking into it as if there were tealeaves. 'Why are you here, Martin?'

'I heard about the rissoles and wine.'

'Seriously.'

'I am serious. Can't an old man visit his longlost sister? Bury the hatchet?'

'Martin.'

'Just some business.'

'Something to do with your job?'

'Something.'

'Something dangerous?'

'I hope not, I'm wearing my good clothes.'

'Would you like to be serious for once?'

'I'd really prefer not to.'

She poured herself another glass of wine, then another one for her brother. That was the end of the bottle.

'Sure, fill it with water and get Brian to turn it into wine. He seems to be able to walk on water already.'

'Yes, he can. And don't be like that. I love him.'

'That's good. He seems OK.'

When they were down to a few drops in their glasses, Kate said, 'There's a bottle of vodka in the cupboard.'

'That's no place for a bottle of vodka,' said Murphy. She got the bottle, and Coke from the fridge. 'Do you not have Diet Coke?' Murphy asked.

She did. He felt better. This time he poured and mixed.

'Jesus,' said Kate. 'That could kill a horse.'

But she drank it nevertheless, and then, after they'd been silent for a while he realised that there were tears on her cheeks. He reached across and took her hand.

'He was so innocent,' she whispered. Murphy nodded; he squeezed her hand. 'It was different with Ken. He knew what he was getting into, what could happen.'

They sat for a while longer. They could no longer hear Brian's voice from upstairs.

'If I ever found the man who killed my son,

what do you think I should do?'

She looked at him in the dim light. She wiped at her tears. 'What do you mean?'

'I mean, if I knew where he lived, should I, like, go and kill him? Or forgive him?'

'You mean if he was just living there, hadn't been arrested or charged or tried or convicted or whatever?' Murphy nodded. 'How would you know it was really him, then?'

Murphy sighed. 'Your faith in the judicial system is touching.'

'My boyfriend's a solicitor, it has to be.' They both managed to smile. 'If you were certain it was him?' He nodded again. 'And me being a good Christian lady with children of my own to think of?' She paused. 'Well, I'd wait for a dark night, until he was coming home drunk from the pub or something, and I'd knock him down in my car and then reverse over him to make sure he was dead. Or I'd hang out in a bar until I met someone who was willing to shoot him in the head. Marty, I love this country and I love the fact that we're at peace, and although I don't like the fact that most of the terrorists on both sides who made all of our lives miserable for so many years are now free, I'm prepared to accept that they are as long as it means all of the trouble is over. But certain things I will not forgive, and I will not forgive what was done to my nephew, and neither will you.' She forced herself to smile. 'And now I'll climb down from my soapbox.' Murphy stroked her hand. She said, 'Why do you ask?'

He shrugged. 'Beats talking about the weather.'

Later, when he was going to bed, he bumped into Brian coming out of the bathroom. 'Thanks for letting me stay,' he said.

'Don't thank me, Martin. It's not my house. Not yet.' And he gave a fake maniacal laugh. He dropped it quickly when he saw that Murphy wasn't laughing. He wasn't laughing because he was very drunk, and he didn't understand the joke. Brian quickly said, 'Downstairs, when you said about us getting married, and I kind of jumped up, it wasn't because I don't want to. I'm taking her out to dinner on Friday night and I have a band set up and I have the ring and I'm going to surprise her, so you sort of discombobulated me. Do you know what I mean?'

Murphy nodded. Then he ran into the bathroom and threw up. Between hurls he shouted back, 'It was something I ate! It's not because you're getting married!'

'*Shhhhhh*,' said Brian.

22

Kate had a six-year-old blue Laguna. She handed over the keys somewhat reluctantly, and would have demanded to know the whys and wherefores in a lot more detail if she hadn't been suffering from a killer hangover. She was in her dressing-gown, standing in the driveway, her hair scraped back, trying to release the child-seat from its tangle of straps in the back and cursing because it wouldn't come away.

'Should I get the scissors?' Murphy asked, laughing.

'It's not funny,' Kate hissed. 'I feel like death.'

'You've only yourself to blame,' he said, waving his finger.

'I've only *you* to blame, more like.'

He felt fine. Experience had taught him that being sick six or seven times the night before always helped with the next day's hangover. It was comforting to have that kind of self-knowledge.

'You'll be back by this evening?' she asked as she finally freed the blue and white checked seat. She turned it upside down.

221

Crumbs and crisps fell out. 'I need it back. And it'll be in one piece?'

'Yes, of course I will. And yes, of course it will.'

'Did you sort that stuff out?'

'What stuff?' She gave him a look. 'You got me drunk, I didn't have the chance. I'll do it when I get back tonight. Honest.'

'Honest? Yeah. Right.' She gave him a hug then and held on to him for a long time.

He said, 'If you're sick down my back I'll . . . understand.'

'Don't, please.'

'Go on inside and get yourself an egg sandwich. That'll sort you out.'

She pushed him away and pretended to be sick.

'How was the lovely Brian this morning? Did he give you a hard time?'

'He didn't say a word.'

'Why, because he's huffing?'

'No, because he understands. You're the huffer.'

'Yeah — people in glass houses.'

She stood in the driveway and watched him go. She waved. He waved back. He thought she was probably right, after all. He didn't have the copyright on grief. But with the passing of time their positions had changed. She had chosen not to renew the copyright,

whereas he had gone out of his way to do so.
Horses for courses.

★　★　★

Instead of aiming for the outer ring, which was faster but extremely boring, he drove down through the city centre, then on to Holywood and Bangor. He then cut across to Newtownards. He kept one eye on Scrabo Tower, dominating the skyline, then turned left away from it and drove along the edge of Strangford Lough. It was bright, but there was a strong breeze driving the waves hard against the shore and they sprayed up and over the road, forcing him to drive with his wipers on. After about fifteen minutes and a couple of wrong turnings, he found the lane he was looking for. It was about a mile long and although Tarmacked, the surface was now badly rutted and scarred by the passage of heavy agricultural vehicles and time.

At the end of the lane was a rusting metal gate with a red *Private Property* sign attached to it. However, the sign was mud-splattered and there was no lock on the gate. Murphy opened it, drove through, then got out and closed it again. He drove on up, and after about two hundred metres he rounded a bend and found a single-storey white-washed farmhouse facing him. Immediately a dog began to bark, and as he drew the car to a stop, sideways on to the building, he saw a curtain move. He noted that while the farmhouse appeared to be at least a hundred years old, the windows were new and double-glazed; there were twin security cameras mounted high up on the walls; the barking dog did not sound like it was a poodle. When he opened the car door there was an angry scampering off to his left and he turned just in time to see a Rottweiler bearing down on him, snapping and snarling. He quickly closed the door. Big paws thumped hard against the paintwork and then teeth and gums and dark evil eyes were up close against the glass.

The front door opened and a woman with short grey hair stepped out. She didn't attempt to discourage the dog, and had to call above the barking: 'What do you want?'

'To be able to speak *dog* like Dr Doolittle.'

She thought she'd misheard. She moved closer. 'What's that?'

Murphy had to dodge his head this way and that so that he could look at the woman; each time the dog followed him a split second later, spitting its anger against the glass. 'I said, call off the dog, Betty, I come in peace.'

She said, 'Clarissa — *no*.'

And Clarissa stopped barking and sloped away.

Murphy waited until he was sure the animal was at a safe distance, then wound down his window. 'You call *that* Clarissa?' The woman was peering at him, trying to place the face. 'I suppose it's like that Johnny Cash song — 'A Boy Named Sue'. Give him a girl's name, makes him tough.'

'I'm sorry, I — '

'Betty.' He raised his chin and turned slightly to the left so that she could get a good look at his face. He smiled as well, which seemed to do the trick.

'Martin Murphy,' she said.

'Long time no see.' He faced her full on again. 'You're looking well.'

She rolled her eyes. 'And look at you. You look like you've been eating for two.'

'You mean I've put a couple of pounds on.'

'You needed to. How long has it been?'

'Too long. Is he here?'

'He's down at the lake.'

'You have a lake?'

'It's not like Lake Tanganyika. It's only small.'

'Still. A lake's a lake. How have you been, Betty? Retirement suiting you?'

'Suits me.'

'And Alan?'

'He didn't volunteer.'

'I know, but . . . '

'He's had a couple of heart-attacks. So don't go upsetting him.'

'Me?'

She gave him another look and then pointed towards a muddy track, leading up over a hill about a quarter of a mile away. 'Just follow that — you'll find him.' Murphy nodded. She said, 'It's good to see you.'

He nodded and started the engine again.

★   ★   ★

Alan Kincaid was fishing in his own lake, wearing thigh-high boots, although the water only came up to his knees. Murphy parked at the top of the hill and walked down. Kincaid appeared not to be aware of him, but when Murphy opened his mouth to speak he suddenly went, 'Shhh . . . '

He then quickly began to reel in his line. It went taut, then slack, then taut again and he reeled some more, then it went slack again and after several moments, he tutted. Without turning towards him, he said, 'How are you, Murphy?'

'How did you know it was me and not some crazed killer intent on revenge?'

He patted his pocket. 'Betty phoned me on the mobile.'

'Ah. Defeated by new-fangled technology.'

'She says you've put on weight.' Then he turned in the water and looked at Murphy. 'But not much.'

'Sure that's women for you, overly critical.'

'You can say that again.'

Kincaid began to wade towards the shore. Murphy supposed he was past sixty now, but not by much. He looked older, though. His skin was sallow and drooping off his face; when he reached the bank he made several attempts to haul himself up, but kept losing his footing. Eventually Murphy reached down and took a firm grip of his arm and helped him up. He had been a big, muscular man. And now he wasn't.

Kincaid set down his rod, then opened a yellow tackle box and withdrew a packet of cigarettes. He offered one to Murphy, who shook his head. 'What's wrong?' asked Kincaid. 'You've never given up?'

Murphy shrugged.

Kincaid sat down on the grass, and indicated for Murphy to join him. It was only mildly damp. They looked at the lake for a while. Betty had been right. It wasn't Lake Tanganyika. It wasn't much more than a large pond.

'Spend a lot of time here, then?'

'Much as I can.'

'Never got fishing.'

'Neither did I. I was going to drain it. Thought I'd try and catch all the fish first. I'm still trying.' He smiled. Then it faded and he said, 'I knew you'd come. Not when, exactly, but I knew you'd come.'

'So it's true.'

'In so far as anything is really true.'

'What's that supposed to mean?'

'Well, Martin, it's like any history, isn't it? We take one thing to be true, and then you find out fifty years down the line that in fact it wasn't true at all. But I suppose you can't afford to wait fifty years.'

Murphy shook his head.

'How did you find out?'

'Does it matter?'

'It might.'

Murphy had to acknowledge that that was true. 'There's a group called Confront in London; they look into old cases, try to kick up a fuss and bring bad guys to justice. They seem to be pretty well-connected as they were able to pull some strings; they were able to tell me about O'Hagan being alive and living in London.'

Kincaid looked a little surprised. 'London? I didn't know that.' But then he shrugged.

'What else did they say?'

'Not much.'

'Who's their source?'

'I don't know. Why didn't you tell me?'

Kincaid finally lit his cigarette and took a long pull on it. Then he coughed. He looked at his cigarette, shook his head, then said simply: 'I couldn't.'

'What do you mean you couldn't? We were colleagues, friends! All you had to — '

'I wasn't allowed. Marty — it's complicated.'

'Not from here it isn't,' Murphy snapped. He could feel the anger building on him. 'The bastard killed my son!'

'I know what he did.'

'They were picked up. You had a confession. And then they walked.' Kincaid nodded. 'So why wasn't I told? Why wasn't I brought in?'

'Why do you think? Christ, Marty, how is it always? It wasn't my decision. It was political.'

'How is it political? What the fuck have politics got to do with it?'

'OK! Enough!' Kincaid threw his cigarette down. It hissed for a moment on the grass. 'If I could have — '

'I don't want to know about fucking *ifs* Alan.'

'I know. I know.' Kincaid slipped his hands together and looked back out over his lake. The breeze was making little racing patterns on the surface. Murphy thought it could be quite a magical place in the summer, like much of Northern Ireland, but now it just felt cold and hard. 'Look, Martin, ceasefire negotiations were at a critical stage, and it was made clear to me that if Riley and O'Hagan were charged it would endanger the peace process. I didn't like it then, and I don't like it now, but my hands were tied. You'd already been transferred. I thought it was better to let sleeping dogs lie.'

'Did you really.'

'Marty, it wasn't like that. C'mon, I did everything I could. But they wouldn't move.'

'But not a hint, not a whisper.'

'I know. I'm not proud of it. What they did to your — '

'Don't go there.'

'OK.'

Kincaid's mobile rang. He took it out, looked at the number, gave a slightly exasperated shake of his head, then answered it.

'Betty, I'm busy. I know. I'm fine. There's nothing to worry about. No, I'm not smoking.' He turned towards Murphy. 'Martin — am I smoking?'

'No.'

'See? No, he wouldn't lie to help me out. He's a police officer.'

Their eyes met.

Kincaid said softly, 'No, I'm all right.' Then he cut the line.

'Tell me about O'Hagan,' Murphy said.

Kincaid lifted his tackle box, which was lying open, and began to poke through the items within: not apparently looking for anything in particular, just for something to do with his hands, and to avoid looking directly at Murphy. 'Well,' he said, 'as far as I can recall he lost two brothers when he was still in shorts, blown up by their own bomb. Even back then the Provos were moving towards politics, but O'Hagan was a hardliner from day one, and vicious with it. Well, you know that.'

'Yes, I do. How was it that he ended up in my house with a knife at my son's throat?'

'I don't know.'

'But there was an investigation.'

'Yes, and it was inconclusive. You know that as well.'

'What wasn't I told? Or what didn't come out?'

'Nothing, Martin — at least, nothing at the time. You know as well as I do, this is a tiny little country and everything's connected.

231

Nobody knows precisely how they came to be in your house, whether someone betrayed you from inside us, or you made a mistake, or they just stumbled upon it. It happened.'

'OK.'

'So then, with the ceasefire coming up, the IRA had to suck up to all the little renegades and their off-shoot groups and make sure they didn't cause trouble, and part of the deal for doing that was getting them off on whatever charges we'd picked them up on.'

'Why the move to London?'

'He fell out with the boys.'

'He wanted to keep the campaign going?'

'No, he knew it was over. But he's like the half of them, got used to the good life, didn't want to give it up. He was making most of his money from drugs, wasn't handing enough over to his bosses, so had a close encounter with a punishment squad. Went over to the Big Smoke and set out his stall there.'

'So that's all he is, a dealer. He's not still involved in the other stuff?'

'Not as far as I'm aware. But I've been out of it three years, Martin. He might be. Or he might have seen the light.'

'And the evidence against him?'

'Dead man's confession — not much use.'

'What about DNA?' Kincaid shook his head. 'But you're certain it's him.'

'It's him.' Kincaid closed the tackle box and shifted towards him. He gave Murphy a long, hard look. 'What are you going to do, Martin?' he asked.

'I don't know.' Murphy stared down at the water. 'What do you do when you catch a fish?'

'What do you mean?'

'I mean, in this wonderful PC world we live in, do you throw it back in or do you crack its head on a stone and gut it?'

'I throw it back in.'

'I thought you were trying to clear the lake.'

'I was. But I'm slowly coming to the conclusion that there's too many of them. So now I throw them back.'

'You give up too easily.'

'I tried. Best I can do. What's your position on the throw-them-back or bash-their-brains-in question?'

'Well, I'm in two minds.'

Kincaid nodded. Then he stood and lifted his rod again. 'Problem with killing them is you get blood on your hands, and I never really liked blood.'

Murphy stood beside him. 'It's fish blood, it's cold, it's not the same.'

Kincaid raised an eyebrow. 'This conversation,' he said, 'is loaded with deeper meaning.'

'No,' said Murphy, 'it's loaded with fish.'

★ ★ ★

He gave Kincaid a lift back to the farmhouse. As soon as she heard the engine Betty came hurrying out onto the porch with Clarissa snarling beside her. Murphy gave Kincaid a hand with his fishing rod and tackle box.

Betty said, 'Are you going to stay for a cup of tea, Martin?'

Murphy glanced at Kincaid, who nodded. But he shook his head. 'No thanks, Betty, I have to be hitting the road.'

'And you got what you came for?'

'Yeah. I suppose.'

'He misses work something dreadful,' she said.

Kincaid came and stood with his wife and put his arm around her. 'Like I would miss that place.'

'All those hellions out running around, all the time he spent putting them away.'

He gave her a squeeze. 'Listen to her. You'd think she worked there as well.'

'Maybe she did,' said Murphy. 'Maybe she was undercover.'

'That's it,' said Betty, smiling up at her

husband. 'That's exactly it.'

'Lucky your cover was never blown,' Murphy said, and climbed back into the car.

★ ★ ★

Kate drove him to the airport. He told her not to bother with the short-stay car park or with walking him in.

She said, 'You didn't think I was going to mention it, did you?'

'Mention what?'

'The footprints on the side of the car. The scratches.'

'They're not footprints. They're paw prints. A dog jumped up. It wasn't my fault.'

'Brian will go mental when he sees the scratches.'

'No, he won't. He's too nervous about you saying no.'

'Ah. Yes. The secret proposal. I found the ring weeks ago.'

'Maybe it's for someone else.'

'I don't think so. And I heard you shouting about it when you were pissed.' She put a hand on his shoulder. 'Are you all right? Did you really find out what you were after?'

Murphy nodded.

'And does that make you happy?'

'Not really, no. It makes me wiser.'

'Do you want to tell me?'

'Not really, no.'

She sighed. 'Have it your way. But look after yourself, all right?' He nodded glumly and looked towards the terminal. 'You'll come to the wedding, won't you?'

'I'll try.'

She shook her head and laughed. 'What, you've so many fish to fry you haven't time for your own sister's wedding?'

'Something like that.' He winked, lifted his bag, and climbed out of the car. Before he had gotten very far she remembered something and pumped the horn. He came back and crouched by her window. 'Thought I'd gotten away with it,' he said.

'You didn't go through your stuff.'

'I know. Sorry. Dump it.'

'I'm not dumping it. Someday you'll want it.'

'Why the fuck would I want it?'

'Because someday you'll get married, and you'll have another baby, and it won't be the same baby, it'll be a different baby and you'll love it just as much, and when it gets older you'll want to show him or her the stuff you had when you were a kid.'

He stood up. He said, 'You don't half talk some shite, sis,' and turned away again.

23

Lawrence was out walking his greyhounds, paying no heed to the rain, when Murphy appeared beside him. It spooked him a bit at first because the Irishman seemed to come out of nowhere and he had the hood of his anorak drawn in so close against his face that it distorted his whole appearance and made Lawrence think he was going to be mugged. He stopped dead in his tracks, tensed up, ready to fight it out, but then he did a kind of a double-take and said: 'Murphy — you nearly gave me a heart attack. Where the fuck did you come from?'

Murphy pointed behind him. 'Over there.'

Lawrence looked but didn't see anything but bushes and trees.

'Christ, well don't do it again.'

Lawrence shook his head and walked on. Murphy fell into step beside him, then stopped again as one of the dogs stopped to go to the toilet.

'I hope you're going to pick that up,' Murphy said.

'Yeah, right. Like I'm going to walk around with a bag full of shit in me hands.'

'If I was still a cop I could arrest you for that. And the dog.'

'I bet you would 'n' all.'

'I could make a citizen's arrest now. You and the dog.'

'You talk such crap,' Lawrence said, giving the dog a good stiff yank on the chain as he finished his business.

'I walk the walk, and I talk the talk.'

They bantered for a while about football, and then when they paused while another of his dogs went to the toilet Lawrence said, 'Andrea told me. Must be harder still, losing a kid.'

'Yeah, well.'

'He shouldn't have told you in front of the group. That's just . . . what's the word? Callous.'

Murphy nodded. He looked a bit sheepish on it, and shifted his eye-contact from the man to the dogs. 'I've been . . . you know, coming round to your way of thinking.'

'About the shit? You bet. They should be able to shit anywhere. It never did me any harm.'

'I mean, about the group.'

'What about it?'

'That there's no amount of talking or watching or organising a bloody petition that's going to get my boy back.' Murphy took a deep breath and fixed his eyes back on Lawrence. 'I need a gun.'

If he was surprised, it didn't show. Instead Lawrence snorted. 'What're you telling me for?'

'Because I saw who you were hanging out with at the dogs the other day.'

'Aw, man, that's just the dogs. We all get tarred with the same fucking brush.'

'No, it's more than that, you know it is. You know them. You're well in. You could . . . you know, have a word.'

'But you were a cop — you must know people.'

'Yeah, well, I kind of burned my bridges.'

Lawrence yanked the chain again, and they walked on. He didn't say anything for a while.

'What do you think?' Murphy finally prompted.

'You're not planning a bank robbery or a hi-jacking?'

'No.'

'A man's gotta do what a man's gotta do?'

'Something like that.'

'And you're prepared to go out there and do it, and you don't give a damn for the consequences?'

'Consequences? I'm dealing with the consequences every minute of every day. Doing this will light up my life.'

Lawrence nodded slowly. 'I might know someone.'

'I'd appreciate it.'

'It'll probably cost you.'

'That's not a problem. You — well, you don't seem surprised.'

'I'm not. So — leave it with me.'

'Thanks,' said Murphy.

'Thank me if I get it,' said Lawrence. 'I'm not promising.'

★ ★ ★

Murphy was due out on patrol with Confront that night. When he checked the rota he saw that he'd been paired with Andrea again, but he got a call from McIntosh to say she'd cried off with a toothache and he was going to cancel it because there were no other members available and it was group policy not to undertake surveillance work without a partner. So Murphy decided on a quiet night, watching the man who had killed his son.

Watching him eat dinner in a fancy restaurant with his fancy wife, who looked a lot better now that she didn't have a towel wrapped around her head. It was an Italian restaurant called *Bella Linguini*. Watching them wasn't difficult, as they chose a window seat. Murphy sat in his car outside. Between the second and third courses O'Hagan appeared to answer a call on his mobile, and a moment later he emerged from the restaurant and approached a car which had only recently parked on the opposite side of the street. A black guy wound down the window and shook hands with O'Hagan, then O'Hagan's hand slipped into his jacket pocket and with some difficulty he pulled out a plastic HMV bag. He passed it into the car, and received in return a different but identical bag. He put this new bag in his jacket, then returned to the restaurant and the other car drove off. Murphy called in the plates.

Half an hour later Carter called back. 'Vehicle licensed to one Vincent Canby, home address in Hackney. I took the liberty of checking his records — he's a dealer.'

'In CDs?'

'In what?'

'What kind of a dealer?'

'What do you think? Why are you watching a drug dealer?'

'I'm not,' said Murphy.

'Do you want to meet for coffee and update me?'

'Not tonight, Josephine.'

O'Hagan and his wife were being given their coats. Then they were at the door. 'Have to go,' said Murphy.

'Who *are* you watching?' Carter asked.

'No one,' said Murphy, then added, 'Just another scumbag.'

He cut the line, then followed the O'Hagans home. He watched the lights go on in their house, one by one, and then, nearly an hour later, go off, one by one, until just the front bedroom was illuminated. O'Hagan was going to bed with his wife. Perhaps, after a few glasses of wine, they might make love. Murphy watched as an indistinct silhouette appeared briefly against the curtains, and then disappeared as the light was flicked off.

He wondered how O'Hagan slept, if he ever thought about what he had done. Or perhaps what he had done to Murphy's family was but a drop in the ocean of his crimes. Perhaps his capacity for violence had horrified him to such an extent that he had renounced it and moved to London to reinvent himself and do good, like supplying drugs in CD bags to the poor addicted of Hackney. Murphy had known all sorts of terrorists in his time; some really had seen the light, though most used it only as an aid to getting out early. Many terrorists, though, were so completely convinced of the righteousness of their actions that they would probably never, ever lose a moment's sleep over the atrocities they had committed. He was certain that O'Hagan fell into the latter category, and that he slept like the baby he had killed.

★ ★ ★

Two hours after the lights went out, Murphy slipped out of his car. He jumped over the short hedge at the foot of O'Hagan's garden then hurried across the grass and into the protection of the gable wall. He moved up the side of the house, and into the small back yard. All the lights were off back here as well. He approached the kitchen window and peered in. Then he tried the door. It was locked. It didn't matter. There was no panic. He took out his key chain, and flipped on the tiny light that was part of it. He removed a screwdriver from his pocket and began working quietly and methodically at the door.

In ten minutes he was in.

He stood in the kitchen for a while, allowing his eyes to become accustomed to the gloom. Then he moved across the room, carefully stepping between a table and chairs and the three stools which sat beside a breakfast bar, and tiptoed through an open door into the hall. Again he stood here until he could pick out shapes in the darkness. He crept down the hall; there were rooms to his left and right. The door to the left was open, the door to the right closed. He chose left: a living room or lounge. He could see the outline of a TV with the red standby button still on; a CD player and CDs in a metal stand. Photographs in frames above a hearth. He went in and gently closed the door. Then he switched on the light.

He approached the hearth, and examined the photos. O'Hagan with a darts trophy. O'Hagan and his wife just married. His wife, one of a group of young nurses. A portrait-style photograph of O'Hagan, his wife and either his or her parents. He turned to the CDs and ran his fingers down the stand, turning his head slightly so that he could read their titles: Fleetwood Mac — *Tusk*. Meatloaf — *Bat out of Hell*. Barry Manilow — *Live at the Copacabana*. He presumed these were the wife's: further down, the choice was heavier, with an emphasis on Irish bands of the late 1970s — Stiff Little Fingers, Rory Gallagher, Thin Lizzy, the Boomtown Rats, and yes, the album of Undertones classics he'd been playing just the other day. Maybe he did what Murphy did, maybe the old punk songs came out when he was drunk, maybe he blasted out the volume until his wife shouted, 'Turn that racket down!' from upstairs. Except Murphy had no wife, not any more. O'Hagan had stolen her in the same way he had stolen their son. Permanently and irrevocably.

Murphy walked back down the hall and through the kitchen to the back door. He set about repairing the lock. When he was finished he locked the door from the inside, then moved to the front door. He unlocked it and left it half open while he returned to the living room. He picked out the Undertones CD from the stand, and slipped it into the player. He turned the volume up to ten. Then he pressed play.

He was at the door of the lounge when 'Teenage Kicks', began and he was hurrying down the front garden by the time Feargal Sharkey started to sing. He was back in his car in time to see the light go on in the bedroom and was driving past the house and away before the first light came on down-stairs.

No sign of a break-in, nothing stolen.

A ghost in the house.

24

'Do you think we're becoming friends?' Carter asked.

'No,' said Murphy.

They were back in the West End Subway café. Across the road, *Rip Her To Shreds* did not appear to be gaining in popularity. The matinée show had ended, but only a few lost-looking groups of grim-faced Japanese had emerged. Carter had a coffee, Murphy a Diet Coke, but his stomach was rumbling.

Murphy took a sip, then said, 'Why do you ask?'

'Well, we meet here ostensibly to talk about work; you tell me about your day, I'll tell you about mine, but we never really get anywhere. I don't say much because I haven't been able to find out anything useful, and you don't say much because you choose not to.'

'It's how I work.'

'It's how you're allowed to work. So we end up with a lot of small talk about nothing in particular. Just chatting away like friends. I'm not knocking it, it's just not very productive. If I was in charge — and I'm not obviously — you'd have to make a detailed written report every day so that I could follow the progress of the investigation. How can I help you if I don't know what the hell you're up to?'

'I don't need your help.'

'It's going that well, is it?'

'It's all in the report.'

'*What* report?'

'The one I'll give you when it's all over and the bad guy has handcuffs on.'

Carter sighed and stirred his coffee. 'You're like some kind of private eye.'

'Which kind?'

'I don't know. Like Kojak or Columbo or something.'

'Neither of whom were private eyes.'

'You know what I mean.'

'I wish I did.' Murphy glanced up at the counter. The Subway was busy: all the tables were taken and there was quite a queue. He could still feel his stomach rumbling.

'Look, do you think we're any nearer to nailing this?' Carter said. 'I ask because I'm interested, and also, if I don't find out what the situation is I'll have my balls squeezed in a clamp when I go back to the office.'

'Well, it's kind of hard to say.'

'Could you try?'

'I have some irons in the fire. That's what I do. Then I see if any eggs hatch. From those irons. You know what I mean. I sow the seeds.'

Carter shook his head. 'If you're hungry, go order.'

'Can you hear my tummy?'

'No, but you keep looking up at the menu. Just go and do it, will you?'

'Do you want anything?'

'Information.'

'I'll see if it's on.'

Murphy joined the queue. He didn't really need to look at the menu. They'd been here so often he knew it off by heart. And each day he'd ordered the same thing. A kid in front of him was asking his mum what a sub was. She glanced at Murphy and rolled her eyes and he thought briefly about making the crack about U-boats, but decided against it. Humour was a very personal thing.

The queue moved on. Carter was on his mobile. Murphy wondered what O'Hagan was doing right now. He glanced at his watch. Four twenty-five. Maybe smoking crack cocaine, or thinking about what dinner he might make for his wife, or calling a priest to exorcise the house or an electrician to take a look at the wiring. He would have to check the wife out. Maybe she was also a former terrorist. Maybe they had met at summer camp in Libya. Or perhaps she didn't have a clue. She thought he was just Matt O'Hagan the Irish charmer. That was the sort of thing Confront could do — tip her off, let her know the full horror of what her husband had done. But no. He wasn't interested in hurting the wife, even if she was a terrorist. He wasn't concerned with terrorists and terrorism in general. It was about an individual. One man. Some kind of a man.

'Sir?'

Murphy focused again. The queue had turned out to be one large family group; they'd now picked up their order and taken it outside, and the teenager behind the counter was looking at him expectantly.

'Oh — right. Sorry. I'll have the uh, usual, the uh — £2.99 tuna sub, cookie and Coke deal . . . except make that a Diet Coke.'

'I'm sorry, sir, we have no cookies left.'

Murphy glanced down at the display shelf beside the till; it was divided into three, with the first section devoted to doughnuts, the second to crisps and the third would have held cookies. Now it just held crumbs.

'Oh, right. Well, I'll take a doughnut instead.'

'The doughnut isn't part of the deal, sir. You can substitute the cookie with the crisps.'

'I don't fancy the crisps. I want the doughnut.'

'The doughnut isn't part of the deal.'

'Yes, I heard you. I mean, what I really want is the cookie, and what you're advertising up there is the cookie, but you don't have the cookie, and I'm just asking you if I can have the doughnut instead. It doesn't seem to me that there's a hell of a lot of difference between a cookie and a doughnut.'

'You can have the cri — '

'I don't want the crisps. I'm salt and vinegar intolerant. I want the doughnut.'

'The doughnut's not part of the — '

'I know it's not! OK — look. Tell you what. Forget the crisps. Forget the doughnut. I'll pay for the sub and the Diet Coke, and you just give me back what I'm losing out on the cookie, OK? Is that OK?'

The boy shrugged. 'Up to you,' he said.

Murphy counted three pound coins one by one onto the counter. The boy swept them off into his hand and rang them into the till. He took out Murphy's change, put it down before him with a receipt and then turned to organise his meal. Ordinarily Murphy wouldn't have looked at the change, but when you're pissed off it's the little things that provoke evil fascination.

Three pence.

Three 1ps.

'Excuse me?'

The boy, with his back to the counter, either didn't hear or was deliberately ignoring him.

'I said, excuse me?'

Now the boy turned, with an empty soft drink cup in his hand. 'Sir?'

'What's this?' Murphy nodded down at the change.

'Your change, sir.'

'Three p?'

'Sir.'

'Are you taking the piss?'

'Sir?'

'Are you taking the fucking piss?'

'Sir?'

'Three fucking pence?'

'That's the difference between — '

Then he lost it, reaching across and grabbing the boy by his shirt and half-dragging him across the counter.

'Three fucking pence!' he yelled. 'Do you think that's fucking funny?'

'Sir, please . . .'

He could see the shock and horror in the boy's face, and was aware of his own mad tension bursting against him, but he couldn't do anything about it. 'That's the trouble with you fuckers,' he hissed. 'No fucking initiative, no fucking brains. Can't you see, if you'd just gone a little way towards meeting me,

251

been a bit more pleasant about it, you might have had a customer for life? That I might have eaten all my meals in here, that I might have told my fucking friends, and *their* friends, and your boss would have seen all the business you were doing and how profits were shooting up and he would have realised what a hot wire you were and you would have been manager in no time and then area manager and then a director and then managing director and then profit sharing and shares and then some big fucking super international conglomerate would have bought you out and you would have been a multi-millionaire overnight and all you had to fucking do was give me the fucking doughnut?'

The boy's eyes were scrunched up; he was on the verge of tears. Nevertheless he began to say, 'But it wasn't part of the — '

And Murphy's fist shot back, ready to punch him hard, ready to really knock him out, but then his hand was grabbed and someone was saying, 'Murphy . . . Murphy!'

He struggled to free his hand. The boy needed to be taught a lesson. He needed to know that . . .

'*Murphy!*' Carter was white-faced, and his grip was hard. 'Come on!'

Carter began to drag him backwards.

Murphy let go of the boy's shirt. The boy staggered back. Carter waved a finger at him. 'It's all right . . . it's all right!' he said. 'Police!' And then he had a card in his hand and he was holding it up. 'We have him now!' and he began to frogmarch Murphy out of the shop, and the surprising thing was that now he didn't have it in him to resist. He could have flattened Carter and made a run for it. Or decked him and then gone after the boy. The boy had a fundamental misunderstanding of how capitalism could best work to his advantage. He had to be told, he had to be . . . but it didn't matter, it didn't matter. Murphy's legs felt suddenly weak and his arms tired and he allowed himself to be propelled through the door and a few yards up along the street.

Then Carter threw him up against a wall. 'What the fuck are you playing at?' he yelled. 'Christ!'

Murphy slumped forward, Carter pushed him back. Murphy slammed two hands into Carter's chest, knocking him off-balance. He staggered back between two groups of tourists who quickly skipped away from the trouble and didn't look back. Carter stood, his eyes wide with disbelief. Murphy shook his head. He stared at the pavement. He took a deep breath. Then another. 'Sorry,' he said.

Carter came forward, then turned and stood with his back against the wall right beside him. 'What the fuck is up with you?'

Murphy shrugged. 'It's that time of the month.'

Carter stared at him, not getting at all the fact that he'd already sought cover in a joke. 'What do you mean?'

'Nothing. *Nothing!*' Murphy pushed himself off the wall. 'Those fucking people just piss me off.'

'I could tell.'

Murphy laughed then.

Carter said, 'Is there more?'

'More what?'

'You know. You're fucking wound up like ... ' He sighed. 'Murphy, is there something wrong, other than the usual stuff that's wrong? Has something happened? Did something happen — something in Ireland?'

'Nope.'

'Something to do with the case, then.'

'Nope.'

'What then?'

'I had an argument about a doughnut, Carter.' He kicked at something invisible on the pavement.

'It's more than that.'

'Yes, it is. There's a cookie involved as well. It's a mystery. The disappearing cookie. The disappearing cookie and the decline of western civilisation. Sorry.' He moved up to Carter again and playfully punched him on the arm. 'I fucked up, all right? It could be worse.'

'You're sure?'

'I'm sure.'

Carter nodded. He straightened his tie. Murphy turned and started to walk back towards the Subway.

'What the fuck are you doing?' Carter asked incredulously, hurrying after him and then standing in front of him.

'I'm going to get my sub. I paid for it.'

Carter shook his head. 'I don't fucking believe you.' He placed a hand on Murphy's chest and pushed him gently backwards. 'You wait here,' he said. '*I'll* get the fucking sub.'

25

Murphy entered Dr Jeffers's office at 2.15, exactly on time for his appointment. He said, 'I'm not late, am I?' to Susan.

'No, you're fine, I'll just . . . ' She went to buzz him in, but then hesitated and said, 'I hope you don't mind, but I heard about what happened to your son. I just wanted to say sorry.'

'Not your fault,' he said.

'I know, but just . . . well.' She smiled, he nodded. She pressed the button and he went on through to Jeffers's office. The psychiatrist was behind his desk, dressed in a smart, dark-blue suit with a thin red tie, and engrossed in a report. He held up a finger as Murphy took his seat, then read on for another thirty seconds until, evidently finished, he nodded to himself and closed the file. He looked up at Murphy and said, 'Well, how are we?'

'We?'

'It's a figure of speech, Martin.'

Murphy nodded. He looked to the window. It was a grey London day. He folded his legs. He unfolded them. He looked at his fingernails, then back to Jeffers. 'I'm fine,' he said. 'Just fine.'

Jeffers opened a different file, lifted a pen and began to write, calling out the words for Murphy's benefit. 'The patient is not quite so full of the joys of spring this time.' He glanced up. 'Is he?'

'He? Me? We.' Murphy sighed. 'No, of course I'm not full of the joys of fucking spring. I'm in shock, I think. Finding out about my son. And fainting like that. They must think I'm a right — '

'They don't think anything.' Jeffers smiled supportively. He put his pen down and clasped his hands. 'Martin, as I said at the time, although I'm not sure if you heard me, sometimes I have to make difficult decisions, and whether to tell you about the man responsible for your son's death in private or public was one of the hardest I've ever had to make. But I think in the end, it was right for you, and right for the group.'

Murphy nodded. 'They were great.' He started to say something else, then stopped.

'But?'

'It's . . . well, it's not enough, is it?'

'What isn't enough?'

'The group and . . . look, to be perfectly honest with you I've gone and done something stupid. Well, not stupid — it feels

257

like absolutely the right thing to do, but you're . . . well, you're not going to see it that way.'

'Martin, don't presume that I'm going to see anything in any particular way. Just tell me. What have you done?'

'This . . . it's all covered by . . . it's confidential, isn't it?'

'Yes, of course it is.'

'But I don't want you to even write this down.'

'That's fine.'

'Well . . . ' He took a deep breath, then looked away, then back. 'I've . . . I went to see someone about getting a gun. I mean, this guy O'Hagan, he slit my son's throat, you know? It's not enough to just . . . watch him.'

Jeffers lifted his pen again, but not to write with; he rolled it between his fingers as he searched for the right words. 'That is . . . perfectly understandable, Martin. It's a natural reaction. But do you know what I take from it, other than a desire for revenge?' Murphy shook his head. 'That at least part of you knows that it's wrong. Otherwise you wouldn't be here, telling me. Do you know what I mean?'

'Kind of.'

'Is this someone getting you the gun?'

'I don't know. I think so.'

'Do you want to tell me who it is?'

Murphy shrugged. 'An old police contact.'

'And if he gets you the gun, you intend to go and confront O'Hagan, get him to admit his guilt?'

'No, I didn't really plan on talking to him.'

'So you will find him and you will kill him?' Murphy nodded. 'And then you'll be satisfied?'

He thought about that for several long moments. Then he shook his head wearily. 'No. I'll never be satisfied. I'll never be even. But he'll be dead, and that's something, isn't it?' Jeffers didn't respond. He just kept his eyes on Murphy, silently inviting him to continue. 'Dr Jeffers — you're a psychiatrist, you have all your certificates and your nice office and you do all sorts of good: you talk to people, counsel them, give them the benefit of your experience, you discuss the differences between right and wrong, morality. But when you go home at night, when you're not working, do you still think like a psychiatrist, or like . . . '

'A man?'

Murphy nodded.

Jeffers sat back in his chair. 'That's a very interesting question. It's along the lines of 'physician heal thyself', isn't it? Although when all is said and done, it doesn't matter

259

what or how I think when I go home, because this isn't about me. It's about you.'

'I know — I know. And sorry for asking. It's just . . . you know, he's out there, and I'm sitting at home and I've no one to bounce off.'

'No girlfriend?'

'No girlfriend.'

'No best friends?'

'Sure, but none I can really talk to.'

A buzzer sounded beside Jeffers. He touched a button and Susan said, 'Dr Jeffers, your next appointment is here. Early. But he's,' and her voice dropped to a whisper, 'in a bit of a state.'

'Very well.' The psychiatrist looked back to Murphy. 'I'm sorry, Martin — sounds like an emergency.' He stood.

Murphy stood as well. 'But this is an emergency too.'

'No, it's not.'

'Of course it's a bloody emergency!'

'No, Martin, this will keep. You don't have a gun, and you haven't done anything rash. You're still in control. We have to explore this further. And think of this as well: even if you had a gun and you were to kill him, you're the first person the police would come looking for. It wouldn't just be the end of his life, it would be the end of your own.'

'I don't care about that.'

'Well, other people care. The Group cares, and we will look after you. I promise you that.' He extended his hand, and Murphy clasped it. 'I promise.'

Then he walked him to the door.

26

He was just sitting there, watching something about water buffalo or bison or wildebeest, with Richard Attenborough — *David* Attenborough doing the commentary — and the next thing, there were tears on his cheeks and he could hardly stop them. Getting all emotional over a fucking dead zebra, being torn about by lions.

What was that song? *If they could see me now, tra la la la la la* . . . A half-eaten Chinese at his feet, an empty wine bottle, crying over hippos mating for life.

Fuck.

Why had he ever become a cop? Why had he, a Catholic, joined a largely Protestant police force? Wasn't it just asking for trouble? Wasn't his whole life one big abject lesson in contrariness? Why did he always have to be the square peg in a round hole? Except he wouldn't have called it that. Just for badness he would have said nigger in the woodpile. Was that anarchy? Or was that the third amendment, or the fifth, or whatever fucking amendment guaranteed free speech?

How drunk was he?

Not enough.

He had, quite consciously, put everything he had ever loved in the line of fire. He had thought only of himself, as if the world and its pleasures existed only for him, and then he had been brought spinning back down to earth. A space station, burning up on re-entry.

He would never outrun it.

It would always be with him.

A zebra torn about by lions. Feeding on a bloody carcass.

The doorbell rang and he cursed because he had a vague memory of inviting McBride round. He forced himself up. On the way to answer it he deposited the Chinese and the bottle in the bin. The doorbell rang again. *Hold your fucking horses.* He ran his fingers through what was left of his hair, then opened the door.

Andrea was standing there.

'Hello, stranger,' he said.

'Hi.'

'How's your tooth?'

'What?' And then she went, 'Oh, it's fine. Aren't you going to invite me in?'

'OK.' He stepped back and she came in. He closed the door, then when he turned from it she put her arms around him and kissed him.

When she stopped he said, 'Oh. I thought you'd gone off me.'

'No,' she said.

Then she took him by the hand and led him into his bedroom.

★ ★ ★

Lying in bed, her back nestled into his chest and stomach, her hair tangled, a fresh Diet Coke cold and half-drunk on the bedside table, she said, 'You had tears in your eyes when I arrived.'

'I was cutting onions.'

'I don't smell onions.'

'I know, I threw them out.'

'Why did you throw them out?'

'Because they made me cry.'

'Do you throw everything out that makes you cry?'

'Mostly.'

'I'd better be careful then.'

'You better had.'

She turned and kissed him. 'I'm worried about you.'

'What's to worry about?'

'You know what I'm talking about.'

'I certainly don't. I'm fine and dandy, although I do have a propensity to faint in stressful situations.'

She ran her hand through his hair.

He said, 'Do you think I'm going bald?'

'You've just got a high crown.'

'Is that not just a euphemism for going bald? What you're really saying is 'Whoa, Baldy, your hair sure is shooting backwards'.'

'No — it's a high crown. My sister was a hairdresser. I used to work there in the summers. I know the difference between a high crown and baldness. You have a high crown.'

'So you don't think I'm going bald?'

'It might have gone back a little bit, but I'd say you'll still look pretty much the same in ten years.'

'So I'm not going bald.'

'No.'

'Could I have that in writing?'

She laughed. 'What's this about?'

'Fear of baldness.'

'No, seriously.'

'I don't know.'

She kissed him again, for a long time.

Then he said, 'Do you think I'm overweight?'

'Yes.'

'Oh.'

'Not by much. You're carrying a few extra pounds, but who isn't?'

'But you wouldn't say 'Hey, fat chops,' if you saw me walking down the street.'

'God, no. Do you ever look around you? What's this about?'

'Nothing.'

'You know, my sister used to tell me that men are much vainer than women and I didn't believe her, then I married Lawrence, and you know, it's true.'

'I'm not vain. I'm just concerned about my health.'

'What does your hair have to do with your health?'

'Well, it's all connected, isn't it?' He looked at her, close enough to him so that he could just flick out his tongue and lick the end of her nose. It made her giggle, and she buried her head against his chest so that he couldn't do it again. 'You know, Woody Allen says sex is the most fun you can have without laughing. I think he got it wrong. Laughing's a big part of sex.'

'I think you might have a point,' said Andrea. She looked down at his groin. 'In fact, you definitely have a point.'

'Laughing's not the same as jokes,' he said.

So she nipped his arse and he yelped and squeezed her hard, forcing her head up. He pretended to kiss her, but licked her nose instead and she screamed and dug him in the ribs.

But very soon, they were making love.

∗ ★ ∗

A couple of hours later, past midnight, he heard the soft purr of his mobile sitting on the table beside the now-warm Diet Coke. He turned the phone towards him, recognised the number, then quietly slipped out of bed. He padded across the floor as quickly as he could, then entered the living room, closing the door behind him before pushing the button.

'Hi,' he said quietly, still moving, getting as far away from Andrea as he could.

'Martin? It's Lawrence.'

'Hi, Lawrence.'

'How're you doing?'

'Can't complain.'

'Did I wake you?'

'It being after twelve on a Tuesday night, no, of course not.'

'Do you have company?'

'No — why?'

'You're whispering.'

'It's late and the walls are paper-thin.'

Lawrence laughed quietly. 'Just thought you'd like to know, that thing you were looking for — I have it, if you're still interested.'

'I'm still interested.'

'Thought you might be. You want to come

down and pick it up?'

'Love to. When are you talking about?'

'Tonight. Now.'

'I've no clothes on.'

'Well, put some on. I don't want to hold onto this any longer than I have to.'

'OK, of course, no problem.'

'I'm down the stadium. See you outside.'

'You'll need to give me half an hour to get there.'

'OK. See you then.' Lawrence cut the line.

Murphy looked at the dull glow of the phone for several moments, standing naked in the otherwise dark room. Then he congratulated himself with a quiet, 'Bingo,' and turned back to the bedroom.

★   ★   ★

As he climbed into his trousers, Murphy realised that Andrea was looking at him. Even in the darkness he could see the brightness of her eyes. Which was nice. 'Sorry,' he whispered. 'Didn't mean to wake you.'

'You didn't. The phone.' She reached across and turned on the bedside light. She began to smooth her damp hair down. 'Where are you off to?'

'I do some security work. Someone's cried off. Have to take it where you can get it.'

'When will you be back?' And then she seemed to realise what she'd said; her hand slipped from her hair to her brow and rubbed at it as if she was trying to erase her words. She pulled the quilt up around her and said, 'Sorry. It's got nothing to do with me.'

He found it quite endearing. He sat on the bed and took her hand. He kissed it and said, 'If you're here when I get back, that's OK.' Then he lifted her chin and kissed it as well, and then her lips, and then her nose.

27

He sat in his car outside the stadium, aware of how exposed he was, but knowing there was nothing else for it. This was how he did it. Without the cavalry waiting in the wings, or his every movement monitored on a satellite. There was no reason to change now. Get inside, expose yourself, expose them, walk away. Now Lawrence was on his way; perhaps he was out there now, across the street, watching, making sure he was alone. Maybe he had the gun. Maybe he had it so he could walk up to Murphy and blow his head off because he'd figured out that even an ex-cop couldn't resist one last catch. Or maybe he had finally worked out what his wife was up to. Maybe the phone call had come from right outside Murphy's apartment. Maybe he had watched her go in, and not come out. Maybe he had knelt with his ear pressed against the door, or his eye to the keyhole, watching, listening as his wife disrobed and screamed out Murphy's name in orgasm.

A lot of maybes.

It was dark here. The stadium floodlights

were off. No moon. The rain was thumping across the car with the staccato rhythm of a machine gun that never had to reload. Murphy had the radio on, tuned to Radio 5 Live. He was listening to a phone-in programme about another disastrous performance by Tottenham Hotspur. Most of the callers wanted the manager to go. Some blamed the underperforming prima donnas who were getting fifty grand a week. Fifty grand. More in a week than he got in a year.

Lights swept over the car and he tensed. He turned down the volume. But then the other vehicle was gone again; he followed the brake-lights in his mirror.

When will you be back?

They had slept together twice.

When will you be back?

He had not enjoyed, if that was the word, a steady relationship since he'd split up with his wife. That was a long time. And he wasn't entirely sure if sleeping together twice even constituted a relationship.

Sleeping together. Making love. Having sex.

Was there a difference? Were they all variations on a theme or were there defined, literal boundaries? There had been precious little sleep. There had been virtually no talking, no whispers of affection, no promises

271

of everlasting devotion, nothing one might confuse with love, and the making of. Which left sex, and there had been plenty of that. But was that it? Was it nothing but the rutting of man and woman? Could she just have been anyone? Any port in a storm? And could he? Was he using her? Was she using him? Were they using each other? And if they were, did it matter? And if they weren't, what did it mean?

She was beautiful and funny, and sharp, and damaged.

And he was — well, it was more of what he wasn't, which was balding or particularly overweight. He smiled at that and thought about buying a kebab on the way home. He checked his hairline in the mirror. She was right. It was high, but Snowdon high as opposed to Everest high. It looked fine. What was he getting so het up about anyway?

Then there were lights in the mirror and this time they were coming right up close, full-beam, forcing him to look away. Then they were switched off but the rain was too heavy to see much beyond the dull outline of the vehicle now stopped behind his, and that there was a figure emerging from it and hurrying towards his own car.

'Fifty grand a week for what? When I played for Luton we were lucky . . .'

'*You played for Luton?*'

Murphy switched the radio off as his door opened and Brian Armstrong climbed in, his face already pink and red against the rain, his blue windcheater soaked through. 'Christ,' he said, 'that's wild.'

Murphy looked at him, confusion etched on his face. 'Brian? I thought . . . '

'Yes, I know, I know.' He was unzipping his coat and reaching inside. 'Lawrence phoned me. Little matter of a gun.' He produced a gun, and pointed it at Murphy's stomach.

They call it heightened reality.

When in a different world you can hear the flutter of butterfly wings and the chatter of ants, but here it was just the rasp of an old man's stubble against the cheap plastic of his raincheater; the little catch in his breath from the too many fags that would, one day very soon, catch up with him; the thump of his own heart, the blood rushing through his veins, the pinched feeling at the back of his neck; the scratch on his chest where Andrea had caught him with a nail.

Then Armstrong smiled and turned the gun around. He held it out to Murphy and said, 'Relax.'

And heightened reality was gone in an instant and even as he smiled back at the old man and grasped the weapon, he was missing it already: those were the moments he lived for, when everything became focused and real, and the pain and pleasure were mixed into one glorious cocktail and anything was possible, good or bad or awful.

He turned the gun in his hand. 'I don't understand.'

'This is how we do it.'

'We?'

'C'mon, Martin. This is how we get our revenge. We help each other out. You kill my enemy, I kill yours.'

Murphy opened up the gun. It was loaded. He snapped it shut again and looked back at Armstrong. 'I don't understand. All I want to do is — '

'Martin — this is the only way it can work.'

'*It?* What're you talking about?'

'Use your head, man. The gun isn't for Matthew O'Hagan. I want you to kill Michael Caplock.'

'Michael Caplock?'

'He destroyed my daughter. He *dismembered* her.'

'I know, I know, but this is — '

'Martin, when I tell most people about what happened, I have to say: 'Can you imagine what that's like?' But I don't have to say it to you, do I? You've been there. So you know. So please, take it, do this for me. And then, in a little while, we'll get your guy.'

'What do you mean?'

'O'Hagan. He'll be dead, and you'll have a cast-iron alibi.'

'You'll kill him for me, and I won't have anything to do with it?'

'Not me, someone else. Don't you see? That's the beauty of it. Unless you're actually pulling the trigger, you'll never know.'

'Christ.'

'I know. It's a big thing, a lot to take in. But it makes perfect sense — you must see that.'

Murphy nodded slowly. A fresh set of headlights swept over the vehicle, and then moved on. The windows were beginning to mist up. He moved the driver's window down just a fraction, enough to clear the mist and so that he could feel a vague spray of rainwater across his cheek.

Not a killer, but *killers*. Not a lone gunman, but revengers, working to a plan.

'Who decides who kills whom?' he asked.

'It doesn't matter, Martin. You just do what you have to do, and then you get sorted out.'

Murphy leaned back against the headrest and blew air out of his cheeks. 'This is fucking crazy.' He turned to look at Armstrong again. 'This is how the other four were killed, isn't it?'

'Four?' And Armstrong kind of smiled, and

Murphy knew there were more than four. Perhaps a lot more.

'Just because they don't show up on the news doesn't mean they haven't been . . . well, you know.'

They sat in silence for a while. Armstrong gave a little shiver, so Murphy closed the window again. The old man nodded his thanks and said, 'I should move to somewhere sunny. I'm not built for this kind of weather.' He turned and surveyed the back seat, then tilted his head a little to look at the underside of the roof.

'Nice car,' he said. 'I was thinking about changing mine. Any problems with it?'

'None at all.'

'Did you buy it new?'

'No, second-hand.'

'Can't understand people who buy new cars. They lose a couple of grand as soon as they drive them out of the showroom.'

'Yeah, I know, it's mad.'

'Though I can see the attraction.'

Sitting with a gun in my hand, discussing new cars and retribution.

'Do I get time to think about this?'

'Well, no. Be better if you make your choice here and now. Save a lot of awkwardness later, don't you think?'

Murphy nodded. He turned the gun in his

hand again. 'It's not that I don't like it. I mean, it's brilliant. I'm just . . . I'm not sure if I could just go up to someone I don't know and . . .'

'You do know him.'

'What do you mean?'

'Because they're all the same. They're the scum of the earth. Martin, believe me, I've done it, there's no guilt involved at all. But do you know what there *is*? Satisfaction. Even a tiny bit of pride. We're taking a little bit of control back from them. I know it's hard to absorb, but listen to me, son. They've already fucked up your life, so why make it worse by killing him yourself and getting put away for it?'

'I know, you're right. But Christ.'

'It's a big thing, Martin, and you don't enter into it lightly.'

'I know, I wouldn't. But Jesus, am I the only one who doesn't know? Is this whole thing with the group been like one big audition?'

Armstrong smiled and shook his head. 'No, not really. And no, they're not all involved. It's — well, I suppose it's a bit like your Irish terrorists, Martin. I mean, I'm sure you know more about this than I do, but don't they have both a military wing and a political wing? Just as a bird can't fly without two wings, the two wings have to know what each wing is doing because you can't fly in different directions at the same time.'

'So there's some with a foot in each camp?'

'Some.'

'Jesus, you wouldn't know to look at them.'

'Well, that's the magic of it.'

'What about the funny wee fella always talking about movies?'

'It's better not to say.'

'Or Lawrence's wife, Andrea. Does she get to go out and — '

'Martin — don't. The less you know, the less any of us knows, the better. Just make your choice. Take the gun and do this, or give it back.'

'And what if I give it back?'

'Then no harm done. And I'm just an old man who gets up three times in the middle of the night for a pee, spinning a yarn.'

Murphy weighed the gun in his hand. 'I get up as well,' he said.

'It's old age,' said Armstrong.

★ ★ ★

He drove around. He found himself outside McBride's church and convinced himself that a couple of hours sitting in the quiet might concentrate his mind, and if God happened to turn up he could ask His advice as well, but it was three in the morning and he had to accept that his expectation that the church would be open and that it would welcome him into the sanctity of its sanctuary was somewhat naïve. The door was bolted and padlocked and there was an alarm blinking high up on the masonry. So he sat in his car some more and listened to the radio and played a couple of CDs — Elvis Costello's greatest hits — Christ, even that was fourteen years old — and his Juliet Turner CD.

McBride lived just near by. He could phone him up and tell him to open the church, that he had urgent God business, but what was the point? Then his friend would feel the need to hang around and counsel and support when all Murphy wanted was somewhere to sit and think and mull.

The rain was long over, the streets were damp, the traffic sparse.

London should be like this always.

And it soon will be, the rate Armstrong and Lawrence and whoever the hell else is involved are cleaning the streets.

★ ★ ★

He drove slowly home, the music and radio off now, hearing just the purr of the engine and the hiss of tyres through the rainwater which was taking its time to drain away.

It was just after 6 a.m. when he pulled up outside the apartment. He stashed the gun in the boot, then used the stairs rather than the lift. He unlocked the front door and said, 'Andrea?' quietly, but there was no response.

The bedroom was empty, and the bed was made. When he went into the kitchen to put the kettle on he saw that she'd set out a bowl of Frosties and a spoon for him on the table.

He smiled.

He sat heavily in the chair and stared at the breakfast. Domesticity and a gun. Love in a cold climate. A ghost in more than one house.

Matthew O'Hagan.

Matthew O'Hagan.

28

The Subway café was out, for obvious reasons — the entire chain of them. Carter reckoned there'd probably be Wanted posters up all over the country. And CCTV footage cropping up on the local news about the barbarian who'd nearly caused a riot over a cookie.

'It wasn't about the cookie,' Murphy said.

'Looked to me like it was.'

'It was the principle.'

'The principle of the cookie.'

'It was about capitalism and intransigence.'

'Whatever you say.'

'And I wouldn't have hit him.'

'You gave a fair impression of someone who was about to do just that.'

'I was angry. They promised and they didn't deliver.'

'Murphy — sometimes that's just the way the cookie crumbles.'

Carter laughed, and Murphy threatened to punch him. They were in a Safeways in Hammersmith, each pushing a trolley, looking for all the world like a couple of single dads meeting up for mutual support and to bitch about their ex-wives. Murphy was an old hand at shopping for himself, and had to help Carter release the trolley.

'And what about the pound?' Carter had asked.

'You get that back at the end.'

'Oh — right, I see.' He was playing stupid, but only just.

'I don't even know if you're married yet,' Murphy said.

'I'm engaged.'

'But you live with her, right?'

'Yeah.'

'She has short blonde hair.'

'It's darker now and longer.'

'It's Beth.'

'It's Louise.'

'Who was Beth?'

'I have no idea.'

They were going through tinned foods. Murphy was choosing between two different types of soup when Carter said, 'We're only pretending.'

'What do you mean?'

'I mean, we're not really grocery shopping, are we? We're just meeting up here as our cover, and we'll fill our trolleys as we talk and then just ditch them somewhere when we've sorted everything out.'

'Speak for yourself!'

'You're actually shopping? You don't have a list.'

'I don't need a list. I know what I need, and more to the point I know where it all is.'

Carter looked about him. 'How could you? You don't live anywhere near here.'

'Carter — I use Safeways all the time; they're all laid out the same. Well, most of them are, depending on the shape of the building.'

Carter rolled his eyes, and lifted two cans at random. 'I think you've been undercover for too long.'

'I'm not undercover now. I'm shopping. What about the gun?'

'Analysed every which way, there's nothing on it besides your fingerprints and his. Do you believe him, the way he told it?'

'Don't see why not. Did you ever see *Strangers on a Train*?'

Carter thought for a moment, then shook his head. 'I saw *Murder on the Orient Express*.'

Murphy lifted a tin of Heinz Baked Beans, the sugarfree kind. 'No, *Strangers on a Train* — two guys meet on this train, right, they talk about the people giving them grief, and they hatch a plot to kill each other's enemy and get away with murder. That's basically what Armstrong, and Lawrence, and God knows

283

who else are doing. But it's like the Jerry Bruckheimer version — *Stacks of Strangers on a Whole Pile of Trains*. They all take their turns at killing, and there's nothing to connect any of them.'

'Apart from Confront.'

'Apart from Confront, or at least part of it.'

'So we pick them all up and one of them will crack.'

Murphy pushed his trolley on, turning the corner into a frozen-food aisle. 'No, we don't,' he said. 'Not yet. We have to force them out into the open.'

'Giving you a gun was kind of out in the open. We have Armstrong, we have Lawrence, let's just squeeze them.'

'We don't have Lawrence, he can deny everything. Armstrong — so he gave me a gun. It's clean, isn't it? No, we have to play along for a while yet.'

'And how are you going to do that without . . . ' He trailed off, and gave Murphy a look. 'Murphy, you're not — '

'I have to kill Michael Caplock.' He leaned into a fridge and produced a packet of frozen vegetables. 'Did you ever try these? They're like steamed, but you do them in the microwave.'

'I never did,' said Carter. 'And what's

Michael Caplock going to have to say about all this?'

'Do you really care?'

Murphy pushed on with his trolley.

★ ★ ★

When they were in the checkout queue Carter said: 'So if it's this *Strange People on a Train* thing . . . '

'*Strangers on a Train*, to the *n*th degree.'

'Whatever. If that's what it is, and you're supposed to be killing Michael Caplock for Brian Armstrong, who is he, or they, killing for *you*? Far as they're concerned, Walker's already dead.'

'I gave them some bullshit about a terrorist I had a run-in with.'

'What sort of bullshit?'

'Does it matter?'

'Well yes, if you're fingering someone and they kill him and it comes back to haunt us.'

Murphy moved his trolley forward. Carter followed.

'The thing is,' Murphy said, 'sometimes to make it work you've got to use personal stuff. Makes it real. So I told them this guy was involved in the murder of my son.'

'And was he?'

'No, of course not. They never caught those bastards.'

'But this guy's got form anyway.'

'Yeah. He's a cunt of the highest order.'

'What's he called?'

'What is this, *Twenty Questions*?'

'If I don't know who he is, how am I going to protect him?'

Murphy gave a short, sarcastic laugh. 'Yeah. Of course. Should have thought of that myself. Should have been the top of my list of priorities. You should apply for one.'

'I should apply for one what?'

'A discount card.' He reached forward and plucked an application form from a pile sitting in a plastic holder at the foot of the checkout. 'Saves you a packet. His name's Matthew O'Hagan.'

'And he's living here in London?'

'Yes, he is.'

'And you're going to put him in the line of fire.'

'You catch on fast.'

'Michael Caplock and Matthew O'Hagan. This is both unethical and immoral.'

'You think? What about 'nothing ventured, nothing gained'?'

'That'll sound good in court.'

Murphy shrugged. 'Yeah, right.'

'Meaning?' Murphy remained silent. Carter

shook his head. 'The thing about you, Murphy, is you're so fucking cryptic. And sometimes cryptic can be a right pain in the arse.'

'You like everything spelled out in a report.'

'Is that so bad? Without reports everything else is chaos.'

'Anarchy.'

'Exactly.'

'Anarchy in the UK.'

'Yes.'

'Great song,' said Murphy.

'What is?'

'Never mind.'

* * *

Outside, Murphy pushed his trolley in one direction, Carter in the other. When he got to his car Carter opened the boot and began to load in the half-dozen bags of groceries he'd managed to accumulate. Thompson got out of the car to give him a hand.

'If I'd known you were actually going to do some shopping, I'd have asked you to get me some stuff.'

'Sorry.'

'And I've a discount card in my wallet — could have saved yourself a small fortune. My wife swears — '

'Could we just get the fuck out of here?'

Carter slammed the boot closed, then got back in the car. Thompson smiled, then climbed in behind the wheel. As he started the engine he glanced across at his pensive-looking colleague. 'Did you say anything to him?'

Carter shook his head.

'This guy Kincaid, he seems pretty straight.'

'I know.'

'If Murphy goes native on us, then it'll be our arses as well as his.'

'He won't, he's fine.'

'He's lying to us.'

'He's not lying to us. That's just how he is. It's always on a need-to-know basis.'

'Well, we need to know what the fuck he's up to.'

Carter slapped his hand suddenly against the dash. 'And I'm telling you he's fine, so just shut the fuck up and drive.'

Thompson started the engine. 'On your own head be it,' he said, and put the car into reverse.

29

Michael Caplock had no idea how they had found out. All he knew was: a week after moving in, a letter got pushed through his front door. He didn't bother picking it up for a couple of hours because the post had already been and he supposed it was just some flyer for a local restaurant or laundry or something. Then when he was on the way to the bin with a full bag in his hand he scooped it up and then it flapped open of its own accord and he saw the first words, and he knew they were on to him, because it was no way to start advertising your restaurant:

Murdering Bastard.

He hadn't been there long enough to make friends with the neighbours, but he'd said hello to them. He'd helped one woman guide her pram up from her basement apartment across the street and she'd been chatty, even mildly flirtatious, and he'd laughed and joked with her right back. Then one day he'd been going out while the old man next door was arriving home with his shopping and he'd smiled across and the man had said, 'That's a cold 'un,' with some sort of regional accent he couldn't quite place.

Get out while you can, we know who you are.

Not 'I', but 'we'. Could be one person, trying to sound more impressive, or the whole street or neighbourhood, firing a warning shot across his bows. Caplock put the rubbish in the bin, then returned to his front room with the letter still in his hand. He peered out of the window — across, up, down, nothing different. He hadn't exactly been expecting a lynch mob, just . . . something. Somebody watching perhaps, or a cop car. Yes — a cop car. They were, of course, the only real suspects. London was a vast and anonymous place, and after his release from police custody he'd reverted to using his mother's maiden name of Olsen; the house was in that name, ditto his utility bills, so there was no reason for anyone to suspect that he was Michael Caplock.

You will burn in hell.

Was that a threat? Or a statement? Or both? He should take the letter down to the local station and make a complaint. Or contact one of those organisations that protected people who were falsely accused of crimes. Shame those neighbours into admitting their scurrilous act of intimidation, let them see the error of their ways, let them welcome him with open arms.

On the other hand, of course, he could just hack that woman with the pram.

Kill her, fuck her, cut her up and put her in a suitcase and float her in the Thames. It was always an option. Show them what he could do and get away with.

No!

He had turned the corner, he had promised himself not to do anything like that again. It was sick, sick, sick, but also — wonderful, wonderful, wonderful and for a few moments, standing by the window his hands grew moist with anticipatory sweat. There was a sudden gnawing feeling in the pit of his stomach and he felt the heat sweep over him, the heat which always . . .

No!

He had promised himself — he had sworn. He had different medication now. It was working. It *was* working.

Calm. Calmer.

It was the cops, it had to be the cops. They were still conducting their enquiries; the case was not closed. He had been obliged, over his solicitor's protests, to provide the police with his address and contact numbers, and to report to them once a week. They were the only ones who knew.

It was way beyond harassment.

He stood by the window in exactly the same position for an hour, watching. It was only when his left leg went into a crampy spasm that he realised how long he'd been there. He winced, flexed, then limped around the room until the circulation righted itself. When he returned to the window he saw the girl across the street, struggling once again with her pram. What was she thinking of anyway, choosing a basement flat with such narrow and twisting steps?

Caplock lifted the *Guardian* he'd bought that morning but hadn't yet read, then slipped out of his front door. Only the girl's top half was visible now, the rest hidden beneath ground level, and she was facing away from him, so he was able to slip away to the left, then cross the road further up and walk back down on her side of the road, with the folded paper under his arm, as if he'd just bought it in the corner shop. When he drew level with her he said, 'Can I give you a hand?'

She turned, the beginnings of a nodding smile on her face — and then she froze, and he knew that she knew. She shook her head quickly and said, 'I'm fine.'

So push it a little further.

'It's no trouble.'

He took a step closer, standing between the

railings at the top of the steps, effectively barring her way even if she managed to get the pram any further up. She glanced up again, saw the size of him, the way he was silhouetted against the sun, and her face blanched.

He liked that. Being able to inspire that kind of fear.

'No, really. In fact, I've left the cooker on . . . ' and she began pushing the pram down again. The baby within started to cry at suddenly being rocked hard against the steps. 'I'd better . . . '

He moved — more like swayed — almost following her. If he just gave her a moment to get her key in the door it would be so easy to push her hard through it; she'd land on her stomach, and then he'd be on her before she could scream, or even if she did, with the traffic, with them being virtually under-ground, with the house upstairs vacant, God he could do it and nobody would disturb them. Just the baby, in its pram, crying maybe. And let it. He wouldn't harm a hair on its head. He had no problem with babies. He knew what he was about to do wasn't right — but he wasn't sick. You didn't do anything to babies. Wasn't their fault. Suffer the little children? Suffer their fucking mothers. Sluts.

She had the key in the door, but she was flustered, couldn't get it to turn. He was still standing there, looking down; he looked both ways along the pavement. Nobody.

If I . . .

No!

What was he even thinking of? On his own doorstep. Madness. Madness. There would be other times, other opportunities. The cops were trying to scare him with their letter, trying to get the neighbours to force him out. But he was stronger than that. They couldn't force him out. He was an innocent man. Did he have any convictions for *anything*? No, he did not. He must be strong. Show them that he was a good man. Take his medicine. Then one day . . .

'Well — any time,' he said, and smiled as warmly as he could. He turned and crossed the road, whistling. He was happy. *See? I'm in control.* When he got back to his window, he lifted the letter and tore it into little pieces. They would not hound him out. People were moving in and out of these houses all the time. It was that kind of an area. Sure, they might think he was in some way dangerous now, but in a few months, who would remember? Who would remember?

30

When Murphy arrived for the next meeting of Confront, Jeffers was already preparing to call the group to order. Armstrong was sitting in the back row. Andrea was at the front, but the chairs on either side of her were taken. She smiled across. He smiled back. She blushed and quickly looked down at her own paperwork. Murphy moved in beside Armstrong. As Jeffers made his opening remarks, Murphy whispered, 'I'm thinking of — '

'Not here. Outside.'

Murphy sat back and listened. He didn't contribute anything to the meeting besides the occasional nod or he groaned along with the rest of them when some killer was mentioned, or clapped when Jeffers announced progress in a particular case. He caught Andrea's eye several times, and she caught his. It was eyeball footsie. When they broke for coffee, they moved around each other, talking with different little groups, sometimes with their backs actually touching, but they didn't speak.

He went for a refill. On the other side of

the table Armstrong was deep in conversation with McIntosh and Peter Marinelli — but it was about soccer, not sadists. When Murphy turned with his cup, Jeffers was standing in front of him. The doctor said, 'Tsk-tsk,' and raised an eyebrow.

'Tsk-tsk?' said Murphy.

'You missed your last appointment.'

'I phoned to cancel. I left a message.'

'You phoned after hours so that you wouldn't have to talk to anyone.'

'It was the only chance I got. I had a job I couldn't turn down.'

'I was worried about you.'

'Well — I appreciate it. But I'm fine.'

Jeffers glanced quickly about him, then moved a little closer. 'And the other thing — that's fine as well?'

Murphy nodded. He took a sip of his coffee, looking at Jeffers over the rim of his cup.

'Did you go any further with it?'

'You mean, actually getting a . . . ?' Jeffers nodded. Murphy shook his head. 'No, you were right. It was stupid. *This* is the way to go.'

Jeffers smiled. 'That's a good man,' he said.

★　★　★

After the group was over Murphy walked out with Armstrong. The latter's car, an ancient-looking Metro, was parked about thirty metres along. As they moved towards it Murphy said, 'I've decided. I'm going for it tonight. I'm going to do it tonight.'

'That's good.' Brian took out his keys. 'What time do you reckon?'

'Time? Does it matter?'

'Not really, no.' He stopped then, still short of the car, and gave Murphy a sympathetic look. 'Just, well, it's your first time. I know you were a cop and everything, but this is different. You're going to be nervous. It's understandable. But if something goes wrong and you need to be picked up, or you need to get rid of the weapon or someone to confirm the kill without you having to hang around, that can be arranged.'

'No, I'll be fine, I know what I'm doing.'

'Good. I'm sure you do.'

Armstrong unlocked the door, made to climb in, then hesitated. He turned and extended his hand. Murphy grasped it.

'You're doing the right thing, you know,' Armstrong said.

'I know.'

'And if you have any dark moments after, don't ever make the mistake of thinking this puts you on a par with them. It doesn't. It *can't*.'

Murphy let go of his hand. 'I'll remember that.'

★ ★ ★

When he'd gone Murphy looked around to see if any other members of the group were still hanging about, but there was no one. He crossed the road and walked a couple of hundred yards up towards the pub where he'd gotten drunk with Andrea.

She was sitting at the bar.

'It's not a good sign, this,' he said, 'drinking in the middle of the day.'

'I'm not drinking.' She showed him her drink. 'Sparkling water.'

'That's nice.' He nodded at the barman. 'I'll have a pint. Of beer, that is. Lager.'

'What're you doing later?' Andrea asked.

'Later when?'

'This afternoon, through to say about three tomorrow morning.'

'Why, what did you have in mind?'

'Sex, sex, something to eat, more sex, then Frosties.'

He smiled. 'Nice touch, the Frosties.'

'I thought you'd appreciate it. So, are we on?'

'I can't.'

'Oh.'

'I'm working.'

'Right through until three? What about this afternoon?'

'It's a double shift.'

'Oh.' She took a drink. She nodded to herself. 'Please yourself.'

'It's not like that,' he said.

'Isn't it?' She wouldn't look at him.

'No. Of course not. You think given a choice between going to bed with you and guarding a warehouse full of cigarettes I'm going to choose the cigarettes?' She shrugged. 'I can get you some, if you want. Half-price. I have to make some profit.' He smiled. She didn't. He put his hand on hers, on the bar. 'C'mon, give us a smile.'

'I don't feel like smiling.'

'C'mon, don't be like that.'

She shrugged. She glanced up at him and said, 'Sorry,' then looked away again. 'You have a job to do. And so have I. I shouldn't let myself get distracted.'

'I'm free tomorrow,' Murphy said, 'all day. All night.'

'I'm not. Lawrence wants me to go shopping with him. That's what I'm doing.'

He looked at her. 'Well, that's OK. If you want to go shopping, you go shopping.'

'We made a mistake,' she said. 'We've been stupid. You're right — we should knock it on the head before one of us gets hurt.'

'Andrea, I never said anything about ending it.'

She stood; she took another sip of her drink; she pulled on her coat.

'I know you didn't, but it's bloody obvious.'

'Andrea, for godsake, just because I can't — '

'Look, you've made your position clear. I understand — so just leave it, OK?' And then she stormed away.

Murphy almost went after her, but then he stopped. He sat down on the bar stool and lifted his drink. 'Bloody women,' he said.

'Tell me about it,' said the barman. 'That'll be seven fifty, including hers.'

31

I don't need medication. I'm fine.

Caplock was examining his reflection in his bedroom mirror.

Look at me. Anyone could tell.

He flexed his muscles. Until the age of twenty-nine he'd been a weakling. *In a good light you could see right through you*, his dad had said, not meaning anything by it but wounding him to the core. He'd started going to the gym not long after, and like all the things in his life — the internet porn, the collecting of *Marvel* comics, the taking of steps three at a time, the twenty-five-minute teeth-brushing that left his gums raw and bleeding, he became addicted to it. *Now look at me, Daddy, look at the muscle, look at the definition* — except his dad was long gone. But he was still watching, he knew that. Watching to make sure he took his medication: *That's a good boy, Michael, that's a good boy.* And if he saw the medication, then he also saw him take the steroids that had helped him to bulk up. *Don't be afraid to ask for help*, his dad had always drilled into him, so he had — help from the steroids, help from the doctor who told him he was borderline schizophrenic.

Borderline! How could you be borderline?

If I'm only borderline, why the pills that make me feel like I'm walking through tar? No answer from the doctor that made any sense, and no comment at all from his dad, watching invisible at his shoulder.

Caplock turned to look at himself side on. Then at his back. Then full frontal again. He wondered: was his head too small for his body now? You could enlarge any part of your body, except for your head. Maybe he should wear a polo neck, perhaps that would help with the size thing. He turned and peered out of his window at the basement apartment across the road. There were lights on. The curtains were thin, but he couldn't see her moving about.

No boyfriend, no husband.

He wanted to call over. Say, 'Did you get one of these letters through the door? They're sending them to everyone.'

She'd hesitate, thinking she'd jumped to the wrong conclusion, that he was actually . . . And then he'd hit her hard and she'd be out cold.

Do it, do it quickly.

Leave no clues — and of course they'd come to him first, that was obvious, but there was a saying, wasn't there — what was it? Oh yes — hide in plain sight. All he had to do was be careful. Not leave any clues. Scrub and scrub and scrub so that there was no skin, no DNA, no blood. Take her somewhere. Bury her. What about the baby? Keep the baby. *Feed* the baby. That would fuck up their whole time of death routine, wouldn't it? Introduce enough doubt so that they'd have to let him walk again.

The doorbell rang downstairs.

He said a mildly annoyed, 'Fuck,' and turned to look for his dressing-gown. He found it, tied himself into it, then walked down the stairs, aware that he still had half an erection. He cupped it through his dressing-gown. He didn't have a spyhole to see who it was, but the door was on a strong enough chain; he opened it a fraction and peered out.

A man smiled at him, then kicked the door in.

The chain snapped off its moorings, and the door hit him flush on the chin; he was vaguely aware of stumbling backwards, of a blast of cold air, and then of being on the carpet, everything swimming in and out of focus. Then the air was cut off again as the door was closed and re-secured, and then there was that man again in his dull green zip-up jacket, standing over him, saying something, but it was all like rushing water in a storm drain, he couldn't work it out at all, and then he saw the gun and it was aiming down at him. He managed a vague, 'No,' and then just as he started to focus properly and the rushing in his ears was lessening, the man pulled the trigger.

Bang.

* * *

'Open your eyes, you sick bastard.'

Heaven or hell? Caplock kept his eyes closed: he could smell burning — synthetics — his carpet. Then he was kicked, hard, in the ribs.

'I said, open them!'

He opened them. The same man, the same gun. The man knelt beside him and instinctively Caplock tried to roll away, but the man grabbed him and hauled him back. He put the gun against his head, then he thought better of it, and put it into his mouth.

'Now you listen to me, muscle boy,' the man hissed. 'You know who you are, and I know who you are, so there's no need for us to fuck around, is there?' Caplock stared wide-eyed; the man dug the gun further into his mouth, almost causing him to throw up.

'Is there?' he spat.

Caplock shook his head.

'Good boy. Then listen to what we're going to do. You may not appreciate this right now, but I'm actually saving your life. I'm supposed to be killing you, and to tell you the truth there's only a few things would give me greater pleasure, but I'm not, I'm saving your sorry arse. And you know all you have to do? All you gotta do is fucking lie here and act like you're dead. Can you do that?'

He tried to talk around the gun. 'I donth unther —'

'Shut the fuck up!' He rammed the gun hard against his crowned teeth. Caplock felt something give way. 'Do you fucking hear me?'

He nodded.

'In about ten minutes the police are going to be swarming round you. There's going to be an ambulance. And after a while you'll be taken out of here with a blanket over your head or maybe they'll zip you into a body bag, and all you've got to do is lie there and count your blessings that you're still in the land of the living. Do you get that?'

He nodded again. He could feel blood running down his chin.

The man finally took the gun out of his mouth.

'Lie on your stomach.'

'Lie . . . ?'

'Just fucking do it.' He turned. 'If you do this right you'll be taken to a safe house and you'll be relocated. Do you hear me?'

'I hear you.'

'Good. Then act fucking dead.'

'But why are — '

'*Do it!*'

He was whacked hard across the back of the head, a fist — no, the butt of the gun. And then there were footsteps down the wooden floor of the hall; the front door opened and then . . . well, maybe he was gone. Or maybe he was standing there, daring him to turn. Caplock could hear the traffic outside. A radio somewhere. The door creaked in the breeze; it banged against the wall. He was dying to turn. But he couldn't.

He wanted to live.

He really did. He loved life and all of its glorious opportunities.

So he closed his eyes and rested his head beside the hole in the carpet which stank of burning underfelt and melted synthetics.

Time passed. Five minutes he'd been lying there. Then ten.

Still he didn't dare move, then true to the man's word, the *Irish*man's word, there was a police siren and rapid footsteps and then they were all around him and one of the cops was saying under his breath: 'Stay where you are, don't move a fucking muscle.'

★ ★ ★

Murphy was staring into the blackness of the river, the gun still hidden in his jacket, when he heard footsteps behind him. He turned, looking panicked, then saw that it was Armstrong.

'Relax,' the old man said.

'I am, I am.' But he clearly wasn't. He clutched the railing. 'Jesus, I think I'm going to be sick.'

'Be sick. There's no shame in it.'

'You don't understand. I fucked it up,' he said. 'I think I fucked it up.'

'No, you didn't.'

'I fucking did.' He spun away from the railing, then kicked out at it. 'I had him in my fucking sights and I should have pulled the trigger but I hesitated and I know fucking better than that. He made a grab for me and I shot him and he went down but I don't know if I . . . I don't know. I just panicked, I ran . . . I don't know whether I got him or not. What if he's not dead? What if he can identify me? Have you any idea what happens to a cop who goes to prison?

They'll tear me — '

'He's dead.'

'What?'

Armstrong smiled paternally. 'You got him, Martin. We just drove past. They were bringing him out in a body bag.'

'Swear to God?'

'Swear to God.'

Murphy put his head back and blew out. 'Well, thank Christ for that.' He even managed a relieved laugh. 'You're sure?'

'As I can be. Did anyone see you?'

'No, I don't think so. I don't know. It was all so quick. If you'd seen the look on his face. I've never seen anyone lose colour the way . . . '

'Shhh,' Armstrong said. 'Slow down.'

'I know . . . I know. I'm sorry.'

He looked beyond Armstrong for the first time. There was a car parked about a hundred metres up, its engine running; he could see there were three people sitting in it, two in the back, one behind the wheel, but he couldn't make out who. Murphy shook his head. 'Were you following me? How did you even know . . . ?'

'Well, you said tonight, so we just kept an eye out. Moral support. Or immoral support, depending on your point of view.' He smiled.

Murphy clutched the rail again. 'Jesus,' he said, 'I really am going to be sick. Was it like this for you, the first time?'

'Every time. Martin — it's not like a hobby. It's not even like going off the top diving board or doing your first parachute jump. This isn't something you get used to.'

Murphy nodded, then opened his jacket and showed Armstrong the butt of the gun. 'So what will I do with this?' he asked.

Armstrong reached across and took hold of it. He turned it in his hand. He felt the barrel and checked the bullets.

'Well,' he said, then took the gun by its barrel and hurled it out across the water. There was a dull splash. 'Out of sight, out of mind, eh?' He turned then and put his hand out. 'Well done, son,' he said.

Murphy shook his hand.

'I'll see you soon.'

'And O'Hagan?'

'Don't worry about O'Hagan. He's as good as dead.'

'Thank you. When do you think — ?'

'There's no rush, Martin. It'll be a few weeks anyway. Let things settle down. Then, when it's done, we might give you a call if there's someone else needs sorting out. Do you think you'll be up for that?'

Murphy gave him a long look, then nodded

slowly. 'Yes, I will. Definitely. I feel . . . better already.'

'And that will grow, Martin, it will grow.' Armstrong winked, then turned and began to walk towards the waiting car.

Murphy called after him: 'Don't suppose there's any chance of a lift?'

Armstrong stopped, then turned towards him and gave a slight shake of his head. 'Better not.'

'Of course,' said Murphy. 'I understand.'

Armstrong smiled then and hurried back to his car. Murphy turned and looked out over the river. He was aware of the car driving slowly past him, but he didn't turn to look.

He didn't need to.

32

'We followed them to the greyhound stadium. Got lucky with the floodlights — look at that. Couldn't have done better if you'd lined them up and asked them to say cheese.'

Carter had a colour print in his hand.

Murphy said, 'You get this from the lab?'

'No — they're backlogged, so we threw it into Boots.'

'I hope you got a receipt.'

Carter gave him a wan smile and turned the photo so that Murphy could see it properly. He pointed at Lawrence, and then at Armstrong. 'These two I know, but these two?'

'Marinelli's a patient of Dr Jeffers, and McIntosh does the surveillance rotas. Don't know much about them beyond that and whatever's in the files.'

Carter nodded, then moved the rest of the photos off the table as a waiter arrived with their drinks. They were in a Pizza Express off Leicester Square. The boy in the red tunic said, 'Have you gents had a chance to look at the menu yet?'

Carter ordered, then Murphy. Carter said,

'Do you want to share a garlic bread?' Murphy shook his head. 'Why not? Who're you kissing later?'

'I'm not kissing anyone.'

'He's not kissing anyone,' Carter said to the waiter, 'so we'll take the garlic bread.'

'I don't want the garlic bread.'

'Fine — I'll have it.' He nodded at the waiter, who hurried away. 'So who is she?'

'So who is who?'

'Whoever you're seeing.'

'I'm not seeing anyone.'

Carter raised an eyebrow. 'Yeah, right. Well, if it's worth anything, I think it's a good thing. It's about time.'

'What's a good thing, what's about time?'

'You going out with someone.'

'I'm not . . . oh, just shut the fuck up, would you?'

Carter smiled. 'You'll share the garlic bread then?'

'No. I don't want any. There is no ulterior motive. I just don't want any garlic bread.'

Carter turned the photograph over in his hand and examined it. His eyes flitted from left to right, and back, left to right and back, like the carriage on a manual typewriter, or like he was enjoying a rally at Wimbledon. He raised the photo to get better light from the window, then peered over the top of it at Murphy.

'You know something?'

'What?'

'That pizza you ordered, it's full of garlic. If you were holding off on the garlic bread because you might be kissing someone later, you're on a hiding to nothing with that pizza.'

Murphy shook his head. 'You're so full of shit,' he said. But a couple of moments later he called the waiter over and changed his order. Carter gave him another look. 'What?' Murphy scowled. 'So I changed my mind.'

'Who is she?'

'She isn't anyone.'

'How did you meet her?'

'I just met her.'

'So she does exist.'

'Yes, Carter, she exists. I'm entitled to a private life.'

'You're entitled to holidays, but you never take them.'

'Well, maybe I will if you don't leave it.'

'Your prerogative.'

'That's right. Can we drop it now?'

'Of course we can.'

So they dropped it. For all of thirty seconds.

'So,' Carter asked, 'is she pretty?'

'It's none of your business.'

'So she's not.'

'Well she is, as a matter of fact.'

'Is she an older woman?'

'What do you mean, older woman?'

'Your age.'

'Christ.'

'So she is.'

'She's a grown woman, she's not some flirty wee tart.'

'Are you talking about my fiancée?'

'No, Carter, that's just your own insecurity coming through. I've never met Beth.'

'It's not Beth.'

'Whoever.'

* * *

When they were finished eating Murphy said, 'What about Caplock? He playing ball?'

'Yeah, he's scared shitless.'

'He's a big fucker, isn't he? I came through that door and I wasn't sure if I could keep him down. But he didn't have the balls to even try it.'

'Isn't that the way with those muscle boys? No heart.'

'You put out the press release?'

'We put it out, same as with Walker. Nobody's really interested these days. It's a crying shame. You could count the number of enquiries on the fingers of one hand. There was a piece in the *Standard*, something on the TV news, but a couple of bombs went off in Spain, and the Americans have invaded somewhere new and the Arsenal manager's talking about resigning, so they have enough on their plate.' Carter lifted the photo again. 'So what are we going to do about these guys?'

'We watch them, wait for them to make a move on O'Hagan.'

'And what if they aren't the ones who make the move? What if there's some other members of Confront who make the move?'

'It'll be them.'

'How do you know?'

'I don't, just a hunch.'

'A hunch? That's going to look good in my report.'

'I think if you're involved in something like this, and you've never done it before, there's probably a tendency to overstate your case.'

'So you don't think there are any others.'

'Maybe one or two, but not . . . well, nowhere near double figures, say. It would be too hard to keep together. I mean, look at that fucking Bravo Two Zero nonsense. They're all meant to be sworn to secrecy yet they've all written fucking books. People fall out, disagree, they talk, it gets out, it's the nature of the beast. This sort of thing, you keep it small or you're fucked. Besides, we can't watch *all* of them. We don't have the resources.'

'You can say that again. We'll be lucky if we can cover this lot. But we will. And we'll need to put someone on O'Hagan as well, just in case they do call in someone else to do it.'

'I'll be doing that.'

'You're sure?'

'Sure I'm sure. I've done all the ground-work, I know his routine.'

'Maybe you'd be better on one of the shooters.'

'All paths lead to O'Hagan. I want to be there when whoever it is goes for him.'

'Why?'

'Because it's my case and I want to be there at the end.'

'It's not *your* case, Murphy.'

'You know what I mean.'

The waiter came across and asked if they wanted dessert. Carter said, 'I'll have some, but he's saving himself.'

The waiter looked at Murphy. 'Sir?'

Murphy sighed. 'He's right. I am saving myself.'

The waiter nodded and began rhyming off the various desserts available. Murphy drummed his fingers on the table and stared out of the window, stared at nothing. He *was* saving himself, only he wasn't sure for what, or for whom, or even if he could ever, ever be saved — because of what he had done, and what he had yet to do.

33

It was like waiting for Christmas, but with added guns. Three weeks, four weeks, five, and then the rumblings started from upstairs. Carter brought word that the surveillance couldn't be extended for ever, prefacing it with a theatrical *don't shoot the messenger* which extinguished at least some of Murphy's anger. So surveillance on Lawrence, Armstrong, Marinelli and McIntosh was temporarily withdrawn, and instead a reduced squad of Carter, Murphy and Thompson concentrated on O'Hagan. They covered him in shifts. O'Hagan didn't have a regular job, and his drug dealing appeared to be low key, low rent. He had few visitors, didn't go out very often, and when he did it was invariably with his wife to their favourite restaurant or to the cinema.

'Maybe that's where the big deals go down,' Carter said, 'in the restaurant. It's Italian, so there's your Mafia connection.'

'Yeah,' said Murphy.

'Or in the back row of the movies. Isn't there a song about that? 'Sittin' in the back row . . . ''

'The Drifters,' said Murphy.

'More your era than mine.'

They were in Carter's car, and had been for several years. Murphy put a CD in. He had listened to Carter's three CDs about twenty times; it was time for a change. Carter tended to like whatever easy-listening jazz-tinged concoction that was currently en vogue. Jamie Cullum. Katie Melua. Norah Jones. But it sounded like elevator music to Murphy.

'You must frequent some high-class elevators,' said Carter, then frowned as Murphy's CD started. He gave it all of thirty seconds. 'That's shit,' he said.

Murphy flipped it to the next track. 'Try this one.'

Not even thirty seconds.

'That's shit as well.'

'What about this?'

This time he was more generous. Twenty-five seconds. 'Jesus, man, what's his problem? He needs to get a life.'

'Listen to this — listen to the chorus.'

'That's a shit chorus. Take it out. Please. Before I kill myself. Who the fuck is it?'

Murphy took out the CD and put it back in his jacket. 'Doesn't matter, you don't like it.'

Carter shook his head. 'No — please. I

really want to know. I want to know what to buy my worst enemy for his birthday. I think the Samaritans should send it out to their clientele. Cut their workload in half — they'll all be swinging from lamp-posts before track one's over. Murphy, your taste's in your fucking arse. C'mon, who is it?'

'You have forfeited your right to know.'

'What?'

'Forget it. You don't like it. Move on. Catch the next elevator.'

Murphy was staring up the street at O'Hagan's house; the lights were on upstairs. He checked his watch. It was a little after ten.

'Are you still doing your little patrols with Confront?' Carter asked.

'Have you any idea how condescending that sounds?'

'Sorry. Didn't realise you were so touchy about your pals.'

Murphy shook his head. He wondered if O'Hagan or his wife slept soundly these nights, or lay awake thinking about the ghost.

'Well?'

'Well what?'

'Do you still go out on your little patrols?'

Murphy sighed. 'Not so many. I told them I'm working nights.'

'How'd they take that?'

'They're fine. I do more during the day.'

'But no more gossip between hitmen?'

'Nah. McIntosh puts the rota together, seems to like to keep us all apart. Makes sense, if you think about it.'

'Yeah, in a crazy killer kind of a way. There they go.' Carter nodded at the O'Hagan house, where the lights had gone off. 'Nighty night, sleep tight, don't let the bed bugs bite.'

Murphy looked down the tree-lined street, where nothing was stirring. It was a pleasantly cool evening, there wasn't much traffic. He liked these kinds of houses, three or four floors, mostly well-maintained. Three boasted For Sale signs. One had clearly just been taken off the market — there was a sign lying flat in the front garden of the house just to his right with a smaller red SOLD sign attached to it. He wondered how much they were worth, and then how much somebody being shot to death in one would bring down the value.

'Christ,' he said, 'this is like Bob Dylan's never ending tour.'

'Why?' Carter asked.

'Because it's never-ending. Dummy.'

Carter started humming to himself.

'You're humming,' said Murphy.

'No, I'm not. I was just thinking that of all the people we think have been killed by Confront, there's never been a single witness.

321

The victims have either been single, or they've been taken out when they're away from their partners.'

'So what are you saying?'

'I'm saying that every night we're numbing our arses out here while O'Hagan's in there with his wife, the chances are they're not going to strike. They don't want any witnesses and they don't want to take the chance of injuring or killing someone innocent. So maybe they'll wait until his wife's at work or out shopping or something and then hit him.'

Murphy thought about that for a while, then said, 'Fair point.'

'So what should we do? Call it a night?'

'Yeah. Suppose so.'

Carter started the engine. Murphy opened his door. 'What are you doing?'

'I thought I'd hang around for a while.'

Carter sighed and cut the engine. 'Right,' he said.

'You don't have to stay.'

'I know.' He sat back, folded his arms, and closed his eyes. 'Let me know when nothing happens.'

★   ★   ★

Carter wasn't exactly sleeping, but when he opened his eyes he found that Murphy was smiling at him. 'What?' he said.

'You're humming again.'

'I wasn't humming. And if I was, it's that fucking annoying song.'

'Which one?'

'The one you played. With the la-la-la kind of chorus.'

'You liked that one?'

'No, I didn't like it. But it sticks in your head.'

'Sticks in your head it must have something to recommend it.'

'Yeah. Well. I don't know about that. It's catchy. So who the fuck is it again?'

Murphy shrugged and looked back down the street. It was after midnight. There was nobody about. He took the CD out of his jacket and said, 'Will I put it on again?'

Carter sighed. 'If you insist.'

'You find that sometimes, things you don't like first time round kind of grow on you.'

'What, like you and me?'

'No, Carter. It's pretty much confined to music. Sometimes movies. Occasionally food. But rarely people. And never you.'

'Cheers, mate.'

Murphy smiled. The first song came on. He glanced to his right and saw a cat making confident progress across one of the gardens. It paused for a moment, sniffing imperiously around the For Sale sign lying flat in the grass, then looked up at the house that had been sold, as if wondering whether that meant a new cat would be moving in. Then it padded away. The music stopped abruptly as Carter hit the eject button. Murphy was too slow — Carter had the CD out and was holding it up towards the nearest streetlight to get a better look at the label. Murphy made a grab for it.

Carter said, 'In a minute . . . '

Murphy made another attempt to get it. 'Just *leave* it!'

'Not yet.' Carter was examining the writing, his brow furrowed. He looked from the disc to Murphy and back. 'What the fuck? *Love Songs, Martin Murphy. Love Songs. Martin Murphy.* These are *your* songs?' Murphy shrugged and slumped back into his seat. 'This is you fucking singing? It is, isn't it?'

'So what if it is?'

'You've made a fucking CD?'

'I recorded some songs.'

'And you can buy this in the shops?'

'No, of course you bloody can't. Do you think I'd be sitting bloody here if you could buy it in the bloody shops? I recorded it at home, and burned a couple of copies, now do you mind?'

He held out his hand. But Carter held on to it.

'No way. I want to listen to this. I had no idea. Jesus, Murphy, you're a dark horse.'

'Yeah well.'

'It's really good.'

'You said it was shit.'

'Well, I didn't know it was you. And you're right, it does grow on you. I'm going to put it on again, but only if you don't take it back.'

'OK.'

'And can I take it home and listen to it?'

Murphy sighed. 'If you want. And if you promise not to take it down the office and make a fucking eejit out of me.'

'Promise.' Carter pushed the CD back into the player. 'This is great. It's like sitting in a car with Elton John.'

'Please.'

'Or Meatloaf.'

'If you're going to take the piss I'll — '

'OK, OK — relax, relax.' Carter hummed along with it. 'Or Lionel Ritchie . . . '

★ ★ ★

Thompson took over at 2 a.m. As soon as he climbed into the car Carter said, 'Tommo, listen to this,' and went to play the CD again, but this time Murphy beat him to it.

He whipped it out and stuck it back in his jacket.

'Hey,' objected Carter, 'you said I could borrow that.'

'I lied.'

'What is it?' Thompson asked.

'Nothing,' said Murphy, and then added for good measure, 'Mind your own fucking business.'

Thompson went back to his own car.

Murphy said, 'How come he gets to watch O'Hagan all on his lonesome, but I get stuck with you?'

Carter shrugged and said, 'Statistics.'

'And what's that supposed to mean?'

'Anything you want — that's the wonder of statistics.' Carter shook his head. 'He doesn't. There'll be someone along in a while to join him.'

On the way home Carter said, 'Is that what you'd really like to do, you know, music?'

Murphy shook his head. 'It's just a hobby. I kind of missed the boat.'

'It's never too late, though, is it?'

'In my experience, it's always too late.' Murphy took the disc out of his pocket and slipped it back into the player. 'With my luck, I'll be discovered just after I've popped my clogs.'

When Carter dropped him off he left the

disc in the player. 'It really does grow on you,' Carter said.

'Yeah well.'

As he climbed out of the car he suddenly saw Andrea hurrying towards him. She slowed as she saw him, trying not to appear too eager. Murphy tapped his hand down on the roof of the car and said, 'All right, Charlie, see you tomorrow.'

Carter looked confused for just a moment, then caught enough of a glimpse of the approaching figure to understand; he nodded quickly and started the engine. As he drove off, Andrea was just coming to a halt beside Murphy. She was wearing a T-shirt and tracksuit bottoms and trainers. He said, 'Jesus, it's a bit late to be out jogging.'

'I wasn't, I . . . look, I'm sorry.'

'Sorry for what?'

'For this, for coming, for . . . *hanging around*.'

'You've been hanging around?' He was smiling.

'No — yes. I . . . I was just slopping around the house. Lawrence was out at the dogs, and I just felt like seeing you so I jumped in the car and came here. I didn't know you were working. I should have gone home, but I just sat in the car. I've been there for hours.'

Murphy took her in his arms. 'That's really sweet.'

She tried to untangle herself. 'I don't want it to be *sweet*.'

'Relax, would you?'

'I'm sorry, I just . . . Christ, I'm dying for a pee.'

Murphy burst out laughing.

★ ★ ★

When she was in the bathroom he shouted through the door, 'If there's a spider in the bath, just ignore it.'

'I hadn't noticed, thanks. It's huge.'

'I know. I've been feeding it up.'

'That's not funny.'

'It's not funny when it jumps either.'

'Jesus.' He heard the toilet flush. A few moments later the door opened and she hurried out. 'I think it was about to pounce,' she said.

'It's a good thing I'm here to protect you.'

She smiled, then reached up and touched his face. 'Are you OK with this?'

'With defending you from a spider?'

She gave him a look.

'Of course I am.'

'Good. Then why don't you put some music on.'

Murphy nodded and turned to his CD collection. He had another copy of his own songs sitting on one of the speakers, but decided that going for two converts in one night might be pushing his luck. As he knelt beside the untidy pile of discs he'd most recently liberated from one of the boxes in the spare room Andrea came and stood behind him.

'Do you want a drink?' he said.

'No.'

'What do you want to listen to?'

'I don't know. I'm not sure if I even do.'

'But you . . . '

'I know. But a lady has a right to change her mind.' She knelt down beside him and kissed his lips. He kissed her back. 'I think I just wanted to get you on the floor.'

'All you had to do was ask.'

'I know. But I'm shy.'

'Are you?'

She nodded.

'Aw. That really is sweet. But it obviously worries you.'

'No, it doesn't.'

'You won't acknowledge it.'

'What are you, my shrink?'

Murphy nodded. 'Yes, I am. You have deep-seated concerns about something or other. We should take our clothes off and discuss it.'

She pulled her top up over her head. 'You're the doctor.'

★ ★ ★

When they had made love and were lying on the carpet with CDs spilled all around them, he said, 'Do you think Lawrence suspects?'

'It's hard to know. There's not much communication.'

'But you're still telling him you're going out on Confront business?'

She nodded. She snuggled in against him and stroked his chest. 'Do you think you just get used to living with people and all their faults? You just settle for what you have.'

'I suppose. You shouldn't, but you probably do.'

'Was your life just perfect before what happened happened?'

'At the time I would have said yes. Looking back? I don't know. You could drive yourself mad thinking about it.'

'Do you — do you have somewhere to go — to see your son? You know, a grave.'

Murphy shook his head. 'Ashes.'

'Did your wife keep them?'

'No, we scattered them.'

'Where?'

'Secret place.'

'OK.'

'What about you?'

'There's a cemetery not far from where we are. I go most weeks. I talk to him. About everything. About us.'

'And what does he say?'

'He doesn't say anything. He's dead.' She laughed quietly to herself. 'There. The first joke I've made about my dad. You must be good for me.'

Murphy smoothed down her hair. 'It's a step forward. But . . . '

'But what?'

'Better joke next time.'

She tried to slap him, but he held her firm, then he kissed her and then they made love again.

★ ★ ★

Later, when they'd made it as far as the bedroom and he'd finally put some music on — Leonard Cohen, but not his miserable early period, his up-tempo happy elder years — he said, 'I've been spending time watching O'Hagan.'

Andrea nodded, lying in the crook of his arm. 'That's allowed.'

'But I'm worried that we're going to lose track of him. The other day I was there and he was with a couple of estate agents.'

'Jesus, how close were you?'

'I wasn't *that* close.'

'Then how do you . . . '

'Because they'd just sold a house across the road. The sign was lying in the garden, they lifted it and took it with them when they left.'

'So now you think he's moving house.' She pushed herself up so that she was resting on her elbow. Her make-up had been melted off in the fury of their lovemaking and he could see the crows' feet now and the blackness beneath her eyes. But it didn't diminish her in any way. The contrary. It illuminated her.

'He might be.'

'I wouldn't worry about it. I'm sure he won't be difficult to track down. He'll have to let so many people know — you know, the bank, the telephone people. Jeffers can get that kind of information.'

Murphy nodded, but in a half-hearted way.

'What?' she asked.

'Well, what if he goes back to Ireland? What if the IRA or someone are after him and he has to disappear? He could be gone for good. I just don't want to lose him.'

'I know. Don't worry. I'm sure everything will be fine.'

They lay quietly in the darkness for a while. Eventually she said, 'What are you thinking now?'

'I'm thinking three times in one night would be pretty much a record for a fat bald bloke in his forties.'

'You are none of the above. But I think three times probably would.'

'Do you think I should go for it?'

'As long as you don't expect some kind of certificate at the end.'

'Certificate? Jesus, woman, if I survive I'll expect a gold medal.'

She laughed, then kissed him and said, 'On your marks . . . '

34

In the morning, long after she'd gone, this time with less of the guilt, none of the hangover, and with a lingering kiss, Carter phoned and said Thompson had spotted Lawrence's car driving past O'Hagan's house about an hour before.

'Uhuh?'

'Thompson also says you called him first thing and told him to plant a For Sale sign in O'Hagan's garden.'

'I didn't tell him to plant it. I told him to lift it from the house across the road and rest it against the gate so it'd look like O'Hagan's house was up for sale. I didn't ask him to plant it. That would have been too obvious, and rather time-consuming. Did he plant it?'

'No, he didn't fucking plant it, but do you mind telling me what you're playing at? What if he'd been spotted?'

'If he'd been spotted, yer man would have said, 'Hey, love, there's a drunk in our garden putting a For Sale sign up'.'

'You really think so?'

'Well, what else is he going to think? 'Hey,

love, there's an undercover cop putting a For Sale sign up in our garden'?'

Carter tutted. 'And the point of this is what?'

'To make them think O'Hagan's on the move. To speed things up.'

'But the sign's already gone. O'Hagan threw it back across the road.'

'After or before Lawrence drove past?'

Carter sighed. 'After.'

'I rest my case.'

'Never mind your fucking case, how come Lawrence chose that particular time to drive past?'

'Because I'm smart. I fed the information to him and he felt the need to check it out himself.'

'How did you feed it?'

'Through a third party.'

'A third party, shit.'

'Meaning?'

'You're shagging his wife.'

'I'm . . . '

'Murphy, that was her last night.'

'How the hell would you know that?'

'Because I'm not fucking stupid.'

'It doesn't mean I'm — '

'Jesus, Murphy, have you no sense?'

He let that sit for several long moments. *Keep a lid on it. Calm.*

'My mum used to say I haven't the sense I was born with.'

'I don't give a flying fuck about your mum. You can't go around . . . ' Carter didn't finish it. He didn't need to.

'I do what I do, I get the results, and it's none of your fucking business who I'm sleeping with, or not, as the case may be.'

'You're still denying it! What are you getting together for late at night then? Chess, is it?'

'That's it. Got it in one. You know, when you get to a certain age, you can have a mature, mutually supportive relationship with someone which doesn't involve making love.'

'Murphy.'

'Carter.'

'Do you think she's involved?'

'In the killing? No, I don't.'

'You're sure about that?'

'Yes, I'm sure.'

There was a full thirty seconds of silence. Then Carter said, 'So what do we do now?'

'Now we watch them like the crime fighters we are.'

★ ★ ★

They watched that day, and the next. On the third day after the For Sale Sign Incident

336

Murphy attended the next meeting of Confront. Andrea wasn't there. During the coffee-break he stood with Armstrong and a young woman with a Polish-sounding name who'd lost her husband in an armed robbery at an all-night garage and a new member called Johnson who hadn't yet had an opportunity to tell his story.

Armstrong listened attentively and offered his usual paternal advice to the young Pole, but didn't talk directly to Murphy until Jeffers called on the meeting to resume and the others drifted back to their chairs. Then he reached across and took another biscuit. He raised it to his mouth, but before he bit into it he stopped and said quietly, 'You should go and see a movie or something this afternoon. Or get your hair cut.'

Murphy's eyes widened. 'Today?'

Armstrong nodded, then bit into his biscuit and moved past Murphy to take his own seat.

★ ★ ★

Murphy hurried away from the church building, his mobile clamped to his ear. 'Carter . . . this afternoon.'

'You're sure?'

'I'm sure.'

'What do you want, the heavy mob called out?'

'No, we can handle this ourselves.'

'Murphy.'

'Carter — it's amateur hour, they've just been lucky so far. I'm going there now. I'll relieve Thompson, get him over to McIntosh. Who's on Marinelli?'

'Jamieson.'

'Armstrong's just left here.'

'I know, Patterson's with him.'

'Do I know Patterson?'

'He's new, but he's fine.'

'OK. What's Lawrence doing?'

'We're down at the stadium with his dogs.'

'OK, just don't lose him.'

'Yeah. As if. Don't forget — you trained me.'

'Aw, away and fuck. You — ' And then he stopped, because he was parallel with the pub where he and Andrea had met up twice now, and there she was, sitting at the bar. Murphy cursed to himself, then snapped, 'Keep me posted,' into the phone, and cut the line. He turned quickly to cross the road away from the bar. He didn't have time for her, not today of all days.

He made it to the other side, but then, 'Martin!' He kept walking. 'Martin!'

Fuck.

He stopped and looked back: she was about thirty yards away, waving at him. He raised his hand, but hesitated before moving back towards her.

Make it quick. Make it quick.

He dodged back across the traffic and hurried up.

'Sorry,' he said. 'Didn't hear you with all the — ' But as he drew near he saw that her left eye was half-closed, swollen, blue turning black. 'Jesus,' he said. 'What the . . . '

'Lawrence.'

Christ.

He took her by the arm and led her back into the pub. She'd left most of a Bacardi on the bar. He ordered a whiskey, then waited until the barman had served it and moved away again before he put his hand to her face and turned her head gently to get a proper look at the damage. She winced instinctively.

'It's not as bad as it looks,' she said.

'I'd say it's exactly as bad as it looks.' He sighed. He shook his head. 'Tell me.'

'He just knew. He was waiting up when I got back. He phoned one of them to check the rota and they told him I wasn't on last night. And then he saw me and it doesn't take a . . . well, sometimes you can just tell when someone's had sex. Three times.' She managed a smile.

'What did you say?'

'I denied it. But he didn't believe me. I don't blame him.'

'For not believing you?'

'For not believing me, and for hitting me.'

'Don't say that.'

'Well. Look what I've done to him.'

'You haven't done anything. Or if you have, you've been put in a position . . . ' Murphy took a drink. 'Fuck. I don't know. These things just happen, you know, and they're horrible. Does he know it's me?'

She shook her head.

'Well, that's OK then.' But he followed it with a smile. He took her hand. Then he looked at his watch. 'I'm sorry, but I'm going to have to go.'

'But — '

'I know, but I promised and if I don't I'll get the royal order of the boot.'

'But I've nowhere to go.'

'You've left?'

'No, I've been thrown out, Martin.'

'And is there no one . . . ?'

She was looking at him. A tear appeared in the corner of her good eye. She turned to the bar. 'It's all right. It's me that's fucked up. You go and do your job. I'll find somewhere.'

'Andrea, it's not like that.'

'Yes, it is. Go on, fuck off.'

The barman looked up. He was a different barman to the one who'd heard Andrea and Murphy argue previously.

Murphy stood his ground. He took his keys from his pocket and set them on the bar. 'Here.'

She swept them off onto the ground. 'Fuck your keys.'

He picked them up and put them back down beside her. 'Please.'

She looked at them. 'I have friends. There's a dozen places I can go.'

'I don't want you to go anywhere else.'

'It would only be for a couple of days. I'll go back to him. I love him.'

'I know that.'

She nodded. She lifted the keys. 'When will you be home?' she asked.

35

O'Hagan was doing DIY, painting the ground-floor exterior window-frames of his house red.

It had always amazed Murphy, the way killers could go about their daily lives as if they were ordinary people with normal concerns. Hold down responsible jobs, walk in the park with their children, choose wallpaper with their wives. Breakfast-lunch-blow someone's head off — dinner-bedtime story for the kids, goodnight.

O'Hagan, in his paint-splattered overalls, gave every indication of being a man entirely at peace with himself. He whistled. He said, 'Good morning,' when men walked past the house; less formal when it was a good-looking girl: 'Hiya.' Or, 'Howse it goin'?' In his head, probably, he wasn't a killer. He was a soldier who had done terrible things in time of war. But war was over. Peace and reconciliation. Love thy neighbour. Love thy enemy.

Bring my son back to me.

Murphy sat in the car across the road and down; he had his son's photo behind the sun visor. Every couple of minutes he flipped it down for a look, then back up again. He had his police issue gun sitting out on the passenger seat, with a newspaper loosely covering it. It was 2.45 p.m. He'd been there for an hour and a half. O'Hagan had stopped for two cups of tea. There was no sign of his wife. Carter had followed her to work one day and discovered that she worked in a private clinic just down the road. She'd stopped for a last fag just outside, and he'd stopped and asked for directions. She spoke like an Essex girl. Perhaps she knew nothing about her husband's past. Carter could just as easily have said, 'Give us twenty fags and by the way, do you know your hubby cuts children's throats?'

But that wasn't Carter's job. It was Confront's, or would have been.

He called Carter. 'Where's Lawrence?'

'He's still with the dogs.'

'Christ.'

'I know, it's like watching paint dry.'

'Carter, I *am* watching paint dry.'

He checked in with Jamieson, Thompson and Patterson. No movement. For another forty-five minutes he watched O'Hagan paint. Although no authority on decorating, Murphy decided that O'Hagan was taking his time not because he was a perfectionist, but because he was lazy. And because he *had* the time. There was no rush. He was perfectly at ease with himself. Little bit of this, little bit of that. Cruise through life.

For the first time in a long while Murphy thought about his ex-wife, Lianne, and Norman, her . . . well, he found it hard still to think of Norman as her lover. *Lover. Luh-ver.* Her man. Her big strong ex-SAS hero. Her protector. He had been sent to guard her against gunmen, and they had fallen in love. Where were they now, Scotland? America? Or just down the road somewhere, lying low? He had never stopped loving her, and deep down he knew that she still loved him, but that was bugger all use to him. It was as if he was trapped under ice: only inches from happiness, but utterly cut off from it and doomed to stay there for ever.

Or until the thaw.

I arrest you, in the name of the thaw.

'He's on the move.' It was Carter. 'He's left the dogs in kennels here, we're in the car park.'

He called Patterson. 'What about Armstrong?'

'He's driving.'

'This way?'

'Not as far as I can tell.'

'OK.' Jamieson reported that Marinelli was in his office, talking to clients. McIntosh was at home; Thompson could see him in an upstairs bedroom window, working at his computer.

Five minutes later Patterson called back. 'Armstrong's turned around and we're now moving towards you.'

Two minutes after that Carter reported that Lawrence was also coming his way.

'OK,' said Murphy.

He picked up his gun, checked it over and set it down again. He flipped down the sun visor, then flipped it back up. He lifted his gun again. He pulled the newspaper sharply across as a woman walking her dog stopped by the car. It was all right, she had her back to him. Her dog, a miniature *something*, was going to the toilet in the middle of the pavement. The woman had a plastic bag in her hands, but she looked both ways, and seeing that nobody was coming in either direction she decided to walk on. But in pulling the dog away she glanced up and her eyes met Murphy's and she hesitated for a moment, but she'd made her decision and pressed on with it. He didn't blame her. He believed in clean streets, and he was aware of the diseases and infections that could come with leaving it, but on the whole he preferred people not to be walking the streets with bags of shite in their hand. It was a real conversation killer. If he was a beat officer, he would turn a blind eye to it, unless of course it was O'Hagan.

The death penalty.

O'Hagan was sitting on his top step, smoking another cigarette. The woman with the dog had crossed the road now and was passing his house. O'Hagan said something. She stopped. She laughed. He came down the steps and reached down and petted the dog. She smiled. O'Hagan was a charmer. A loveable Irish rogue.

'Patterson? What about Armstrong?'

'Even when the road's empty he's not driving much above twenty. How old is he? He's driving like one of those doddery old — '

'Just stay with him. Carter?'

'We're definitely coming your way. Five minutes, tops.'

'Patterson — how long do you reckon?'

'This rate — fifteen.'

The woman walked on. O'Hagan stood watching her until she turned the corner, then he shook his head, smiled to himself and returned to his painting.

Not a care in the world.

If only he knew. If only he fucking knew.

Murphy had his hands on the steering wheel, but didn't realise how hard he was gripping it until he saw his knuckles burning

346

white against skin; when he let go of the wheel it was slimy with sweat. He squirmed in his seat. He was a veteran at surveillance. He didn't exactly get himself into a zen-like state of calm, but he could cope. This was different though. This was — Christ, *this time it's personal.*

He heard the big booming voice of the movie voiceover. American, of course: '*This time it's personal.*'

But it was.

He lifted the gun again. He checked it.

'Armstrong's stopping!'

'Where are you?'

'We're still miles away. He's stopped, he's getting out . . . he's got one of those tartan trolley things old people have. He's going shopping!'

'What do you mean?'

'He's going into a fucking Waitrose.'

Murphy looked over at the house. O'Hagan, with his back to the road now. Who was shot like that — Jesse James, was it? At least in the movie.

This time it's personal.

'Sir? What should I — '

'Leave him.'

'Leave him, sir?'

'He's not going anywhere. Come back here. Jamieson?'

347

'Marinelli's still with clients.'

'OK, leave him — come back here. Thompson?'

'McIntosh's on his computer. His wife's just coming out of the house now, with their kids. She's getting into the car . . . '

'OK, well he's not going to get a taxi. Drop him — get back here. Carter?'

'We're about a quarter of a mile away. Murphy, when do we stop him?'

'With his gun out and the moment he sets foot on O'Hagan's property.'

'And what if he shoots before we — '

'He won't. That's my job.'

'We should have back-up.'

'We have you Carter. And the rest are on their way.'

'But what if — '

'Where are you?'

'There's two . . . three turnings before yours. You'll have a visual in just a few seconds.'

'OK, don't crowd him, don't crowd him.'

'He's passed the first turning . . . '

Murphy looked up at O'Hagan. He was just climbing back down the short ladder he'd been using to get to the top of the window-frames. He picked up a tray of paint and headed back into the house, leaving the front door open. Murphy looked in his mirror.

Lawrence's car, Lawrence's car . . .

'He's past the second . . . just coming up to yours now.'

Lawrence's car, Lawrence's car. He's whacked Andrea, nearly blinded her . . .

'Fuck it! He's not turned! Murphy — he's not — '

'I hear you. Relax, stay with him. He'll come from the other end.'

'OK, OK. I know the layout — he can turn here, cut through. We're just coming up . . . oh, fuck it, Murphy, he hasn't turned. He's . . . for fuck's sake, Murphy, he's picking up speed, he's turning right. I'm after him. Murphy, we're going away from O'Hagan's. There's a one-way system here. If he gets into that . . . he's into it, I'm going with him. He's bottled it, Murphy. He's not doing it.'

'Could he have spotted you?'

'No! I don't know! I've been so careful.'

Murphy wasn't sure when he became fully aware of the motorbike. He'd seen it in his mirror, coming down the road behind him, but he was watching for Lawrence's car and hadn't paid any attention. Then when he'd checked O'Hagan's house and saw him go inside with the tray he'd seen it again at the very end of the road, indicating right. But now it was right back behind him, purring down.

But still he didn't connect. Thompson was on, asking what he was supposed to do; Jamieson echoed it. Murphy turned in his seat, looking over his left shoulder, then his right, trying now to get a fix on the bike, but he only caught glimpses of it. Then suddenly it was there, right beside him, speeding down the pavement, and all he really saw of the rider as it went past was that his black visor was down and that his leathers were: strikingly familiar.

'Oh Jesus fuck!'

'Murphy?!'

'Get back here now!'

Murphy scrambled out of the car, gun in hand, and began running even as the biker gunned his machine up the short flight of steps onto O'Hagan's path. He jumped off, kicked out the stand with practised ease and was reaching inside his jacket as O'Hagan reappeared at the front door with a fresh tray of paint in his hands.

There was just the briefest moment when they stopped, each surprised by the encounter.

Murphy bolted across the road, narrowly avoiding a car, then vaulted over O'Hagan's low garden wall. He could see the biker in the doorway and then there was a shot, and he cursed — but it was the biker who staggered back and for a moment Murphy thought he was covered in his own blood — but then he saw it wasn't blood, it was paint, red paint. The biker recovered quickly and followed O'Hagan back into the house and down the hall. He was raising his gun just as Murphy made it to the door.

'Jeffers!'

The good Dr Jeffers stopped. He turned slightly, glanced back at Murphy and looked surprised for just a moment: but his gun never left O'Hagan, who was lying at the end of the hall, paint-spattered but also bleeding from a bullet wound in his arm, or maybe his shoulder.

Jeffers pushed his paint-sprayed visor up.

'Dr Jeffers — put down the gun!'

'Murphy?' And then he seemed to understand what was happening. 'Murphy, this isn't how we do it, but I understand why you're here. You have to do it yourself.'

Murphy kept the gun trained on Jeffers, but he saw beyond him that O'Hagan was trying to crawl out of the hall and out of sight into the kitchen. 'And you stay where you are as well!' he bellowed. 'Stay where you fucking are!'

O'Hagan froze. His face was a mask of shock and horror. 'Please,' he whispered, 'I haven't . . .'

Jeffers centred his gun on O'Hagan.

'I said drop it!'

Jeffers glanced back. 'Then do it yourself! We can't stand here for — ' And then he saw what Murphy was holding in his other hand. His police ID. Jeffers almost laughed. 'You think that makes a difference?'

'Put it down!'

'Murphy, he killed your son.'

'I know what he did.'

O'Hagan was looking at him now, his mouth open in surprise, the pain forgotten.

'He cut his throat.'

'I know what he fucking did. Now put it down before — !'

'Before what? Murphy, this is the right thing to do, and if you won't — '

'I *won't*. Now — '

'Then I will.'

He turned, and as his finger squeezed the trigger, Murphy shot once; Jeffers gave a little jump, then his knees buckled. As he fell he dropped his gun. He clutched instead at his arm, but Murphy could see that it was more than just his arm; it was a side-on shot that must have gone straight through and into his torso. Jeffers put his arm out to try and get the support of the wall, but there was no strength in it and he slid down to the floor. Murphy stepped forward and pushed the gun away with his foot.

Along the hall, O'Hagan tried again to pull himself away.

'I've told you already,' Murphy hissed, raising his own gun again. 'So much as an inch . . . '

O'Hagan stopped. He stared, mesmerised, back at Murphy.

Jeffers coughed blood; he tried to sit up. Murphy crouched down beside him. 'Just stay where you are.' He raised his phone. 'I need an ambulance.'

'Martin . . . *Martin* . . . '

Jeffers's fingers, thickly coated in blood and paint, grabbed at Murphy's shirt, but couldn't get a grip.

'Just stay still. There's an ambulance on its way.'

'No, listen. *Listen.*' He coughed again and blood came up; his breathing was laboured. 'You . . . asked me once . . . what I did when I went home . . . when I wasn't a psychiatrist . . . when I was a . . . man. And you were right — you were right. I did my job, but at night . . . my wife . . . animals like that . . . ' He raised his hand and pointed weakly at O'Hagan. 'Animals . . . Martin, now you have to do it . . . '

Jeffers finally got a grip on his shirt and pulled at him, knocking him off-balance and causing Murphy to fall towards him. He put out his free hand to support himself, but the blood and paint made it slide up Jeffers's sleeves and across the bullet-hole. Jeffers let out a shout, but held on. He hissed into Murphy's ear. 'He sliced your son's throat. Take my gun — take *my* gun and shoot him. Kill him, Murphy . . . No one will ever know.' He scrunched Murphy's shirt with all the strength he had left. 'No one will ever know.'

Finally he let go and slumped down; he coughed again and groaned.

Murphy looked at Jeffers's gun, lying just a few feet away, speckled with paint. In all the time he had known about O'Hagan he had not decided what to do about him. Whether to go *this* way, or that.

He had kept all options open.

He was a creature of stealth and opportunity. And here was the opportunity.

He picked up the gun and walked down the hall towards O'Hagan, who scurried backwards until he came to a wall and couldn't go any further.

Murphy stood over him, and trained the gun on his face. 'You killed my son,' he said.

It was the closest he'd been to O'Hagan. He could see now how pinched and tired his face was. The white stubble. The uneven teeth. The bags under his eyes. The eyes themselves: in another reality he might have recognised them, he might have remembered them as cold and cruel and lethal from the day his son was murdered, but he didn't. They were just eyes, blue and wide with the anticipation of death.

'Why?' Murphy asked. His finger curled around the trigger. He thought of his son Michael: ashes scattered in a secret place, his photo slipped in behind a sun visor.

O'Hagan had nothing to say. There *was* nothing to say.

Apart from: 'I'm sorry.'

'You're sorry?'

'Please. It was a long — '

'Don't! Don't fucking say it. It was yesterday, you fucker, and tomorrow!'

O'Hagan closed his eyes, waiting for it.

Murphy could no longer hear his son's voice. Somewhere, over the past few years, he had lost the sound of it.

My son has left the building. And unlike Elvis, he's left nothing behind. Not old enough for a legacy.

Any lingering sweet thoughts hopelessly overwhelmed by the horror of his death. At this man's hands.

Sorry.

Sorry.

Sorry.

'Murphy.'

He didn't need to turn. Carter stood in the doorway.

'Murphy.' Soft.

From O'Hagan: 'Please God.'

'*Murphy.*'

O'Hagan was struggling to cross himself.

Movement behind him — but the gun stayed on O'Hagan's face. The finger pulsed against the trigger; it squeezed, but not enough . . . just a fraction more, just the tiniest little fraction.

'I'm sorry,' O'Hagan whispered.

'Murphy.'

Jeffers was judge, jury and executioner. *No one will ever know*, he'd said. But he was wrong.

Murphy lowered the gun. *I would know.*

He turned back to tell Jeffers, but Jeffers was dead.

Carter moved up to Murphy and held out his hand, and Murphy put his gun in it. He didn't look at O'Hagan. He just turned and walked out of the house. He stood in the fresh air and breathed in. Except it wasn't fresh, it was full of blood and smoke and burning.

'What . . . what are you doing?'

Murphy turned towards the road. O'Hagan's wife was standing by the gate; she had shopping bags in either hand.

'Me? Just standing here, missis.'

'What were you doing in our house?' She moved up the steps. 'Who are you? Where's Matt?' And then she saw the blood on his shirt and her mouth dropped a little bit. 'Oh Jesus.' She let go of the bags and dashed past him.

He could have stopped her. He just . . . didn't. He should have warned Carter. Again, he just . . . didn't.

She charged through the front door, saw Jeffers's corpse and Carter bending over her husband, his own hands thick now with blood. Carter wasn't aware of her, so that when she screamed it shocked him to the core and his natural reaction was to raise his gun and shoot.

Protect yourself at all times.

And when you shoot, shoot to kill.

So he did.

36

Armstrong played his old man whimsy, Marinelli and McIntosh sweated and denied, Lawrence said he was only interested in dogs, then Murphy walked in on them, one by one, and at first they presumed he'd been arrested as well but then he sat down opposite and smiled and showed them a photo of Jeffers lying dead and said, 'Care to comment?'

And they broke pretty quickly after that.

McIntosh first, because he was a natural record-keeper. He'd organised legitimate surveillance and the paperwork to go with it for Confront, but then used both to compile files for those members of the group more interested in guns than petitions. It was all sitting in his study, on his PC, and he knew it wouldn't be difficult to access once they brought a computer expert on board. So he said, 'I did some organising, but I never shot anyone.'

Then Marinelli, not repentant at all. He said, 'They fucking asked for it,' before his solicitor could stop him.

Armstrong said his wife had Alzheimer's, he was heading the same way himself, that he'd never go to trial, and finally that Jeffers took advantage of him.

And then Lawrence, just him and Murphy and a uniformed cop in the corner of the room, without even the tape recorder running. He offered Lawrence a cigarette, and he took it, warily.

'Christ,' said Lawrence. 'What am I going to tell my wife?'

Murphy sat on the edge of the table. 'You still have a wife, do you?'

'Of course I do — Andrea!' And then he stopped. 'Why, what have you heard?'

'I heard you've been slapping her around.'

'She's been screwing someone else.'

'Yeah, I heard that as well.'

'Where did you . . . ?'

'It's all over the internet.'

'The . . . '

'Relax, Lawrence. It was kind of common knowledge at Confront.'

'So you know who it was?'

'I might. Tell me about Jeffers.'

'If you know who she's — '

'Tell me about Jeffers, we'll see where it takes us.'

Lawrence sighed. He took a long drag on his cigarette, then rubbed one hand vigorously across his temple. 'This is so fucked up.'

'You're telling me. Who approached who?'

'Well, Andrea and I were both patients.'

'He saw you together?'

'Not after the first time. Andrea was more amenable to what he was saying, he was already starting to organise the group, and I said I wasn't interested because — well, you know why, it being a talking shop and all that. He'd given me — not just me, all of us — his home number in case we needed him after hours, and one night when I was really down, felt like topping myself, it just all got too much, I called him and he told me to go round to his house. I was surprised when I got there because he was pretty drunk, and then we both got drunker, and then it all came out. He really was a mess, and so angry, but he couldn't do anything about it because he knew the difference between right and wrong and he was a psychiatrist and he had a moral duty to do this or that — just all this shit. It was obvious what he wanted to do, what I wanted to do, so we decided to do it and it felt great, I'm telling you — great. But then, you know, you took out Caplock . . . ' Murphy gave him a look. 'No, of course you didn't. You've been playing us like fucking fools.'

Murphy shrugged. 'So once you'd done one, there was no turning back.'

'I wouldn't put it like that.'

'How would you put it?'

'There was just always a worse case, and an opportunity to do something about it. We were getting results and we were getting away with it. You couldn't blame us. It's like gambling — you know, you get addicted, and the stakes get higher and you take more risks.'

'Like what?'

'Like your guy, Walker. He would have been way down the list, but then because of him Andrea got smacked and I just lost it and went and did him myself. I shouldn't have done that, it was a mistake. Was that what tipped you off, killing Walker?'

'Walker's alive.'

'Christ. Martin — this is bad, isn't it?'

'Yes it is, Lawrence.'

'I would never have guessed that you were — you know, *undercover*.'

'Well, that was the idea.'

'We got on OK though, didn't we?' Murphy just looked at him. 'Is there anything you can do for me? Anything at all?'

'How many do you think were killed, since this started?'

'I don't know. I mean, they were spaced out over a couple of years. The way Jeffers set it up, there could be some I don't know about.'

'Take a rough guess.'

'Thirteen? Maybe fourteen. Ah Martin, you know it ran so well, so efficiently, I thought we could keep it up for ever. That stuff about your son — that was all made up, wasn't it? Christ, you're some actor, aren't you? We really fell for it.'

Murphy didn't respond.

'Which means O'Hagan — he was one of yours too. Jesus, and I thought we were good at organising things.' He shook his head. 'I know we've had a row, and I know she's been seeing someone else, but I love my wife. I really love her. Do you think you could tell her that?'

Murphy stood. 'Sure I'll tell her, Lawrence. Next time I'm fucking her.'

He walked to the door before Lawrence could respond, and was out of the room before Lawrence could attack him. The cop in the corner threw Lawrence back in his seat, and ignored him as he broke down in tears.

37

Although Lawrence had admitted his role in the murders quite freely when the tape was off, he shut up shop as soon as his solicitor arrived. He denied everything, but they'd get him all right, you could tell that just from the look on the solicitor's face when he saw the extent of McIntosh's records, and then later again when they brought in a whole stack of stuff Jeffers thought he'd deleted from his home computer.

Lawrence wanted to see his wife, but she wasn't at home and she wasn't at her friends' and then Murphy, who'd spent the night in the office, sleeping under his desk, suggested to Thompson that Lawrence send a text message to her mobile. Although it was pretty clear the suspect wasn't allowed permanent access to his own mobile phone, it wasn't at all clear under what circumstances it could be returned to him, how long he was entitled to use it for, and whether a text message entitled him to the same amount of privacy as a normal phone call or could immediately be scrutinised or recalled by the investigating officers. Fortunately neither Lawrence nor his solicitor were of the texting generation, so they had to be guided through it by Thompson, who was, so they had direct access to the messages. Lawrence eventually sent three — the first two imploring Andrea to get in touch, which were ignored, and a third basically saying: *I'm under arrest for murder, please come.*

After a while the response came back: *I'll be there in an hour.*

Murphy, dead tired, drove home, then waited around the corner from his apartment until he saw Andrea emerge. She was wearing a smart blue skirt and top and black shoes with decent heels. Her sunglasses made it difficult to judge if the bruising around her eye had gone down much.

She stood at the kerb and put her hand out for a taxi. Three passed her by, then the fourth pulled over and she climbed in. Murphy stayed where he was until the taxi was out of sight, then hurried up to his apartment. He took out the spare keys he kept at the office and let himself in. The set he'd given to Andrea were sitting on the floor where she'd pushed them back through the letter box. He checked the kitchen table. She hadn't left any cereal out for him. He looked at the answerphone — no blinking light. Of course not. Nobody ever phoned him. And he had not phoned Andrea. He'd left her alone for thirty-six hours.

You have to be cruel to be kind.

He spent a couple of hours in bed, then after he'd showered and changed, he started to box up his stuff. They had another apartment ready for him. He moved after nearly every case, and he had it down to a fine art. A lot of his musical equipment, he hadn't even bothered to unpack after the last move. He promised himself that when he got to the new place he would make a point of setting up one of the rooms as a small recording studio. He had been encouraged by Carter's reaction to his CD. Annoying at first, but it grew on you. Much like Carter himself. Which reminded him: he phoned.

'How're you doing?' he asked.

'How do you think?'

'You're still there?'

'I'm still here.'

'And how is it?'

'It's a shit-hole. First-class service, they cater for your every need, but it's still a shit-hole.'

'There's a good reason for it. Relax and enjoy it.'

'Murphy, I'm in a nut-house.'

'You're undergoing psychiatric evaluation.'

'Exactly. The nut-house.'

'Man, I've been there half a dozen times. Just chill — it'll do you the world of good.'

'That is no recommendation at all coming from you, not previously known for being particularly stable.' Carter sighed and said, 'This is really going to fuck with my career, isn't it?'

'No, you'll be fine.'

'She was unarmed and I didn't shout a warning.'

'It was the heat of the moment. It happens.'

'That's not what the papers are saying. They're going mental.'

'Forget the papers. Besides, think how much worse it would be if you'd actually killed her.'

'I know that.'

'In fact, if anything fucks up your career it'll be the fact that you *didn't* kill her, because they'll have you down as someone who not only forgets procedure but can't shoot straight either. Plus she's bound to get — what? — the best part of a million in compensation and they'll take that directly out of your overtime.'

'Did you phone to cheer me up, or what?'

'Something like that.'

They were silent for a few moments, then Carter asked quietly: 'And how're you doing?'

'Just fine.'

'How do you feel about Jeffers?'

'I don't feel anything. It happens. The others are talking away — we're up to nine people who took part in the killings. See? I told you it wouldn't make double figures.'

'You think we'll get to charge nine?'

'I don't know. Lawrence anyway, and Armstrong, and probably the Scottish one for keeping the records, the others I'm not so sure. No weapons, no witnesses, no DNA. They can accuse each other all they want, but if we can't make it stick . . . well, you know.'

'I know. But Murphy — you did the right thing.'

'What do you mean?'

'Not shooting him.'

'If you say so.'

'And with all the heroin we found, he'll be away for a couple of years.'

'Yeah, I know.'

'You're not going to hang around waiting for him, are you?'

'What if I do? What if I made the wrong decision? What if this just eats away at me for years and then they let him out and I really do go after him?'

'Well, Murphy, with my luck I'll probably still be working with you, so I'll be there to stop you.'

'How would you stop me?'

'I'd shoot you.'

'With your aim?'

Carter laughed. They left it there, a little said, a lot unsaid. That was the way it was, the way it always would be.

★ ★ ★

That night McBride came round to watch the Man United match. When he saw the boxes scattered across the lounge he shook his head and said, 'Where are you off to this time?'

Murphy shrugged. 'I don't quite know. There's some sort of delay in getting the keys, so they're keeping it to themselves until everything's ready. Somewhere equally palatial, though.'

McBride nodded around the apartment. 'Yeah, right,' he said. 'See if you can get somewhere a little more awkward to find. I just finally worked out how to get here — two different Tube lines and a bus. It's not a challenge any more.'

'I thought you just closed your eyes and God directed you.'

'Well, He usually does. But He's been putting his prices up lately, so I'm trying to handle the small stuff myself.'

McBride had brought some beers. Murphy was all out, so they split them. United were two down within twenty minutes. 'I'm feeling a bit sad,' said the priest.

'They *are* crap,' said Murphy.

'No, it's not just that, it's watching football, drinking beer — and having to look at that exercise bike standing lonely and neglected.'

Murphy looked at it. He made a bold, life-changing decision: 'I'm finished with it, mate. You can have it if you want, you probably need it more than I do.' McBride, who was a bit sensitive about his weight, returned his attention to the TV screen. 'What I mean is, you'd probably get more benefit from it than I do.'

'I know what you mean.'

'I don't think you're fat.'

'Who ever said I was fat?'

'No one. I'm just saying . . . ah, fuck it. Have a crisp.' He was handing the priest the bag when the doorbell rang. Murphy took a handful for himself, then sauntered down the hall to answer it.

Later he thought, *I should have a spyhole.*

When he opened the door, Andrea was standing there. She looked absolutely perfect, as good as she ever had. The bruising around her eye had faded, and what was left was expertly covered. Her clothes were sharp and new-looking and her hair had that just-left-the-salon look.

'Andrea,' he said.

She punched him once, hard, across the nose and he staggered back, already bleeding.

'Bastard,' she said.

Then she turned on her expensive-looking heels, and walked away.

We do hope that you have enjoyed reading this large print book.

Did you know that all of our titles are available for purchase?

We publish a wide range of high quality large print books including:
Romances, Mysteries, Classics
General Fiction
Non Fiction and Westerns

Special interest titles available in large print are:
The Little Oxford Dictionary
Music Book
Song Book
Hymn Book
Service Book

Also available from us courtesy of Oxford University Press:
Young Readers' Dictionary
(large print edition)
Young Readers' Thesaurus
(large print edition)

For further information or a free brochure, please contact us at:
Ulverscroft Large Print Books Ltd.,
The Green, Bradgate Road, Anstey,
Leicester, LE7 7FU, England.
Tel: (00 44) 0116 236 4325
Fax: (00 44) 0116 234 0205

THE HORSE WITH MY NAME

Colin Bateman

Ex-journalist Dan Starkey is stuck in a grimy Belfast bedsit. His life is a disaster, and his only solace is the pub round the corner. He needs to get out more (particularly since the sessions at Relate with his wife Patricia have been cancelled and she's hooked up with new man Clive). He really, really needs something to get his teeth into. Fellow ex-journalist Mark Corkery provides that something. Corkery, whose secret persona is The Horse Whisperer, an internet horse-racing gossip, wants him to investigate Geordie McClean, the man behind Irish American Racing. Simple enough, surely? But Trouble is Dan's middle name — and trouble is what he finds.

MURPHY'S LAW

Colin Bateman

What Detective Martin Murphy really wants is to get back on the streets, doing what he does best — fighting crime. But his medical file (already thick and growing fast) says he should be retired. Then his boss, Murdoch (one realistic eye on retirement, the other fantastically set on late-life promotion), offers him one final chance: to infiltrate a gang of diamond thieves. They are tough, violent and ruthless. And Murphy will fit in perfectly.

THE ROSENBERG PRINCIPLE

Colin D. Peel

In coal seams buried far beneath the ground, giant fires burn uncontrollably. Adam McKendrick has the expertise to extinguish them. An assignment in Indonesia leads him to another fire, born in the dying flames of Hitler's Reich. McKendrick uncovers a radical form of international terrorism. Now he must protect Lucy Mitchell, whose work has put her life at risk. Can McKendrick save Lucy from an organization developing the world's deadliest bioweapon, and prevent their vision of a new world order?

WEB OF DISCORD

Norman Russell

Set in the Victorian era, the sequel to *The Hansa Protocol*. Returning from a court appearance, Detective Inspector Box finds himself investigating the violent death of Sir John Courteline, the great philanthropist. It looks like an act of private revenge, but Box soon uncovers a widespread conspiracy. Pursuing the killer's trail of signature deaths across London and Cornwall, Box's investigation finally leads him to the bleak wilderness of Eastern Prussia, where the scene is set for an awesome final confrontation.

STEEL RAIN

Tom Neale

Special Agent Vincent Piper of the London FBI Field Office is a newcomer to this vibrant city. There is anger simmering beneath its surface. He's only here to patch up his marriage . . . But when his daughter Martha is murdered in a terrorist bomb attack in the city, Piper realises he's staying. He knows who planted the lethal device: all he has to do is find him . . . Sarah, his daughter's tutor, and the mysterious Celeste, help him piece together his shattered life. Piper invests his trust in them, but what exactly are their motives? Before he can find out, he has a man to kill.